For the wonderful readers and writers who make up The Friendly Book Community x

AUTUMN DREAMS AT MERMAIDS POINT
CHARACTER LIST

Alex Nelson. Tom's half-brother, Emily and Max's uncle, son of Archie and Philippa Nelson.

Amber. A classmate of Emily Nelson.

Andrew Morgan. Married to Sylvia, Laurie and Nick's father. Owner of The Mermaids Cave, a large gift shop on the seafront.

Andy Sullivan. Owns and runs the local fish and chip shop.

Anna Nelson. Tom's late wife and mother to Emily and Max.

Archie Nelson. Tom and Alex's father. Married to Philippa, grandfather of Emily and Max. Known in the family as 'Pop'.

Aurora Storm. Pop star who staged a number of mermaid sightings around the Point as part of a viral campaign for her comeback album.

Barbara Mitchell. Part of the local knitting circle.

Becca. A school friend of Emily Nelson.

Belinda Nelson. Tom's mother, Archie's first wife. Happily living in Portugal with her partner, Eduardo.

Ben. A new school friend of Max's.

Bev. Part of the local knitting circle, known to have a sharp tongue.

Bryan Bannerman. A property developer.

Carlotta. Barbara Mitchell's cat.

Claire. A family friend of Tom and Anna Nelson.

Dan. Molly's husband, Samuel's father.

Darren. Friend of Nick Morgan.

Dennis Rouse. Head of DR Talent Agency. Aurora Storm's agent.

Donald Turner. Patient at the surgery.

Dr May. Provides GP Locum service for Doc Gadd.

Eduardo. An artist and Belinda Nelson's partner.

Emily Nelson. Tom and Anna's 15 year-old daughter.

Fraser. A GP who replaces Tom at his London surgery.

Freddie. Ben's father, married to Miranda.

Gareth Beckett. Nerissa's late fiancé. Died in a road accident whilst on a military deployment twenty-five years before the books are set.

Isobel Kennett. Nerissa's predecessor at the surgery.

Ivy Fisher. Laurie's one-time best friend.

Jake Smith. Investigative journalist and new arrival in the Point. Hero of *Summer Kisses at Mermaids Point.*

Jo Nelson. Alex's ex-wife.

Katie. Helps out in the café sometimes.

Keith. Works on a fishing trawler.

Kitty Duke. Part of the local knitting circle.

Linda Smith. Jake's mother. Recently widowed wife of Nigel Smith.

Lorelai 'Laurie' Morgan. Runs a café next door to her parent's gift shop. Heroine of *Summer Kisses at Mermaids Point.*

Luca. Owns and runs the local delicatessen.

Malcolm Gadd. Mermaids Point resident doctor, known to everyone as 'Doc'. He lives in and runs his surgery from an imposing white building situated at the end of the seafront.

Margot Beckett. Gareth's mother.

Max Nelson. Tom and Anna's 12 year-old son.

Merrow Morgan. Andrew and Nerissa's mother (deceased).

Michael Gadd. Doc Gadd's great-nephew.

Michelle. Bev's daughter-in-law.

Miranda. Ben's mother, married to Freddie.

Moira Henderson. Head teacher of Emily and Max Nelson's secondary school in London.

Molly. Patient at the surgery. Mother of baby Samuel.

Nerissa Morgan. Andrew's younger sister, paternal aunt of Laurie and Nick. Nerissa is the live-in receptionist and housekeeper of the Point's aging doctor, Malcolm Gadd. Heroine of *Autumn Dreams at Mermaids Point*.

Nick Morgan. Runs a tourist boat business from the Point's commercial harbour with his and Laurie's uncle, Tony.

Nigel Smith. Linda's late husband and Jake's father (deceased).

Paul. Married to Victoria. Keen open water swimmer.

Pete Bray. Landlord of The Sailor's Rest, a popular pub on the seafront. Owns the Penny Arcade a few doors down from the pub.

Philippa Nelson. Archie's wife, Alex's mother and Tom's step-mother. Step-grandmother to Emily and Max. Known in the family as 'Mimi'.

Samuel. Baby son of Molly and Dan.

Sebastian 'Bas' Donovan. Works part-time at the surgery as the cleaner, lives with his mother and younger sister.

Shelly. Resident.

Sylvia Morgan. Married to Andrew, Laurie and Nick's mother. Runs The Mermaids Cave with her husband as well as working part-time at the village school as classroom assistant.

Thea. A classmate of Emily Nelson.

Toby. Doc Gadd's golden retriever.

Tom Nelson. Widower of Anna, and father to Emily and Max. A doctor who decides to relocate his family to Mermaids Point. Hero of *Autumn Dreams at Mermaids Point*.

Tony Evans. Sylvia's brother, maternal uncle of Laurie and Nick. Owner of Mermaid Boat Tours, a pleasure boat business which takes tourists on trips around the area and out to the Seven Sisters, a group of nearby islands.

Victoria. Married to Paul. Keen open water swimmer.

Will Mitchell. Barbara's late husband.

1

JULY

'Ah, Gareth, you should see the way he makes her smile. It's like a light comes on inside her.'

Nerissa closed her eyes for a moment, picturing her niece, Laurie, as she'd seen her in the pub the previous evening, head tilted as she listened to whatever Jake was whispering in her ear. It had been a rare night out for the whole family, a chance to welcome Jake's mother to Mermaids Point and introduce her around. Nerissa still wasn't sure what to make of Linda – she wasn't at all convinced it was a good thing for Jake to have her back in his life, especially when his relationship with Laurie was still finding its feet, but she'd held her peace until now.

Shifting to ease the ache in her hip from sitting cross-legged on the ground too long, Nerissa confessed her doubts to the one person she was always able to speak her heart to. 'Honestly, Gar, she's such a mousy thing, it's a struggle to make even the most basic conversation. I don't think Linda's had an opinion of her own all her life.' She sighed, knowing she was being unfair given the little her sister-in-law, Sylvia, had told her about what both Jake and his mother had been through over the years. 'At least she's free of that awful man now. Given time, she might come out of her shell a bit more. If anyone can help her, it'll be Sylvia.'

Nerissa loved her sister-in-law with all her heart, but she knew from personal experience what Sylvia was like once she found a pet project.

Glancing down at the bunch of sunny yellow daffodils in her hand, Nerissa gave a small laugh. 'With any luck, she'll be so busy with Linda she won't have time to try to fix me up with anyone for a bit. I don't know why she's still bothering after all these years.'

She rearranged the bouquet to release one of the golden trumpet flowers which had twisted at an odd angle. Other women might prefer roses or extravagant lilies, but daffodils had been Nerissa's favourite since the first time Gareth had turned up on her doorstep. Tanned and fit after weeks of basic training, he'd presented her with a bunch of daffodils, a nervous smile tugging at his gorgeous full lips. He'd kissed her for the first time that day, down by the caves on the beach where he'd taken her for a walk. He'd told her he loved her that day, too, that he was tired of waiting for her to notice him, that she was his girl now. Forever.

She raised her free hand and pressed it to the echo of the warm glow that had heated her cheeks when he'd said those words. She'd been noticing her brother's best friend from the moment he'd picked her up and brushed gravel off her knees when she'd tripped over by the swings in the park. He'd been eleven to her seven, and had interrupted a noisy kick-about with her brother and the rest of their pals to set her back on her feet and wipe away her tears with the sleeve of his sweatshirt. Her heart had been his from that moment on, though, of course, she'd been too young to understand or articulate anything beyond the feelings of security and happiness she felt whenever he was near.

Those fledging feelings had developed into a full-blown crush once her hormones caught up with her heart. Her early teens had been an excruciating torture of unspoken adoration and blushes whenever he popped over to the Morgan family home – which had been practically every day, especially during the holidays. When he'd announced at twenty-one that a life on the fishing boats wasn't for him and he was off to join the army, the scandal of it had rushed around the village like wildfire. Nerissa had lain on her bed and wept silent tears into her pillow, thinking him lost to her forever. And then he'd come home on leave to reveal those messy, wonderful things she'd been feeling for him weren't unrequited after all.

Swallowing around the tight ball in her throat, Nerissa laid the daffodils on the square of neatly clipped grass in front of the plain white headstone. 'I love you, Gareth,' she whispered, touching her fingers to her lips before pressing them to the engraved letters of his name. 'Happy birthday, sweetheart.'

Rising to her feet, Nerissa turned away before the first tear dripped down her cheek. Gareth had always hated to see her cry, and though it'd been over twenty years since he'd last been able to brush them from her cheeks, she still didn't like to do it here in the little graveyard behind the parish church where he'd been laid to rest after a road accident during a peacekeeping mission in the Balkans. Such a waste of a life, of the promise of *their* life, *their* future together.

She clutched the diamond and sapphire ring dangling from a chain around her neck, squeezing it until the imprint of the stones hurt. She'd taken it off when the band had grown too tight but hadn't been able to let it go. To let Gareth go.

With the ghosts of memories they'd never share swirling around in her mind, Nerissa ducked her head and hurried along the path to the lychgate guarding the entrance to the churchyard. So fixated was she on the past, she didn't notice the woman coming the other way until they were practically on top of one another.

'Nerissa.' The lack of inflection in the word sent a chill rippling down Nerissa's spine.

'Hello, Margot. How are you?' She winced the moment the stupid, automatic words left her lips.

The death of the man they'd both loved above all others could've brought them together in solace and mutual grief, if only Gareth's mother had been willing. She'd never forgiven Nerissa for him joining the army, even though it'd been a decision he'd made on his own. Gareth had told his mum of his plans for a future with Nerissa before he'd said so much as a word to her. In Margot's mind, it was therefore Nerissa's fault he'd quit the boats and left the village in hopes of giving them both a better, brighter future. Two decades had hardened that initial irrational, if under-standable, need to blame someone for the loss of Margot's son, into a lasting bitterness.

Desperate for a way to cut through the frigid atmosphere between them, Nerissa nodded to the enormous bouquet of white lilies and roses Margot carried. 'Those are nice.'

'They're the ones I always get. The same as for his funeral.' Margot didn't meet her eyes, every stiff inch of her posture radi-ating a fervent desire for Nerissa to go away. Not that she'd ever say as much, because Margot's disdain was as polite as it was cold. Nerissa wished just once she'd let it all out, scream and rail and call curses down upon her head. Perhaps if Margot could give voice to all that resentment, she could finally let it go, instead of allowing it to consume her from the inside out.

Holding back a sigh, Nerissa took a step back and to the side, clearing a path for the other woman to pass through the lychgate. 'I'll leave you in peace, Margot. You know where I am if you ever need anything.'

The only response was the sharp click of Margot's heels on the path as she strode away.

Shaking her head, Nerissa passed beneath the roof of the gate, trying not to think about that awful rainy day when the pallbearers had paused beneath it with Gareth's coffin on their shoulders as they marked the symbolic passage of his life from this world to the next. Margot was never going to change, and it was way past time for Nerissa to stop trying. As she paused at the kerb to check for passing cars, she knew it was a fruitless thought. It wasn't in her nature to let someone hurt if she could help it.

With that in mind, she changed direction and headed the opposite way to her niece's pretty seafront café which had been her intended destination. Both Laurie and Sylvia were waiting for her there with hugs that would ease the ache in her heart and a slice of her favourite Victoria sponge to lift her spirits. As much as she needed that right now, there was someone who needed it more.

After a couple of weeks holed up in Sylvia's spare room, Linda had recently rented one of the small holiday cottages in the centre of the village while she tried to decide if she wanted to make a more permanent move to Mermaids Point. With a little coaxing, perhaps Nerissa could get her to join her for a walk on the beach and on to the café, where they would both find a warm welcome. Though her beloved Gareth had been nothing like the awful bully Linda had been tied to for years, she understood loss better than most. So she would extend the hand of friendship and offer what comfort she could to the recently widowed woman.

And just maybe they'd both feel a little better afterwards.

2

When she reached the old fisherman's cottage, Nerissa lifted the heavy iron knocker and rapped hard a couple of times and waited. And waited.

Stepping back on the pavement, she raised a hand to shield her eyes and studied the windows. The upstairs curtains were pulled closed, which wasn't all that surprising as they were catching the full force of the summer sun, but the downstairs curtains were also drawn shut behind the lacy nets which shielded the windows from nosy passers-by.

A movement at what Nerissa knew to be the lounge window caught her eye – was Linda in there or had the breeze stirred the curtains through the horizontal upper window which had been opened to its fullest extent?

Feeling a bit awkward, Nerissa checked around her to make sure no one was watching her snooping, then went to stand directly beneath the opening. The muffled sounds of a television show drifted out. Nerissa strained her ears, trying to pick up any indication of Linda moving around. The sound changed abruptly, the music switching from a romantic melody to a thumping beat.

Nerissa waited another minute and it switched again to the sound of two men arguing, followed by a rapid burst of gunfire which made her jump. Pressing a hand to her racing heart, Nerissa laughed to herself as she realised it was a rolling stream of programme previews. Linda must've gone out and left the television on. She might even be at the café already.

Nerissa was about to turn away when soft sobs reached her ears. *Maybe it was coming from the television?* Stretching on tiptoe to get closer to the window, she recognised a comedy series she'd recently binge-watched.

The sobbing came again, sounding totally out of place against the snappy dialogue.

'Linda?' Nerissa called, keeping her voice soft. 'Are you there?'

The sobs cut off immediately as the television in the background rolled through to another preview.

Legs aching, Nerissa dropped down to her heels for a moment before stretching back up to the open window. 'Linda? It's Nerissa. Is everything all right?'

A long silence, then a strained terse reply. 'Go away.'

'Sorry, I just wondered if you fancied joining me down at the café...'

More silence.

'Okay, well, hopefully we'll catch up soon. Give me a call, anytime.'

Embarrassed at herself for prying, Nerissa abandoned her spot beneath the window and turned away, pulling out her phone as she started to walk back the way she'd come.

She fired off a quick WhatsApp message to Sylvia.

On my way. Just called to see if Linda wanted to join us and I think she's crying. Can't tell as she won't answer the door, but she told me to go away. ☹

An instant later, the word *typing* appeared at the top of the screen, followed shortly by a reply.

Did you try the front door?

Nerissa stopped on the pavement to tap out a sharp response.

NO! I left the poor woman to it. I already feel bad for snooping around under the window.

Typing...

Go back and see if the door is open. Those old cottages have a latch that works from the outside.

Of course, Sylvia would know that. She seemed to know everything about everything in the Point.

As though sensing Nerissa's hesitancy, Sylvia sent a follow-up message.

Just try the door, Ner, we can't leave her on her own if she's upset.

Against her better judgement, Nerissa retraced her steps.

The front window was now closed, the curtains still drawn tightly. 'This is a big mistake,' she muttered under her breath as she reached for the old-fashioned metal latch and pressed her thumb to it. When it clunked down, Nerissa took a deep breath and forced herself to nudge open the door. 'Linda? I'm so sorry to intrude,' she said as she stepped onto the stone flags of the hallway floor and edged the door closed behind her. 'I just want to make sure you're okay and then I promise I'll go away and leave you in peace.'

Stepping into the darkened interior of the front room, Nerissa's gaze flickered over the array of dirty cups and plates on the table, past the small pile of crumpled tissues on the sofa cushion and met Linda's reddened eyes. Her mousy hair hung limp around her face, and the thickness of the seam on the sleeve of the cardigan she was huddled into suggested she had pulled it on inside out. Moving cautiously the way one might around a skittish animal, Nerissa made her way to the nearby armchair and sat down. With the window closed, the heat was stifling, but Linda didn't appear to notice. Reaching out, Nerissa pressed the mute button on the remote control, cutting off a canned laughter track. Tension settled as thick and unpleasant as the air.

'Is there anything I can get for you?' Nerissa asked, hoping a neutral question might help her ease her way into the conversation.

'I told you to go away.' Linda punctuated the words with a noisy blow of her nose into a sodden-looking tissue.

Nerissa leaned forward and nudged the Kleenex box on the table nearer to Linda. 'I thought you might have learned from the way Sylvia and the rest of the family invaded your home that us Morgans aren't very good at minding our own business.'

When Linda's husband, Nigel, had died unexpectedly six weeks previously, their son Jake had gone home for the first time in ten years to deal with the fallout. Unwilling to let him handle things on his own, the Morgan clan, minus Nerissa, had descended, uninvited, to help him manage the arrangements, and to try and get Linda back on her feet a bit. It had seemed like she was making progress, and they'd all hoped a stay in the Point might give Linda a bit of breathing space and a chance to make some decisions about her future, without being surrounded by constant reminders of what she'd lost. From the state of both Linda and the little cottage, those hopes were misplaced.

'True.' Linda gave just the glimmer of what might have been a smile, and Nerissa felt her shoulders relax.

'If you really want me to go away, I will,' Nerissa promised. 'But at least let me get you a cup of tea or a cold drink first.'

Silence stretched long enough for the knot of tension in Nerissa's shoulders to return and she was about to get up when Linda sighed and said, 'There's some sparkling water in the fridge.'

Nerissa took her time fetching them both a drink, giving Linda a minute or two to collect herself. Once she'd set the glasses on the coffee table, Nerissa circled the sofa and tugged open the curtains a couple of inches to let in a little bit of light and propped the upper window back open. By the time she retook her seat, Linda's face was dry and she was holding the cool glass against one cheek. After a sip of her own water to wet her lips, Nerissa took a breath and hoped she could find the right words.

'Grief is a funny thing, and it doesn't come with any rules.' When Linda remained silent, she stumbled on. 'I... I lost someone very special to me. It was a long time ago now, but some days are harder than others. It would've been his birthday today.'

'I'm sorry for your loss.'

When Nerissa glanced across, it was to find Linda's attention was fixed on her, rather than her glass. 'Thank you. Like I said, it was a long time ago. I just wanted you to know that I understand some of what you're going through.'

'Do you?' Linda's laugh was harsh and bitter. 'I don't expect you do at all.'

Startled, Nerissa took another sip of her water to cover her shock at the ugliness in Linda's tone. 'Well, of course, everyone's experience is different. Gareth and I had barely a year together, not a lifetime shared like you and Nigel.'

'And you loved him.'

Oof. Those four words and the untold story they hid all but stole the breath from Nerissa's lungs. Wishing like hell she'd ignored Sylvia's urgings and carried on her way to the café, Nerissa braced herself for another peek beneath the lid of the Pandora's box she'd inadvertently opened. 'From the little bits Laurie has told me, I understand Nigel could be difficult.'

'Difficult?' Linda laughed that bitter laugh again. 'Bloody impossible, more like.' Her head turned sharply away as though she hadn't meant to uncork the bottle of repressed feelings and didn't know how to stopper it again before she said any more.

Nerissa didn't blame her. She wasn't at all sure she was the right person for Linda to be talking to about this, but then again, who was? Poor Jake had enough on his plate coming to terms with his own grief – not that he'd shown a flicker of emotion. Well, maybe things were different when he and Laurie were alone, but when he was around the rest of the family, it was as if he'd shrugged it off and was determined to focus only on the future. Nerissa didn't blame him for that either, perhaps if she'd done a bit more of that she wouldn't be suspended as she was in a life half-lived. Her hand hovered at the base of her throat, drawn once more to the engagement ring she hadn't worn long enough to develop a tan line on her finger. No, she couldn't do anything to help Jake, but Linda was a different matter. 'Tell me.'

Linda's shoulders slumped, her body curling in upon itself. 'He was so charming when we met. I was sixteen and it was the first time I'd been allowed to go to the Apple Blossom fair without my parents. I went with a little gang of pals from school. Nigel and his friends were a bit older and they pushed in the queue with us just as we got to the dodgems. Somehow they split us up and I ended up riding in the car with him.' She raised her glass and gulped at her water like a survivor crawling out of the desert, not stopping until its contents were drained. 'God forgive me for saying so, but sitting down in that bloody bumper car was the worst mistake of my life.'

'Given everything that's happened, I don't think anyone would blame you for feeling that way.' In the darkest, quietest moments of the past twenty years Nerissa had wished Gareth had never shown up on her doorstep.

Linda's next words were barely above a whisper. 'But then I wouldn't have Jake, and what kind of woman, what kind of mother wishes away a life that gave them a child?'

'Regretting your life with Nigel and wishing Jake away aren't the same thing,' Nerissa responded in a fierce voice, furious with the dead stranger who'd tied Linda up in so many Gordian knots.

'He'd have been better off without us,' Linda muttered.

Reaching across the narrow coffee table, Nerissa grabbed Linda's limp hand and gave it a hard shake. 'Look at me.' It took a few moments, but when their eyes finally met, Nerissa tightened her grip. 'I'm not here to absolve you of guilt for past actions, that's something for you and Jake to sort out between yourselves, but you're free now to make your own decisions about how you move into the future.'

'But that's the whole problem. I don't know *how* to make those kinds of decisions.' Linda placed her empty glass on the table, then covered her face in her hands. 'Nigel did everything, and I went along with it.' Her hands fell limply to her lap. 'I knew I'd made a terrible mistake within the first six months of our marriage, but when I spoke to my parents, they told me I'd made my bed and I had to lie in it. I don't think they really understood how difficult it was, or maybe I didn't explain it well enough...' She glanced across at Nerissa. 'We weren't the sort of family that really talked about those sorts of things.'

Nerissa's heart ached for the woman. Nerissa had grown up in a boisterous, loving family, and though she was a bit more introverted than her older brother, she'd always had someone to talk to, someone who would listen. Yes, she'd been told a harsh truth a time or two by their mother, but she'd never been brushed off in the way it sounded like Linda had been. She wondered what her mum would've made of Linda's situation and a wave of longing struck her. Merrow Morgan had passed away three years ago – long enough to adjust to her not being around, but it was another hole in her life that felt too big.

Focus. Giving herself a little mental shake, Nerissa rose from the armchair and rounded the coffee table to take a seat on the sofa beside Linda, taking her unresisting hand once more. 'I don't want you to feel under pressure to talk if you're not comfortable with it.'

Linda returned her touch with the tiniest of squeezes. 'You are kind. It's just another thing I don't know how to do. I feel... useless. A waste of space. I shouldn't have come here, I'm a millstone around Jake's neck.'

'I'm sure he doesn't feel that way,' Nerissa said, not being entirely truthful, but Linda's confidence didn't seem like it would take another blow. 'But I understand you not wanting to feel like a burden to him. Why don't you let me help you – I know Sylvia would say the same if she were here. You're not on your own, Linda. We'd like to be your friends, if that's something you'd like too.'

Linda swallowed so hard, Nerissa could see the bob in her throat. 'I don't know how to be a friend. Not any more. Nigel never wanted me to spend time with anyone other than him, even when he was at work.'

'Oh, fuck Nigel!'

The two of them shared an equally shocked look before they both burst out laughing.

'I'm sorry,' Nerissa gasped around her giggles. 'I shouldn't have said that.'

Linda raised her free hand to wipe the tears from the corners of her eyes. 'Yes, you should, and I should have too – a long time ago.' Tilting her head back, she opened her mouth and yelled, 'Fuck you, Nigel Smith!'

Nerissa couldn't stop another snort of laughter escaping. 'Bravo!'

With a long sigh, Linda closed her eyes and her hand tightened around Nerissa's palm. Nerissa pressed back, giving what strength and support she could and the time to process what must be a tumult of emotions.

When Linda finally spoke, her words broke Nerissa's heart. 'I don't know who I am.'

'You're free now, Linda. Free to be whoever you want to be.'

As she watched the other woman wipe away the last of her tears, Nerissa decided she needed to listen to her own advice. For too long she'd allowed the past to shackle her, allowed others to mould and shape her life, instead of taking control. And she knew exactly where to start. She'd let Doc dither and delay over making a decision about his retirement for too long. As his live-in housekeeper-cum-receptionist, whatever decision he made would have a profound effect on the next chapter in her own life. The prospect of being both jobless and homeless at the age of forty-three was frankly terrifying, which was why she'd let things drift. It felt hypocritical to sit here urging Linda to seize control of her destiny and not do the same.

Her fingers rose to toy with the ring on her necklace. Change was coming for both of them, whether they liked it or not.

3

'Max? Em? Sorry I'm late guys.' Tom Nelson tossed his keys onto the side table in the hall as he kicked the front door shut behind him with his heel. Silence greeted him, which wasn't unexpected these days.

Tugging at his tie, Tom carried his medical bag into his study, tucked it into the bottom drawer of his filing cabinet and spun the combination lock. Not that he didn't trust the kids – they knew his study was strictly off limits, but he'd been doing it since Emily had first started crawling. A memory of her as a chubby infant, all smiles and rolls of baby-powder scented sweetness sprung to mind, bringing a rare grin to his face which was quickly wiped away by the continued silence to his greeting.

He closed the door of his study, pausing to toe off his shoes in the hallway before padding towards the kitchen. 'Max? Em? Where are you?' he called again.

'In here.' The response when it came was in a much deeper voice than he'd expected. What was his brother doing here?

Perplexed, Tom entered the room to find Alex stirring a bubbling pot on the stove top. Max sat at the battered pine kitchen table, his head bent over something. Bracing himself for another one-sided conversation about his twelve-year-old son's obsession with his phone, Tom was pleasantly surprised to realise Max was focused on his maths book.

'Hey, bud, where's your sister?' Tom bent over to press a kiss to the top of Max's tousled blond hair. It was several weeks past needing a cut and Tom added it to his mental to-do list.

'*Upstairs.*'

The single word response was followed by a long silence and Tom wondered if the two of them had been fighting. They got along great for the most part, but perhaps today was one of those rare occasions when they'd butted heads. He tried a different tack. 'How was school?'

'Okay.'

Normally, the question would prompt a flood of information, terrible jokes Max had heard from one of his friends, an insistence Tom watch whatever the latest hilarious video was trending on TikTok, but not tonight.

Tom rested a gentle hand on Max's shoulder. 'Only okay?'

Keeping his eyes fixed on his book, Max bobbed his head up and down.

Glancing over his shoulder at Alex, Tom raised his brows.

His brother shook his head and mouthed 'later', then banged the spoon he'd been using on the rim of the pot of what smelled like chilli and replaced the lid. 'Another half an hour, I reckon.'

'Sounds good,' Tom replied, tamping down his growing sense of unease. It wasn't completely unheard of for his brother to drop by unannounced, but he was more likely to be found messing around on the PlayStation with Max rather than doing something useful. Alex's idea of domestication had always left a lot to be desired, even when he and Jo had still been together. After the explosive destruction of his marriage eighteen months back, Alex had survived the first year of being single by writing and anonymously publishing an excoriating account of his wife's betrayal, which became a runaway bestseller. The stress of keeping his identity quiet, as well as pressure from his publisher to produce a follow-up book, had turned Alex into a takeaway-eating slob.

An image of the last time he'd been to Alex's flat came to mind and Tom dismissed it with a quick shudder as he looked his younger brother over. Though he still sported the terrible postbreakup beard he'd been cultivating, his clothes were clean and smart. A far cry from the sweatpants and stained T-shirts that had become his recent outfit of choice. Something was most definitely up.

Giving Max's shoulder a quick squeeze, Tom released it and crossed over towards the pastel blue Smeg fridge. How he'd ever let Anna talk him into the ridiculous-looking thing, and all the other matching small appliances...

Shaking his head to chase away the thought before it could take root, he tugged open the door and reached for a couple of bottles of Heineken from the top shelf. 'Beer?' He offered one to his brother.

'Cheers.' Alex took the bottle and retreated back to his spot beside the oven.

'Want a drink, Max?'

Max finally looked up, a hint of his usual cheeky smile lighting up his face. 'Can I have a beer?'

'Nice try.' Tom twisted the cap off a carton of apple juice and poured some into a glass. He set the drink down in front of Max, then pointed to his textbook. 'Why don't you take that upstairs and finish off, and we'll give you a shout when dinner's ready?'

Max folded the book closed, gathered his stuff under one arm, and stood. His expression a serious mask once more, he cast a quick glance towards his uncle. 'It wasn't my fault.'

'It'll be all right, Maxy,' Alex said, sending another warning glance towards Tom, who shut his mouth against his better judgement. 'Take your drink now.'

When Max looked his way, Tom forced an encouraging smile. 'Let Em know dinner will be ready in about half an hour.'

With a little nod, Max traipsed from the kitchen. Tom gave him a count of five seconds before he shoved the kitchen door closed behind him and rounded on his brother.

'What the bloody hell is going on?'

Alex took a sip from his beer like he had all the time in the world. 'The school called me.' He took another sip. 'At about half one.'

Half-one? Tom checked his watch. 'That was five hours ago.'

'Yup.'

Grinding his teeth, Tom tried again. 'Why did they call you?'

Alex set his beer down, then folded his arms across his chest. 'I don't know, Tom, why did they call me? Is it perhaps – now stay with me here – because *you* didn't answer your phone?'

'I didn't get any messages.' Tom reached into his pocket, letting out a soft curse when he pulled out his work phone. He'd put his personal phone in his medical bag before starting surgery and forgotten all about it.

He yanked open the kitchen door and ran towards his study.

'Come on, come on,' he muttered when he messed up the combination on his cabinet lock the first time.

By the time he'd got the drawer open and his phone out of his bag, Alex had followed him into the study and closed the door behind him.

Tom showed the display full of missed call notifications and urgent texts to call the school to his brother. 'I didn't hear it.' With a sick feeling in his stomach, he checked the button on the side of the handset. 'Shit. I'd put it into silent mode.'

'Never mind about that. Luckily enough I was at a loose end today. For a change.' There was no mistaking the sarcasm lacing Alex's tone, and Tom winced, knowing it was aimed inwards and not at him. Poor Alex had been struggling for months now, and he'd been meaning to check in with him.

Tom sank down into his chair. He'd been meaning to do a lot of things and dropping the ball on all of them. *If only Anna was here to help...*

Three years and the wistful, painful, pointless need for her hadn't lessened one bit.

Alex set the beer he'd retrieved from the kitchen on the desk and took the seat opposite him. 'Max had his phone confiscated for looking at – now how did Mrs Henderson put it?' He tapped a finger against his lips. 'Inappropriate images.'

Oh, Christ. Tom grabbed for his beer and took a gulp. 'Porn, you mean? How the hell did he break the settings on his account?' He knew it was only natural for boys to be curious about such things. Hell, their dad had found a dirty magazine under Tom's bed once, although he'd been a few years older than Max was now, leading to the most embarrassing conversation of both their lives. But the stuff he'd had access to then was so much tamer than the horrendous hardcore images plastered all over the internet these days.

'Not exactly.' Alex pulled a face. 'Some of the older girls have been persuaded to share selfies and...'

When he hesitated, Tom went cold all over. 'Not Em?' he whispered, hoarsely.

'I'm sorry, Tom. Apparently it started as a dare between a few of the girls and things got out of hand. One of the boys in Emily's class got hold of them somehow and he sent them to all his mates. They were all around the school in no time. They got sent to Max as part of a group message and he almost got in a fight when he recognised Em in amongst the photos. That's how his teacher found out about it, and he got sent to the head.'

Tom leapt to his feet, equal parts furious with, and devastated for, his daughter. He made it as far as the study door before Alex restrained him with a tight hand around his upper arm.

'Don't, Tom.' When he tried to shake Alex off, his grip tightened. 'You need to calm down.'

'Calm down?' Tom spun on his brother, shoving him back a couple of steps, his anger grateful for a close target. 'There are nude pictures of my little girl circulating the school – and God knows where at this point – and you want me to bloody calm down?' He swallowed a sudden rush of bile. *Christ, what had Max seen?*

Alex raised his hands in a placating gesture. 'Not nudes from what I managed to get the kids to tell me earlier. She's in her underwear.'

'Like that makes it any better!' Tom exploded. The desire to lash out, to strike down anything and everything washed over him in a hot wave. He'd never been a violent man, even shoving his brother was several steps too far. Horrified by his lack of control, Tom whirled away. He needed to put as much distance between himself and Alex as possible – not easy in his little matchbox of a study. Keeping his back to his brother, Tom braced his hands on the wall, pushing against the hard surface as though he could force his anger out through his fingers and into the solid plaster and brick. 'She's my little girl, Ally.' His voice cracked on the last word, a long-forgotten name he'd used when he'd been a teenager himself and Alex a toddler. Though his relationship with his father after he'd divorced Tom's mother, Belinda, had been difficult, he'd never let his antipathy for the man influence his feelings for his much younger brother. It was impossible not to love Alex. He'd been born with a natural charm, and Tom had been the first of many Alex had wrapped around his finger.

A tentative hand patted his shoulder. 'You're about five hours behind exactly where I was, Tommy. The head teacher had to lock her office door until I calmed down enough to agree to bring the kids straight home and not go hunting for those little shits.'

Tom turned to face his brother, seeing his own righteous fury reflected back in hazel eyes turned to flint. Knowing he wasn't alone in this nightmare, that Alex was there to back him up, helped him regain control of his temper. 'I'm sorry.' He dragged a deep breath into his lungs, fighting past the claw of emotion squeezing everything in his chest tight. 'How... how is she?'

Alex retreated to his chair, picked up his beer and took a long drink before replying. 'Heart-broken, confused, terrified.' He made a point of looking Tom square in the eye as he said the last word, and Tom felt the look like a punch in the chest.

'Of me?' He could barely get the question out, the mere idea of it making him want to retch.

'Of your reaction, of letting you down.' Alex scrubbed a hand over his eyes. 'She's utterly broken up about it, Tom, and I know things haven't been great between the two of you since... well, for a while.'

Since Anna died, he'd been about to say. Only he didn't. No one even said her name to him, Tom realised with a sick ache in his stomach. He'd turned Anna into a ghost, even around his closest family. Even around the children. There was no accusation in Alex's tone, but there didn't need to be. Tom carried enough guilt over the chasm between him and his eldest child to bury a mountain.

'I should go and talk to Emily.' Although he had no idea where he was going to start. Sorry would be a bloody good opener, though. Sorry for what she'd been put through today, even more sorry for how much harder he'd made things for her with the selfishness of his own grief.

He reached for the door handle, but before he could turn it, Alex was on his feet once more.

'Give it another few minutes. You can't go and talk to her until you're sure you can be calm about it.' Alex pointed towards the other chair. 'Sit down and finish your beer.'

Tom didn't think it would do any good, but he sat anyway. He could sit for five minutes, for five days, for five years and he didn't think he could be calm about what he'd learnt in the last few minutes.

Ignoring his beer, he reached for his phone and scrolled through the messages and emails from the school. The latest one had come in a few minutes previously, asking Tom to call Mrs Henderson regardless of the hour. He flicked to her name in his contacts and pressed the call button, switching the phone to speaker mode and setting it on the desk in front of him so Alex could hear both sides.

'Moira Henderson.'

'Mrs Henderson, it's Tom Nelson. I'm so sorry not to have contacted you sooner, my phone was on silent mode. No excuse, I know.'

'Good evening, Dr Nelson.' She sounded weary, stressed and a little sad and Tom could relate in bucketloads. 'How is Emily?'

He hesitated for a moment, then said. 'She's in her room. My brother has been catching me up on things and I thought it best to talk to you and have all the facts at hand before I speak to her myself.'

Mrs Henderson sighed. 'It's a dreadful situation, my heart goes out to the poor girls involved.' Tom had always found the head teacher to be a sensible, level-headed woman and his admiration for her only increased as she said those words. 'I'm still trying to get to the bottom of it, but there appear to be two or three ringleaders who've pressured the other girls into getting involved.'

Tom shared a quick glance with Alex. 'Do you know how many girls are affected?'

'Fourteen so far. Nearly every girl in Emily's house group, and a few from other classes in the same year. I've got a horrible feeling there might be more.'

'Jesus,' Alex blurted out before clapping a hand over his mouth.

Tom gave him a look. 'Sorry about that. Alex is here with me.'

A humourless laugh echoed from the phone. 'Don't worry, I've said and thought worse in the past few hours. Look it's only a few days to the end of term, so we've decided to exercise some flexibility across the whole of Year 10 while we continue our investigation and get to the bottom of things. We've issued a handful of suspensions, but please be reassured that Emily isn't one of them.'

'What about Max? I'm still not clear on his involvement in all this.'

'Poor Max.' Mrs Henderson sighed. 'He did rather bear the brunt of things because he was the one caught with the offending material in the first place. He was beside himself with worry about getting Emily into trouble. His phone is locked away in my desk – I meant to return it to him before your brother took him and Emily home, but things had escalated by that point and it slipped my mind. I suggest you have a good talk with him, but there won't be any further punishment on our part.'

'That's some small comfort, and of course I'll have a talk with him. Alex said something about him getting a group text with the photos in it.'

Another sigh. 'One of those WhatsApp group chats, I'm

afraid. We do our best, but it's impossible to police these things. Understandably, there are some girls who don't want to come back in to school. Although we would strongly encourage them all to attend, we won't report any absence. With the support of my teaching staff, we're going to run quiet sessions in the library for anyone who doesn't feel comfortable sitting in their normal classes. I've spoken to the external mental health support team and they're making someone available for the students involved to talk to if they wish. It will be by appointment and entirely confidential. We're also going to run some workshops with Miss Walker, who is our in-house RHSE lead across all the year groups, and we'll be particularly focusing on social media, body autonomy and consent.'

He exchanged another quick look with Alex, not sure if he should be relieved or worried about how seriously the school was taking it. Alex gave him a cautious thumbs up and he nodded. Better it was tackled properly, and it seemed like they were using it as a teachable moment rather than seeking to ostracise or punish the girls involved. 'Sounds like you've got everything in hand. Look, I'd better go and see Emily and find out how she's coping with all this. Do let me know if there's anything I can do to help. I'm going to contact my locum service and arrange cover for the rest of the week so I'll be around.' As he should've been from the start rather than trying to play catch up.

'Thank you. I'll be sending out an email later this evening or early tomorrow morning with details on the arrangements we've made for the rest of term. Do send Emily my best and tell her we're here to help.'

Tom found himself nodding, even though she couldn't see him. 'Thanks, Mrs Henderson. Take care.'

'Goodnight, Dr Nelson.' And with that she ended the call.

Tom sat back in his seat and regarded his brother. 'What a mess.'

'You're not wrong,' Alex agreed. 'Hey, I think the locum thing is a great idea, and if you want me to stick around so you can focus on Emily, I'm happy to keep Max occupied, take him to school, whatever after-school stuff he's got, just say the word. Poor kid's had a bit of a shock so I can have a quiet chat with him when it's just the two of us and you can concentrate on Em.'

Relief flooded through Tom's veins. 'You're sure you don't mind?'

Alex shrugged. 'I've got nothing else going on.'

It was on the tip of Tom's tongue to raise the issue of Alex's next book, or rather what appeared to still be a *lack* of Alex's next book, but that could wait. Perhaps if Alex stayed with them, he'd find a quiet moment in the next few days. 'Spare room's made up, and I can loan you whatever you need this evening.'

'Perfect. I'll shoot home in the morning after I drop Max off and chuck some things in a bag. Look, you go and see Emily and I'll check on dinner. I'll put some rice on and get Max fed. You guys can heat some up later.'

'Sounds like a plan.'

Tom pushed to his feet, weary to his bones, the weight of the loss of Anna a stone in his gut. She would've known what to do, the right words to say. Her natural warmth and empathetic nature had drawn everyone to her – Tom included, even though once he'd worked his way into the fringes of her orbit during their first year at university he'd been hopelessly tongue-tied. For reasons that still mystified him, Anna had taken a shine to him too and they'd had twenty wonderful years together. Not enough. Never enough.

4

Pausing outside Emily's bedroom door, Tom gave himself a mental kick up the arse. He couldn't fall back into the indulgent cycle of his own pain; Emily needed him. Had needed him for the longest time.

Grasping the handle, he raised a hand to knock and hoped he wasn't too late. 'Em?' he said quietly as he pushed open the door. 'Em, darling, can I come in?'

The supine lump under the pretty floral quilt shifted, followed by a breathy sound that ripped Tom's heart in two. Though his every instinct was to rush in and gather her into his arms, he forced himself to remain on the threshold of her room. Emily's trust had been violated in the very worst way, the least Tom could do was try and give her a sense of control now.

'I can stay here, if you'd rather? Or I'll go away and leave you in peace if that's what you'd prefer?'

'Stay.' It was barely a whisper, but more than enough encouragement for him to hope it wasn't too late to cross the gap that had been allowed to grow for too long between them.

Stepping quietly into the room, Tom shut the door behind

him and slid down the wall to sit beside it, legs outstretched. He'd sat in the exact same spot when they'd been trying to sleep train her, waiting silently for her breathing to deepen before crawling out on hands and knees. The memory of those exhausting nights sent a pang of nostalgia through him. It had been so easy in those days to fix Emily's problems with a hug and a kiss. It was going to take a hell of a lot more than that now, but he'd sit there all night if he had to. She needed him and he would not let her down. Not this time. Not ever again.

'I love you, Em. I'm not mad – well not with you. I want you to know that.'

'I'm sorry.' A hiccup-sob swallowed the end of the apology and Tom was up on his haunches before he could stop himself.

'Don't apologise to me, darling. I'm the one who should be sorry, not you.' Tom balled his fists, pressed his knuckles into his thighs until he could swallow down the rush of anger. Not at her – at himself for being absent, for being so damn selfish and wallowing in his grief. 'Do you want to tell me what happened?'

A violent shake of the bit of mussed blonde hair sticking out of the top of the quilt.

Tom bit back a sigh. When Emily had been little, it'd always been him she'd turned to. As she'd grown, he'd taken more of a backseat to Anna, who'd taken on the lion's share of the childcare while he'd worked to build his practice and secure their future. Without the bright sun of Anna to draw them together, they'd circled alone like lonely planets, isolated in the coldness of their grief. 'I spoke to Mrs Henderson just now...'

Emily bolted upright, the quilt pooling at her waist to reveal she was still wearing her school uniform. She must've crawled straight into bed the moment she got home. 'Oh God! What did she say? I'm suspended, aren't I? Amber and Thea made us do it!'

Unable to bear the distance between them, Tom walked on

his knees to the end of her bed. His hand found one of her feet, curled gently around the quilt-covered toes. 'You're not in trouble, Em. Not with me, not with Mrs Henderson either. She said it's up to you whether you go in tomorrow, though.'

Emily shoved aside a tangled hank of hair which had fallen across one of her eyes. 'I can stay at home?' She sounded so relieved, Tom was tempted to agree, even though hiding from the inevitable would only make things more difficult for her in the long run.

'You won't get into trouble if you don't go in, but I don't want you to make any snap decisions about it. There are options – you can have quiet time in the library rather than go to any classes. If you went in, you'd be able to see your friends at least, say goodbye to them before the summer holidays start.'

Emily's face crumpled, and tears welled in her already reddened, puffy eyes. 'I don't have any friends, not any more, thanks to Max!'

'Hey!' Tom gave her foot a squeeze. 'You mustn't blame Max for any of this, he was sticking up for you.'

Arms folded across her chest, Emily glowered through her tears at him. 'If he hadn't been stupid enough to get caught, no one would know anything about this.'

He wouldn't know anything about this, she meant. It was on the tip of Tom's tongue to fling the accusation back at her; after all, if she and her friends hadn't been stupid enough to take compromising photos in the first place— He cut the thought off before it could fully take root.

'I know you're upset, but you can't take this out on your brother. Actions have consequences, Em. Once those pictures started being shared, there was no way you could've kept a lid on this.'

The moment of defiance shattered and Emily once more burst into noisy tears.

Tom dropped his head onto the bottom edge of the bed. God, why was he so rubbish at this? He had tricky conversations every day in the surgery and always managed to find a way to tiptoe through the emotional minefield when it came to things like a difficult diagnosis. How could helping a patient with stage four cancer be so much easier than dealing with a heartbroken teenager?

Get a grip, Nelson. Pushing himself up from the floor, Tom sat on the side of the bed, not too close to Emily, but near enough she could lean in for a hug if she wanted one. 'I know it seems like the worst thing in the world right now, but it'll blow over. You might find it easier than you think, especially if you face it down tomorrow rather than letting it hang over you.'

She raised incredulous eyes to his face. 'You have no idea what you're talking about! They hate me now! I can't go back there.'

She grabbed for the sparkling pink phone he'd given her for her birthday a couple of months back and tossed it onto the quilt between them.

Tom stared at the screen, open on a WhatsApp chat. It was tempting to snatch it up and read it, but he had to tread so carefully. Em's mood was too volatile for her to be thinking clearly, and it would be all too easy for her to see it as a betrayal later if he pried into her personal messages. He pressed his thumb to the home button, closing the app and returning her phone to the front display. He then touched the power button on the side for good measure, locking the phone before he stood to tuck it into his pocket.

'Hey!' Emily protested. 'What are you doing? Give me that.'

Taking her outstretched hand, Tom folded it into his as he sat back on the edge of the bed. 'I'm going to hang onto it until the morning.'

She pulled against his grip, forcing him to let go because the last thing he wanted to do was hurt her.

'You can't do that! It's mine, give it back!' she shouted.

'Enough.' He hadn't raised his voice to match hers, but it was a tone he'd very rarely used around the children since they'd been old enough to be reasoned with.

Emily lowered herself against her pillows, arms folded once more across her chest. 'I hate you.'

Lord, give me strength.

'No, you don't. Lashing out at me isn't going to change the situation any more than blaming Max is. Your friends are upset, just like you are now, so they're saying things they don't mean as well. Give them a day or two to calm down.'

She rolled her eyes. 'You don't have a clue, do you? I only took those stupid photos in the first place because they wouldn't be friends with me otherwise. Now they're never going to want to hang out with me.'

'If that's the kind of people they are, then you don't need them as friends.'

Emily snorted, an ugly, derisive sound. 'You say that like I have any choice. I'm not exactly inundated with people who want to be friends with me.'

Tom frowned, taken aback at her words. When she wasn't angry and upset like she was now, Emily was the soul of sweetness and good humour. As easy with people as Anna had been. The house had always been full of giggly girls, dancing around the lounge to pop videos, sneaking down to raid the snack cupboard during sleepovers. Those had stopped when Anna had grown too tired, too sick to cope with them. And afterwards? The last thing Tom had wanted was a house filled with laughter.

Trying to ignore another wave of guilt battering at him, he recalled the smiley little brunette who had been the instigator of much of the mischief. 'What about Becca? You two were always so close.'

'Her dad got a new job and they moved to Manchester just after Christmas. You really have no idea, do you?'

Shit. How on earth had he missed that?

Because you've been sleepwalking through your life for the past three years.

'Oh, Em, I'm so sorry.'

Snatching up a pillow, Emily clutched it to her and buried her face in the top of it. 'Just go away.'

Feeling useless and defeated, Tom rose to his feet. He stared down, willing her to look up at him, but Emily kept her face buried resolutely in the pillow. The lace edging on the pillowcase caught his eye. He remembered Anna buying it a few years ago when Emily had decided pink bears, rainbows and unicorns were too babyish.

His eyes shifted to the framed photo of Emily and Anna on the bedside table, laughing as they clutched a pair of melting ice cream cones. The bond of love between mother and daughter radiated from the cheap seashell-covered frame they'd picked out on the same holiday. Anna was everywhere, in everything. She haunted every corner of the house as completely as if she were a manifested ghost.

At first, it had been a comfort to keep everything the same. The kids had enough to deal with and it was important they remembered their mother, and Tom had sure as hell needed it. Somewhere along the line, though, it had stopped being a comfort blanket and was now threatening to smother them all. He had to stop living for the past, stop wishing for things to be as they had been when there was no way to turn back the clock.

Placing his hand on the top of Emily's head, he stroked the tangled strands so like her mother's and smiled sadly. He didn't need to keep the house as a shrine to Anna's memory when she lived and breathed in the two beautiful children they'd made together. It was time to move on, make a fresh start.

'Look at me, Em.'

It took a few moments before she raised her red face. She might have her mother's hair, but those shattered hazel eyes were all his, as was the pain and anger he recognised in them.

'I've let you and Max down when you needed me most, I see that now. I'm sorry it has taken me so long to realise it.' Tom bent, pressed a kiss to her cheek and stepped back from the bed. 'Things are going to change from now on. I promise.'

5

It had been one of those mornings in the surgery when the phone didn't stop ringing thanks to a series of random minor accidents and incidents in the village. Coupled with a full appointment book, due in large part to a mystery stomach bug sweeping through the local teenagers, it was nearing two in the afternoon before Nerissa managed to escape from the reception desk into the peace and quiet of the kitchen to fix a bite to eat for her and Doc Gadd.

Neither of them were feeling very hungry thanks to the unwelcome display of symptoms one of the young lads had deposited on the carpet in Doc's office. 'Impressive projection,' Doc had said with a wry laugh as he'd escorted the hapless teen to the spare treatment room, leaving Nerissa to tackle the mess with a bucket of hot soapy water. They'd decided to leave the windows open and transfer the rest of Doc's appointments to the temporary space for the afternoon, and Nerissa had gone through the appointment book and cancelled two emergency appointments with worried parents. They'd seen enough similar cases to know there had to be a common cause, and the treatment advice was a watch-and-wait brief – plenty of rest, plenty of fluids and call any time day or night if the symptoms worsened. And so Nerissa had this small window to rustle up something to keep her, and particularly Doc, going through to the end of the day.

She'd just put on a pair of oven gloves to remove the tray covered in bubbling slices of cheese on toast when the back door swung open.

Toby, Doc's – or more accurately these days as she took care of him – her golden retriever bounded from his basket in the corner and took up guard in front of the open door. A low growl rumbled, warning Nerissa of the identity of the visitor before the two men had taken a single step over the threshold. There was only one person the normally placid dog had taken an active dislike to – Doc's great-nephew, Michael.

'Get out of it,' Michael snapped, aiming a foot at, and thankfully for his sake, missing Toby's flank.

'Toby. Bed.' Nerissa pointed to the corner and the dog slunk away, casting her a look of reproach. She didn't blame him. It wasn't in Nerissa's nature to be mean any more than it was Toby's, but she'd happily bite Michael herself most of the time.

The smell of almost-burnt cheese filled her nostrils and she swung back to the grill just in time to turn it off and catch their lunch before it was ruined.

'As I was saying,' Michael stepped into the kitchen, his back to Nerissa, dismissing her without a word of greeting, 'this part of the building is mostly original, but it wouldn't take much to modernise it – depending on your plans, of course.'

'Hmm.' The older man who'd followed Michael into the kitchen was dressed in a smart, navy pinstripe suit with a white shirt and a flamboyant orange tie the same shade as the silk handkerchief spilling from the breast pocket of the jacket. He had a soft, sleek look about him. Well-groomed, Nerissa thought to herself. 'Oh, hello,' the man turned a polite smile to her, hand outstretched. 'I hope we're not intruding. I'm Bryan, Bryan Bannerman.' He said his name with the kind of self-assurance that said he expected her to recognise it, but she had no clue.

'Nerissa Morgan.' Nerissa raised her oven-glove clad hands in an apologetic gesture. 'As you can see, we weren't expecting anyone.' She cast a pointed look at Michael. 'What are you doing here?'

Michael bristled, his plump cheeks mottling in a way reminiscent of salami. 'I wasn't aware I needed the housekeeper's permission to drop by.'

Bryan Bannerman had the good grace to look away, but not before Nerissa caught a flash of annoyance and disgust at the rudeness in Michael's tone. It made Nerissa feel a shade more kindly towards him, even though his presence didn't bode well. Ever since Doc had been making noises about retirement, Michael had been sniffing around the place like Toby when he caught the scent of something delicious to him – and usually disgusting to Nerissa – when they were out exploring the beach.

As Doc's lone-surviving close relative, Michael had taken on the assumption of an inheritance with an enthusiasm Nerissa found altogether distasteful. You'd think Doc had one foot in the grave from the way Michael behaved. Sure, Doc might be a bit past it in terms of coping with the full-time medical needs of their community, and some of his attitudes, especially when it came to things like women's health, were two steps removed from the dark ages, but he was still fit for his age and fully in charge of his mental faculties. If Michael had his way, he'd have Doc packed off in a tiny retirement flat and the surgery building on the market before the year was out.

'You don't need my permission to do anything, Michael, but we're absolutely slammed in the surgery. I'm grabbing us a late lunch between appointments. If you'd let your uncle know you were coming, we might have been able to rearrange things.'

Giving Michael her back, Nerissa picked up the kettle, filled it just enough to make two cups and switched it on. Petty, but if Michael and his guest wanted tea, they could damn well make it themselves. Or better yet take themselves off down to Laurie's café and leave Nerissa in peace.

'You carry on,' Michael waved his hand like royalty bestowing permission on a lowly subject. 'I can show Bryan around without an escort.'

Show him around?

Nerissa bit her tongue and concentrated on measuring the correct amount of tea into the pot. Doc insisted on loose-leaf, left in the pot to stew until the teaspoon could almost stand up in it.

Not your business, she chided herself silently. Doc didn't pay her enough to get involved with whatever Michael was plotting. And even though she was dying to know what exactly he was up to, she would never give him the satisfaction of asking – not when he'd as likely try to dress her down again for not knowing her place.

Having filled the pot, she set it down on the tray she had placed on the table earlier. 'Best if you keep away from the surgery, we've had some dreadful cases of D & V in this morning. One poor lad did a re-enactment of *The Exorcist* all over Doc's carpet.' Feeling devilish, Nerissa reached for the empty kettle and waved it towards the two men. 'Cup of tea?'

Bryan Bannerman took a step towards the back door, face going pale. 'No! Erm, no, thank you so much for the offer though.'

'Well, if you change your mind, the cups are in this cupboard, so feel free to help yourself.' Nerissa gave him her best just-here-to-help smile. 'Now, if you'll excuse me, I need to get Doc's lunch to him.' She slid the cheese on toast onto a couple of plates, which she added to the tray and lifted it. 'If you don't mind,' she nodded towards the door on the opposite of the kitchen.

When Michael didn't attempt to move, Bryan cast him another confused look before hurrying over to open it. 'Are you sure you can manage the tray?' he asked as he held the door open with his shoulder.

'Oh, I'm fine, thank you so much. It was a pleasure to meet you, Mr Bannerman.'

'Bryan, please,' he replied, inclining his head in a little bow. 'I'm sorry again that we barged in unannounced.' He cast a look back into the kitchen, his smile falling away.

'Of course, Bryan. Well, you take care now.'

As she carried the tray down the little hallway connecting their living quarters to the surgery Nerissa couldn't help feeling a little bit smug about the earful she imagined Mr Bannerman would be giving Michael as soon as they were alone.

She'd left the door to the consulting room propped open and a pleasant breeze ruffled the dark curls which had slipped from the bun pinned at the nape of her neck. Lord, the heat had been stifling for days. She set the tray down on the desk, then proceeded to set out the tea things and Doc's plate, before retreating to a chair set at right angles against the side of the desk with her own lunch.

'Well, this looks splendid, doesn't it?'

One thing she'd say for Doc, he was always appreciative of whatever meal she set before him – even when it was just a bit of cheese on toast.

'I hope it's not gone too cold. I was delayed by some unexpected visitors.' When Doc raised a bushy eyebrow in her direction, Nerissa continued, 'Michael's here.'

'Is he now?' Apparently unperturbed, Doc took a bite of his

toast and chewed it before reaching for the pot and pouring them both a cup of tea.

When Doc seemed disinclined to say any more, Nerissa couldn't help adding, 'He had someone with him, a chap called Bryan Bannerman. Have you heard of him?'

'Can't say I have, my dear,' Doc murmured, attention focused on adding exactly the right amount of milk to each cup.

Nerissa stuffed a square of toast into her mouth before she said anything else, then wished she hadn't as it sat uneasily in her still queasy stomach. Doc had a habit of playing the obtuse card when it came to things he didn't want to discuss. He was so damn polite about it, though, that it was hard for Nerissa to push him. She knew he knew she knew he was stringing her along, the sly old dog, but it still worked nine times out of ten.

Pulling out her phone, she typed Bryan Bannerman into the search engine and had her worst suspicions confirmed when the first entry took her to the homepage of Bannerman Construction and Development. Beneath a guff paragraph touting the humble family origins of the business was a grinning image of the man she'd just met – looking even sleeker and more pleased with himself than she would've thought possible. 'He's a developer.'

'Interesting.' Doc nibbled another square of toast. 'Do you know, I wasn't sure about it when you suggested Red Leicester instead of Cheddar, but I should've trusted you all along.'

Refusing to be drawn into a distracting conversation on the merits of melted cheese, Nerissa set her half-eaten lunch on the tray and sipped her tea while she waited to see if he would say anything else about Michael's unexpected visit. To her growing frustration Doc held his peace as he finished lunch. Fighting the urge to snap at him she stood and gathered their empty plates onto the tray. They had a full afternoon ahead and now was not the time to force a discussion about the future, no matter how unsettled she was feeling. *When would be the right time?* Ignoring the silent self-admonishment, Nerissa forced a smile. 'Do you want any more tea?'

'No, this will do me fine, thank you.' Doc settled back in his chair, both hands wrapped around his teacup. 'Perhaps you'd be so kind as to bring me a glass of ice water on your return, though? I don't think this heat is going to let up any time soon.'

A stickler for appearance, even he'd removed his jacket in surrender to the blazing temperatures and rolled his sleeves in precise squares to just above the elbow. He looked as crisp and fresh as a daisy, his cheeks smoothly shaven and a faint hint of his favourite aftershave carrying on the slight breeze.

By contrast, Nerissa felt as limp and sweaty as the tendrils of hair clinging to her neck. She cast a quick glance at the clock over Doc's shoulder. Even with the delay caused by Michael, they still had ten minutes before their next appointment – plenty of time for her to dash up to her room and refresh herself, maybe even change her blouse and skirt combo to a cooler dress. 'I'll be back in five.'

'Take your time, my dear,' Doc said as she carried the tray towards the door. 'Oh, and Nerissa?'

She paused on the threshold to glance back at him. 'Yes?'

'Don't worry about Michael, everything's in hand.'

How many times had she heard him say that in the past month?

Fighting the urge to scream, Nerissa stomped her way back to the kitchen. She was furious with Doc for being so blasé about everything, and even more furious with herself for letting him get away with it – again!

6

'And that's all he said?' Jake asked as he held open the door to The Sailor's Rest later that evening. There were a few pubs in and around the village, but the sprawling edifice on Mermaids Point seafront was a favourite of the family – and not just because it was the one closest to the café and shop the Morgans ran on the very same street.

Doc had been content to settle in front of the television with a bit of quiche and some salad, giving Nerissa leave to escape for the evening. When her brother, Andrew, had posted the words LIQUID REFRESHMENT! in the family WhatsApp group, followed by a row of beer and wine emojis, Nerissa had responded with one of her favourite GIFs, Lucille Ball grinning as she waved a bottle of champagne in the air, the contents spilling everywhere. Sylvia had added one of two women clinking together enormous glasses of wine. Jake had posted Forrest Gump sprinting with the words 'I'm on my way', while her nephew, Nick, had settled for Father Jack in his crusty armchair yelling 'Drink!'

'Yup.' Nerissa shrugged, the frustration she'd been feeling

since her non-discussion with Doc following Michael's visit bubbling back to the surface.

'And what do you think he meant by that?' Sylvia asked. 'Oh, look, that table by the window is coming free.'

Nerissa watched half in admiration, half in disbelief as her sister-in-law strode across to where two young men were finishing the last of their pints and placed her handbag on the table they were sitting at.

'Thanks, darling,' Sylvia said with a wave and a smile as the boy on the left slid along the bench seat and stood, a slightly befuddled look on his face. If they were considering a second drink, it would have to be at the bar – thus was the power of steamroller Sylvia.

'Thank you,' Nerissa cast a guilty smile at the other man as he too got up – not guilty enough to stop her scooting onto the bench and over to the half-wall.

Another reason they loved this pub was the recent changes the landlord, Pete Bray, had made. It had taken a lot of negotiation with the local council, but he'd gained permission to replace the old sash windows with a set of modern folding windows which could be slid back on either side to create an open-terrace feel without anyone spilling out onto the pavement outside. They also let in some much-needed fresh air on stifling summer days like today.

Laurie and Jake sat next to her, Nick on the other side next to his mother, leaving a space for his dad, who stood at the head of the table.

Clapping his hands together, Andrew shot them all an enthusiastic grin. 'Right, my lovelies, what are we having?'

'Pinot,' Sylvia replied before casting a questioning look to Nerissa.

'Oh, yes please. Make sure it's ice cold, though.'

'Pinot three,' Laurie raised a hand. 'Get a bottle, Dad, and an ice bucket.'

'And one of those buckets of beers, eh?' Nick rose to his feet. 'What do you reckon, Jake? Fancy a bottle, rather than a pint? It'll be colder.'

'I'm in.' Jake shifted onto one hip, reaching behind to pull his wallet from his back pocket. 'Let me get these.'

'Your money's no good, here, son!' Andrew waved him off with a smile.

When Jake looked as though he might protest, Laurie laid a hand on his arm. Though she lowered her voice, Nerissa was close enough to hear her say, 'Leave it. You know what he's like. We'll ambush them with a takeaway later.'

'Good plan.' Looking happier, Jake wrapped an arm around Laurie's shoulders and pressed a kiss to her temple. Keeping Laurie against him, he half-turned to face Nerissa. 'You were telling us about Doc's plan to deal with Michael.'

Nerissa wrinkled her nose. 'If only I could believe there was a plan, but you know what he's like. Never deal with something today which you can put off forever.' She rubbed the back of her neck, more as a self-soothing gesture than in any hope of relieving the tension which seemed to have set up permanent shop between her shoulder blades lately. 'I thought we were getting somewhere after I finally cornered him about his future plans last month, but he's never said another word since promising me he would sort something out and let me know.' She closed her eyes for a brief moment as the jitters of uncertainty began swirling in her tummy. 'Things can't go on like this forever. I just need to know where I stand.'

Sylvia leaned across the table, taking both of Nerissa's hands in her own. 'Don't fret, Ner. Whatever happens, we've got you covered.'

Nerissa squeezed Sylvia's fingers, saying everything she was feeling in that brief touch. She was hugely grateful for all her brother and sister-in-law did for her, but the prospect of giving up what bit of independence she had and moving under their roof filled her with despair. She'd ask Linda if she wanted a roommate before that happened, although if Michael did persuade Doc to sell up to a developer, she wouldn't just be out of a home – she'd be out of a job as well. She couldn't expect Linda to let her move into the cottage she was renting if Nerissa didn't have the means to contribute to the bills.

Before she could dive too deep down another woe-is-me rabbit hole, Nick and Andrew returned laden with two huge ice buckets: the first full of long-necked beer bottles, the other holding not one, but two bottles of Pinot Grigio.

'Andrew, it's a school night!' Sylvia protested, even as she reached for one of the wine bottles.

'Don't worry, my love, I'll see you home safely.' Andrew slipped onto the bench seat before Nick could steal his spot.

'That's what you told me after our first date, and look at the trouble I ended up in!' Sylvia laughed as she said it, already tilting her face up as her husband leaned down for a kiss.

Nerissa felt something twist deep inside her, a yearning for that kind of easy familiarity. Though it'd only been a few months, she'd noticed the same sort of interactions developing between Laurie and Jake, the special emotional shorthand couples had that only made sense to them. Her fingers itched with the need to touch the ring dangling at her throat. Had she and Gareth had the same thing? It was getting harder and harder to remember specifics about their short time together. Another little bit of him stolen away by the cruel sweep of time's hands.

'Nerissa?'

Startled, she focused on the glass Sylvia was holding out to her. 'Sorry, I was miles away.' From the concern in Sylvia's eyes, Nerissa knew she'd given herself away. Not wanting another lecture about leaving the past where it belonged, Nerissa accepted her wine with a small shake of her head. 'I'm fine,' she said, low enough for it to be just between the two of them.

Sylvia eyed her for one long moment before letting something Laurie was saying draw her attention away and Nerissa heaved a small sigh of relief as she too made an effort to join in the rest of the conversation.

They were a bottle down when a familiar voice at her elbow turned Nerissa's attention away from a terrible joke her brother was regaling them with to the man standing on the pavement beside and a little below her, thanks to the pub's slightly raised position from the pavement. It was Andy Sullivan, who ran the fish and chip shop on the high street. 'Hi, Andy, how's things?'

'Can't grumble,' he said with a grin before lifting the front of the large, padded satchel he was wearing cross-body and withdrawing the first of several paper-wrapped parcels Nerissa could see nestled inside it. 'Right then,' he continued, holding out the package towards her. 'Everything is labelled on the front.' He all but pushed the parcel into her hands. 'That's a large cod and chips.'

'Thanks, Andy,' Jake half-leaned across Nerissa to take the fish and chips. 'You're a lifesaver.' He slid the package across to Andrew. 'There you go.'

'What's this?' Andrew asked, unwrapping the food and sending the heavenly sent of fried fish, salt and vinegar into the air.

'Our treat, and it's already paid for,' Jake said in a tone that brooked no argument before he nudged Nerissa. 'Grab the rest, will you?'

'Oh, of course.' She took the next package, then the next,

handing them off to Jake like a game of pass the parcel as he dished them out around the table.

Andy set the last one in her hands. 'Fish cake and a small chips, that must be yours,' he said with a wink because it was the same thing she always ordered.

'Curry sauce?' she asked, hopefully, mouth already beginning to water as the smell of the food intensified with each unwrapping.

'As if I'd forget!' Andy reached into his bag one last time and produced two Styrofoam cups with plastic lids.

Jake leaned across once more, a five-pound note for a tip held out. 'Cheers, for the delivery, Andy.'

'All part of the service.' Andy tucked the money into his back pocket with a grin and a nod of thanks before turning away at someone calling his name. 'And thanks for the extra business.' He gave Jake a quick thumbs up before taking a few steps towards the people sitting somewhere behind them, a paper menu already in his hand.

'Well, this is very kind of you, Jake,' Nerissa said as she popped the lid on one of the curry sauces. Having given up on her lunch she was starving, her appetite very much restored by the sauce's sweet-spicy fragrance.

'It's nothing. Just my way of doing my bit and saying thank you to everyone for making Mum feel so welcome.'

'How is she?' Nerissa hadn't liked to ask earlier because things were still a bit raw between Jake and Linda, and she didn't want him to feel pressured.

A wry grin twisted his mouth. 'She seems really good. Doing a beginner's salsa class this evening, if you can believe it.' The way he said it made it clear he couldn't quite get his head around the idea.

Nerissa laughed. 'She's certainly taking turning a new leaf to heart – and good for her! I haven't had a chance to catch up with her this week, but I'll have to make a point of it now.'

Salsa classes! Nerissa wanted to clap her hands together with glee. Since their chat a few weeks previously, Linda had tried her hand at a pottery class, joined the local knitting circle and – with a bit of encouragement from Sylvia, who worked a couple of mornings a week at the local primary as a teaching assistant – was waiting on a DBS background check to be completed so she could lend a hand with some of the after-school activities. She was even considering investing in a wetsuit in order to join the local open water swimming group. Rather her than Nerissa, but it was just such a joy to see the other woman taking their conversation to heart and trying new things. *Unlike me.* She'd been full of determination to turn over a new leaf and yet here she was still bobbing around in the wake of other people's lives. Maybe she should reconsider the wetsuit idea and jump in at the deep end herself.

'Another?' Sylvia asked as she reached for the unopened bottle of wine.

Nerissa tapped the screen on her phone beside her and checked the time. It was just after seven, so even if she indulged a little, a walk on the beach and a couple of big glasses of water when she got home would stave off any potential hangover. 'Oh, go on then.'

'Good girl.' Sylvia grinned as she poured them both a generous measure. 'You can finish the rest,' she said to Laurie. 'You've got more tolerance than us old ladies.'

Nick laughed. 'Come off it, Mum, you know what a shandy-lightweight she is. She'll be suffering for days if she has another glass.'

'I'm not the one who was cuddling up to the toilet last weekend, was I?' Laurie shot back at her brother as she lifted her glass and held it out for their mother to fill.

Nick protested, 'That was a one-off after Darren's stag night, and I still went out on the boat that morning.' Nick and their Uncle Tony – Sylvia's older brother – ran a boat tour business operating out of the old harbour just over the crest from the main seafront. As well as sightseeing tours to the string of islands situated off the end of the Point, they ran deep-sea fishing trips and helped out the local conservation group when they needed to visit the larger islands in the chain which made up a local wildlife preserve.

'Maybe so, but your face was as green as the Hulk's,' Andrew chipped in as he pulled the beer bucket closer. 'I think I'll look after these now.'

Nerissa laughed as she watched her brother and nephew play-scuffle over the bucket, while Sylvia rolled her eyes and pointedly looked past them.

'Busy tonight,' she observed. 'I guess we weren't the only ones feeling the heat.'

'People have got that Friday feeling a day early,' Nerissa agreed, following Sylvia's gaze towards the bar. 'Ha! So much for a quiet night in front of the TV,' she exclaimed, catching sight of Doc perched on his usual stool by the bar.

Sitting up straighter, she looked past her niece's shoulder and could see Toby curled up at Doc's feet. He looked hot and miserable, his nose tucked between his front paws. He'd probably thought he was getting an extra evening walk, not a short trot to the pub, poor thing. At least someone had put a bowl of water down for him. Deciding she would rescue him as soon as she'd finished her drink, Nerissa leaned back, only for Sylvia to reach across and pat her arm.

'Who is *that*?' Sylvia was pointing somewhere behind Nerissa, making no attempt at keeping her voice down.

Nerissa cast a quick glance over her shoulder and froze as her eyes clashed with those of the stranger who'd just entered the pub. Shock thrilled through her, like a static overload as he held her gaze for a long moment before his lips curled into a smile that threatened to stop her heart. His features in repose were quite stern thanks to a strong jawline and a nose that wouldn't have looked out of place on a Roman emperor's coin. That smile changed everything though, lighting up his eyes and displaying the kind of lines that spoke of an easy sense of humour. When he raised the thick brows curving over his deep-set eyes, Nerissa came back to herself and spun around – horrified she'd been caught staring.

'Well, that was a moment if ever I saw one!' Sylvia crowed, clutching her hands to her heart and swooning back in her seat. 'A proper *their eyes met across a crowded room*, like you normally only read about in books.'

'Stop it!' Nerissa hissed as she grabbed her wine and took a gulp so large Jake had to pat her on the back as she choked on it. 'I'm fine, I'm fine,' she gasped when she could draw in air, wondering whether it might be a good idea to slide off her seat and hide under the table. She cast a glance to her left, or maybe she could vault over the open side of the pub wall and make her escape into the not-very-dark. Damn these long summer nights when the sun didn't set until nearly ten o'clock.

'Oh.' Sylvia's face fell. 'False alarm on the hot man front, he's got a couple of kids with him.'

She would not look around. She would not look around. Nerissa's will power lasted all of thirty seconds before she grabbed Jake's arm. 'Sit still a minute,' she said before using him as a shield to peer around. Sure enough, the man was heading towards the bar with a couple of teenagers following on his heels. She watched as he pointed to a small table in the corner and the older girl led the boy towards it, pulling out her phone the moment her bottom hit the cushion. The man continued towards the bar, taking up position next to Doc. As she watched them shake hands, she couldn't help a little sigh over how friendly he seemed.

'Can I move yet?' Jake asked, laughter in his words.

'Shh, and no you can't,' Nerissa replied because as she watched it became clear it was more than a casual greeting being shared by the stranger and Doc. The old man was patting a spare stool next to him and – even more shockingly – had pulled out his wallet to buy a drink. *What on earth was going on?*

7

'No, it's fine, I'll get these,' Tom protested as Malcolm Gadd produced his wallet from inside the pocket of a smart pair of chinos. The temperature was still pushing the high twenties, and he could already feel a trickle of sweat rolling down his back, but the elder man looked as fresh as if he'd just stepped from the shower. 'I've got the kids with me,' he continued, pointing to where Emily and Max were both hunched over their phones. At least they weren't fighting, unlike the interminable car journey earlier. If he'd had any sense, he would've put the other doctor off for a day or two and given himself time to get the children settled into their holiday let and to find his bearings. But if he'd had any sense, would he be thinking about upending his family and transferring them to a little village in the back of beyond in the first place?

He'd been idly flicking through his latest copy of the *British Journal of General Practice*, earmarking articles he wanted to read and having a nose around in the classified section when the striking image of a sprawling white building framed by a sky so blue it had to have been digitally enhanced caught his eye. The somewhat terse text accompanying the image had further sparked his interest – 'Partnership opportunity supporting small rural community. Current incumbent retiring. Call Malcolm Gadd for more details.'

When he'd done as the advert suggested and called Malcolm, he'd been even less forthcoming, telling Tom he'd only talk to him face-to-face and he'd need to see Mermaids Point for himself.

Mermaids Point. Who could resist a name like that? Not Tom, who was a bit of a romantic at heart.

A quick Google search had brought up a bunch of articles about a pop star and a viral video campaign as well as scores of images of a long stretch of beach and rows of quaint shops and old-fashioned cottages.

It'd been ages since he'd taken the kids away on holiday – there'd been a disastrous escape too soon after Anna's death which he'd allowed some friends to talk him into, and which had put them off the idea of holidays altogether. When they had explained that they had a villa already booked and no-of-course-it-wouldn't-be-too-much-trouble, he'd been in no fit state to make any kind of a decision beyond a howling need to just not be in the place – now a terrible void – where Anna had been their everything. Instead of giving him and the children a neutral space to talk about their feelings, Tom had found Claire, their hostess, just a little too eager to delve into their grief. It had been disappointing, if not altogether surprising when he'd had a message from another mutual friend about an intrusive Facebook post Claire had put up, including photos of Emily and Max without his permission. It was only after he'd hustled the kids out of the villa and they'd been in the queue for the next available flight back to the UK that Max had confided his tearful relief at them leaving because one of Claire's boys had been picking on him.

When he'd suggested a week at the seaside, Tom had used the recent news reports as an excuse for choosing Mermaids Point, saying they could go mermaid hunting. Emily had rolled her eyes, but he'd seen a glimmer of excitement behind the façade – she'd been obsessed with Aurora Storm, the pop star behind the stunt which had put the village front and centre in popular attention – and had seemed impressed he'd secured them a holiday cottage in such a sought-after location.

Malcolm Gadd had helped him find somewhere to stay – a last-minute cancellation he'd heard about on the grapevine. Not that they'd seen much of the cottage. A horrendous accident on the M5 had led to miles of tailbacks. With his temper at breaking point as Emily and Max started another pointless argument, he'd grit his teeth until the traffic crawled level with a motorway services and turned off. Full of McDonald's and with Max ordered into the front passenger seat to give Emily space to spread out, they'd re-joined the queue and limped along for another hour before their exit had blessedly come into view. With only ten minutes to go before he was due to meet Malcolm, Tom had herded the children into the pretty – if tiny – cottage in the heart of the village with instructions to dump their bags and have a pee so they could go exploring. They'd seemed unbothered when he'd mentioned meeting an old colleague and steered them into the pub a few minutes later, their noses glued to their phones, headphones cutting them off from the world around them.

They barely glanced up as he now placed a couple of Cokes and a packet of crisps to share on the table in front of them. He stared at the crooked little crown of hair revealed by a too-short summer trim on Max's bent head and wondered if other parents felt this same helpless sense of disconnection. How was it possible to know these two little souls as well as his own, and yet feel like they were strangers to him at the same time?

Once this meeting with Malcolm was over, he would put everything he had into the next few days. Though they'd only glimpsed it over the railing, the beach looked as encouraging as the pictures he'd seen and was begging to be explored. No phones other than for taking pictures, he promised himself as he returned to the bar, where the older man was waiting patiently for him.

'They'll spend so much time staring at those phones, they'll miss out on life,' Malcolm observed as Tom took the stool opposite him and reached for the blessedly cold pint of lager which had already soaked the beermat beneath it with drips of condensation.

The comment cut a little too close to the bone and Tom couldn't hide a wince as he raised his glass to his lips.

'No offence,' Malcolm added quickly. 'I mean, most kids these days are the same.' He swept a dismissive arm towards the crowded bar in front of them, 'Most of the adults too.'

Tom glanced around and had to agree. Everywhere he looked, people were fiddling with their phones or tablets. He even spotted a couple in the far corner with a tablet propped on a folding stand, sharing a pair of earphones. Each to their own, he supposed, but he couldn't quite get the point of sitting in a pub to watch something when they probably had a decent flatscreen at home.

'I know what you mean. We're all hooked on our gadgets these days. I'm hoping to get them off the phones tomorrow and get out exploring. Is there anything you recommend?'

'Well, there's the beach, of course, and a nice footpath that'll take you right to the top of the Point. The view from there is beautiful enough to make your heart sing.' Malcolm patted his chest and gave him a sheepish grin as he added, 'Even one as old as mine.'

'You look fitter than me,' Tom scoffed, not entirely joking. He and Anna used to run regularly when they were younger, and then when the children had been little, they were always on the go, so it had been easy to keep the weight off. He found himself sucking in the little curve of stomach that threatened to creep over his waistband and added exercise to his list of things he needed to get on top of. The list was expanding as quickly as his mid-forties spread.

As he studied the older man, he struggled to put an age to him. The deep lines on his face and a smattering of liver spots on the thinning skin of the back of his hand spoke of an age the rigidity of his spine and his hawk-bright gaze seemed to contradict.

'I do my best,' Malcolm said, 'but it pains me to admit it, these old bones of mine ache too much at the end of the day.'

'Hey, Doc!' a voice called from across the bar. 'Shelly needs a repeat, can I pick it up in the morning?'

'No problem,' Doc replied, without batting an eyelid. 'I'll leave one on reception for you.'

'Cheers, Doc, you're a life saver!' The man raised his drink, a gesture Malcolm returned before taking a large swig from his pint.

'Now then,' he said to Tom, setting his glass back down. 'Where were we?'

'Does that sort of thing happen often?' Tom nodded towards the man who'd called out who was now laughing at something with his group of mates. He hadn't taken into consideration this aspect of village life – everyone knowing who you were when you were a prominent figure in the community and expecting you to be at their beck and call, even in the local pub.

'Why did you become a doctor?' Malcolm countered, ignoring his question. 'More specifically, why did you become a GP?'

Taken aback, Tom paused to consider the point. He'd loved science at school and always been fascinated by the complexities of the human body. He couldn't point to a defining event in his life like so many of his peers at medical school had claimed to have experienced, nor even remember it being a conscious decision. Being a doctor was just something he'd felt like he'd always wanted to do.

The choice to become a GP rather than specialise had involved a more complex series of factors. He'd met Anna by then and already knew he wanted to build a life and a family with her. The stability of a more regular routine after the madness of junior doctor's hours, as well as the realisation he wanted to establish long-term relationships with his patients, had steered his thinking towards general practice. He'd never been ruthless enough during his surgical rotation to push himself to the fore, and the constant pressure of A & E was one for the adrenaline junkies. Being a GP was a deeper investment and required a lot of things that seemed to come naturally to him. Specialisations each had their own highs and lows, but he got to see a bit of everything, from the nervous excitement of expectant mothers to easing the passing at the end of a life well-lived. It was a privilege even on the days it weighed heavily.

'I like helping people.'

Malcolm nodded as though he'd passed some kind of test. 'Folks round here need more help than most.'

Before he could say any more, a man Tom judged to be in his mid-fifties came and stood next to Malcolm. 'There you are, Doc, mind if I grab a quick word?' The expectant look on his face said he clearly didn't expect Malcolm to mind.

'Hello, Keith. This is a colleague of mine, Tom Nelson.'

'Very nice, I'm sure,' Keith said, barely giving Tom a first, never mind a second glance. 'Now, look, I'm certain it's nothing, but I gave my leg a bump the other day and it's still not right.' Not giving Malcolm a chance to respond, Keith propped his foot on the wooden bar of the doctor's stool, almost kicking the poor dog curled up on the floor, and began tugging his trouser leg up.

Tom took one glance at the ugly wound on Keith's leg before looking away, appalled at the man's lack of discretion, as much as his foolishness in leaving an injury that nasty for so long without getting it looked at. The self-neglect he could forgive – it was nothing new, especially with a certain generation, and he knew pride and fear were a deadly combination in too many men when it came to seeking medical advice. Asking for a repeat prescription was one thing, but expecting Malcolm to run an impromptu clinic in public like this was a step too far.

'Looks a bit ripe, doesn't it, Keith? Hurts a bit and all, I bet?' Malcolm seemed unperturbed about the unconventional setting. All his attention was on the man before him, who visibly deflated the moment Malcolm spoke, as though he'd puffed up all his courage in the moments before he'd approached them, and it was already deserting him.

'Hurts like the devil. I cleaned it up and put a bit of Savlon on it, but the bloody thing won't mend. I can't be off work for this kind of nonsense.'

The edge of desperation in those last words tugged at Tom's conscience. 'We could pop over to the surgery and take a better look, if you like?' he found himself saying.

Keith turned to give him a proper look as Malcolm said, 'That sounds like a capital plan.'

'I... I don't want to put you to no trouble,' Keith said, his cheeks reddening.

Bit late for that.

'It's no trouble,' Tom lied. He cast a sorry glance at his barely touched pint still sweating on the bar, then turned to check the kids still had a drink. The kids! He couldn't just leave them stranded in a pub full of strangers. 'Hang on a sec.'

Emily looked up as he reached their table. 'All right?' she said, a shade too loud because she hadn't taken out her headphones.

Tom pointed at her ears and tried to suppress a grin at the exaggerated sigh only a teenage girl was capable of as she removed the buds. 'I need to give Malcolm a hand at the surgery for a few minutes.'

'Who's Malcolm?'

'The colleague I told you about, remember?' When Emily continued to stare blankly, he sighed. 'Look, it doesn't matter, I just need you and Max to come.'

'But why? We're fine here.'

'I haven't finished my Coke,' Max piped up, having finally looked up from his phone.

'I'll get you another one. I can't leave you here on your own.' Tom swallowed down the sharpness creeping into his tone because none of this was their fault. 'And a pickled egg, if you like?' It was a silly joke, harking back to a time when Max had been nine or ten and insisted on trying one from a jar he'd seen on the bar in a long-forgotten pub they'd been to for Sunday lunch. The more he and Anna had protested he wouldn't like it, the more insistent he'd become, until, in the end, Anna had shrugged and ordered one. With all the stubborn pride he possessed, Max had worked his way through the bloody thing like it was better than the best chocolate in the world, his little face growing greener with every chomp of his jaws. He'd lasted all of thirty seconds before Tom had whipped him off his feet and carted him into the gents just in time for the return trip.

As he'd hoped, Emily started to giggle while Max scowled for a moment before he too started laughing. 'I'll pass, thanks.'

Tom crouched before them. 'I'm sorry, I'll make it up to you, I promise.'

'It's all right, Dad,' Max said in a world-weary tone. 'Helping people is what you do.'

Swallowing an expected lump in his throat, Tom rose to his feet and turned away. They sacrificed so much with so little complaint. He *would* make it up to them.

While the children gathered their things, he moved back to where Malcolm was shrugging into a jacket that had been hanging unnoticed on a peg behind him as he urged the retriever to his feet. Was it possible for a dog to look resigned, because Tom swore there was the same here-we-go-again expression in his eyes as in Max's.

Keith repeated his protests but was hushed into abashed silence by a wave of Malcolm's hand.

'Is everything okay?' A soft voice spoke at his shoulder and Tom turned, wondering who else had come to join their little circus.

He stopped dead, face-to-face with *her*. He'd been trying not to think about her since that unexpected locking of eyes as he'd walked into the pub. Close up, she was even more striking, with wide dark eyes and a decadent tumble of rich black curls spilling around her face and halfway down her back. Those pretty eyes widened, the soft bow of her lips opening in a little oh, and he wanted to...

Tom wrenched his train of thought back so violently he took a physical step back, almost bumping into poor Keith in the process. 'Sorry,' he muttered, not sure who he was apologising to.

'Ah, Nerissa!' Malcolm greeted the woman. 'Perfect timing. Could you be a dear and take Toby? We just need to pop back to the surgery for a few minutes with Keith.' The way he said *we* clearly included Tom.

'You must be a mind-reader,' the woman, *Nerissa*, said with a smile. 'I was just coming to rescue him for a walk on the beach, poor thing.' She ducked down to scratch the retriever beneath his chin. The dog's tongue lolled in a blissful expression and Tom found himself wondering if Nerissa would pet him like that.

Where the hell had that come from?

Coughing to cover the heady rush of embarrassment coursing through him, Tom glanced away to where Emily and Max were waiting. His son was staring at his phone, but Emily was watching him with the same intensity a hawk watches a mouse. The dog came to his rescue, squeezing between Tom and Nerissa, his wagging tail swiping Tom's leg on the way through as he bounded up to the children. Though the subject of a pet had been raised several times over the years, Tom had stood firm on the subject, wanting them to be a little bit older and able to take on the responsibility that came with it. Then Anna had got sick and it'd become another missed opportunity to regret.

Perhaps sensing their hesitancy and unfamiliarity, Nerissa stepped closer and placed a hand on the dog's head. The retriever sat at once, his lolling smile still fixed on the children. 'This is Toby. He's very friendly, if a bit licky at times. You can pet him if you like.'

Max beamed a grin so wide it threatened to split his cheeks. Shoving his phone in his back pocket, he hunkered down to stroke the dog, his awkward moves growing in confidence as Toby shifted to lean his weight against the boy's shoulder. 'Good boy.' Max grinned up at Tom. 'I think he likes me.'

'I think he does,' Tom agreed, his heart feeling like it might burst from his chest. When was the last time he'd seen his lovely lad smile with such unbridled joy?

'I'm fine,' Emily said when Nerissa gave her a questioning look. 'He's a nice dog, though,' she continued hurriedly, as though concerned she might have caused offence.

'He's a menace, but I adore him,' Nerissa said, making Emily smile and Tom want to hug her for her gentle empathy. This stranger didn't know anything about his children, but she was being kind and careful of them, and he was grateful for it. Even more grateful a few moments later when she said, 'I'm taking him for a walk on the beach. Would you like to come with me?'

Max's head snapped up. 'Can we?'

'Sorry, I shouldn't have put you on the spot like that.'

With her addressing the comment directly at him, Tom didn't have any choice but to look at Nerissa. He focused on her chin, not wanting to meet her gaze and get caught in another embarrassing eye-lock. 'It's kind of you to offer, but you don't have to.'

She shrugged, the gesture causing a ripple of wild curls to fall forward. 'It's no trouble. We'll just be heading down onto the beach, along the waterline and back up the steps at the other end and to the surgery.'

'I don't want you to go out of your way,' Tom protested again, but there was no force in it. He couldn't see any harm in it – they'd be in the open at all times and though the sun was drawing down it was still light enough outside. Besides, this slip of a woman wasn't much bigger than Emily, and Tom sensed nothing but a willingness to help from her. It would also give the children a chance to explore a bit rather than being dragged from pillar to post.

She laughed as though he'd made some hilarious joke. 'It's not out of my way.' Turning to the children, she gestured towards the door. 'Come on then...'

Tom watched the three of them – and the dog – walk away. When Max turned his head up to say something to Nerissa, she placed a soft hand to his back, laughing at whatever he'd said. His son seemed to grow before his eyes, like a flower unfurling at the touch of the sun's rays.

'She's part of the deal, you know?' Malcolm said at his shoulder, startling Tom's attention away for a moment.

'I'm sorry?'

'Nerissa.' Malcolm nodded at the last flash of dark hair disappearing out the door. 'She works for me at the surgery. When you take over, I expect you to keep her on.'

'Oh. Well, yes of course. I wouldn't dream of putting anyone out of a job.'

'Or a home, I trust,' Malcolm said with a pat on his shoulder. 'She's the live-in housekeeper as well as my receptionist. You'll be glad of an extra pair of hands, no doubt, with two children to manage.' Barely pausing to draw breath, he turned to Keith, 'Right then, let's get that leg of yours sorted.'

It wasn't until he and Malcolm were helping Keith hobble up the steps in front of a sprawling white building at the end of the seafront that Tom realised both he and Malcolm had been talking as if his move to Mermaids Point was a done deal.

He paused on the threshold to glance up at the pretty window boxes stuffed with sunny marigolds and trailing ivy. It was the kind of welcoming touch a woman would think of. He pictured the stone pots Anna had framed their doorstep with in London now dusty with barren soil, the seasonal door wreaths she'd made now gathering dust in the cupboard under the stairs. As he followed the men inside, he thought of Max, glowing under Nerissa's gentle attention, and knew in his heart he wanted to see his boy smile like that every day.

8

'Wait there,' Nerissa called as they wove their way through the group of people who'd spilled out of the pub onto the pavement. As the children halted obediently at the kerb, she realised she didn't even know their names. Deciding it could wait until they were safely on the beach, she checked the road both ways before smiling at the girl. 'Sorry, I'm sure you're both sensible enough to cross the road on your own, but indulge an old lady. It's not a busy road, but there's always one person who doesn't think and drives too fast. We're heading for those steps, just over there.' She pointed a little to the right.

'You're not old!' the girl said, winning Nerissa's loyalty forever. 'And don't worry, Dad is much worse when it comes to stuff like this, so we're used to it. I can't believe how quiet it is here,' the girl said as they made their way across. 'Even in the evenings, there's always loads of traffic on our street.'

'It'll be bumper-to-bumper at the weekend,' Nerissa replied. 'We get a lot of day trippers as well as people who choose to stay.' She made sure to hold onto Toby's lead as they negotiated the steps. He wasn't a badly behaved dog, but he knew the steps meant the beach and the beach meant he could run, and he was already quivering with anticipation. The last thing she needed was him bumping into one of the children and potentially knocking them down the steps.

The moment her foot touched the pebbles at the base she bent to unclip the lead and Toby barrelled away, tail flying madly. With a whoop, the boy set off in pursuit, leaving Nerissa and his older sister alone.

'I'm so sorry, we didn't get introduced earlier,' Nerissa offered her hand. 'I'm Nerissa.'

The girl eyed her hand for a moment before taking it in a quick grip and release. 'I'm Emily; that's Max.' She nodded at her brother who was chasing Toby up and down the same short stretch of beach, his laughter and the dog's happy barking rising up on the currents of the warm evening air.

'Pleased to meet you. Are you staying in the Point long?' Nerissa tucked the lead in her back pocket as they made their way across the pebbles towards the thin strip of sand which was rapidly disappearing under the evening tide.

'The Point, is that what you call it? I like that. We're here for a week.' Emily pulled her long blonde hair out of its scrunchy, smoothed some escaped strands back from her forehead, and twisted it all up on her head in the kind of messy, nonchalant topknot Nerissa could only dream of achieving. Though she loved her hair, it was too thick and had too much of a life of its own to be tamed by anything other than a plait or a tightly wound bun. A gust of wind sent her curls flying everywhere – proving her point – and she fished an elastic from her pocket and braided the mass with quick familiarity. 'I love your hair,' Emily said, watching her as she settled the plait between her shoulder blades.

'I was just thinking the same thing about yours. It's so smooth and silky.'

'Thanks.' Emily raised a hand to touch her topknot, a sweet blush creeping onto her cheeks as though she wasn't used to compliments. 'Have you always lived here?' she asked as they strolled along, following the track of paw and footprints in the sand.

'All my life. My family has been here for generations. My brother and his wife run a gift shop and their daughter, Laurie, runs the café next door. Her cakes are to die for – you'll have to get your dad to take you in for afternoon tea while you're here.'

'Don't you get bored, though? I can't think there's much to do around here.'

Nerissa considered the question rather than leaping to instant defence of the village she loved. It'd been a long time since she was a teenager, and though she'd always been content here, many – Gareth included – had found the smallness of life in the Point confining rather than comforting. 'I go through phases of loving it and "get me out of here". I had a chance to leave when I was a bit older than you are now, but it didn't work out.'

'What happened?' When she didn't answer immediately, Emily swung round to face her. 'Sorry, that was rude of me to ask.'

Nerissa patted her arm. 'No, it's fine. I was madly in love with a boy who couldn't wait to leave the village. I would've followed him anywhere, but he died in an accident and my life took a different path. I lost my sense of adventure after that. Nowadays, I'm a bit too comfortable in the rut I've made to change. The people I love most in the world are all here, and that's what matters to me.'

'My mum died a couple of years ago and now I don't know

what to do about anything any more.' Shoulders stiff around her ears, Emily turned away to stare out to sea. The last rays of the setting sun had burnished the waves a brilliant gold.

Nerissa felt the pain in the girl's voice like a fist around her heart. Losing Gareth had been devastating, but she'd had the solid bedrock of her family holding her up. When her mum had died not long before Nerissa's fortieth birthday, it had still been far too soon, but having the centre of your family ripped away at Emily's age was unfathomable to Nerissa, even with her own experiences as reference. As the sun dipped further below the horizon, the sea turned from gold to the red-black of a rose's petals. She could mouth a load of platitudes, the same things this poor girl must've heard a thousand times, or she could steer their conversation in another direction. 'I'm forty-three and I still don't know what I'm doing with my life.'

Emily's giggle sounded a little wet, but her voice was steady when she spoke. 'Dad says I can take a year out before I start my A levels.'

Nerissa cast a quick look down the beach to where Max and Toby were still chasing each other around. They weren't far, but far enough away they wouldn't overhear them. 'And is that something you might want to do?'

'I don't know. I think I messed up a couple of my exams – I haven't told him that,' Emily rushed the last bit out.

'I won't say anything.' When Emily stayed silent, Nerissa decided to give her some space. 'I'm going to rescue Max before he and Toby both end up soaking wet.' She placed a gentle hand on Emily's shoulder. 'Catch us up when you're ready. The words we give to the sea are heard only by the waves.' It was something her mum had always said to her when she was growing up and feeling frustrated, and Nerissa had taken them to heart. Whenever she needed to get things off her chest, she either spoke them to Gareth in the stillness of the churchyard, or she came down here to the beach and stood much as Emily was now.

Emily nodded, her attention still fixed on the far horizon.

Jogging a few paces away to give Emily as much privacy as she wanted, Nerissa raised an arm and waved at Max. 'Hey! Not too close to the edge now.' As she drew nearer, she realised her words were in vain because the bottom few inches of Max's jeans were darker than the rest and his trainers made a squishing sound as he ran up, Toby on his heels. 'No! Don't you dare,' Nerissa warned the dog as he braced his legs in a stance she recognised. 'If you're going to shake, you do it over there.' She pointed up the beach.

Toby gave her his best innocent eyes, not budging an inch.

'No!' Nerissa cried, a little desperately as she moved Max behind her just in time to shield him from the sand and salt spray the retriever sent flying into the air as he gave himself a huge shake from tail to nose and back again. She glanced down at the spatters marring her clean T-shirt and capri pants. 'Oh, *Toby.*' To add insult to injury, he had the cheek to stick his nose into the palm of her hand as though expecting a treat!

Max peeked around her, took one look at the mess and started giggling. When Nerissa raised an eyebrow at him, he clapped a hand over his mouth to try and stifle his amusement, but there was no hiding the way his shoulders were shaking up and down. 'Sorry,' he managed, sounding not in the least bit repentant.

'I don't know what's so funny, young man,' Nerissa said, her voice mock-stern as she folded her arms. 'I'm the one who's going to have to explain to your dad about the state you're in.' She looked down at his soaking-wet legs and feet. 'You could've at least taken off your trainers.'

'I didn't think about it until it was too late,' Max admitted, expression growing sheepish. 'Don't worry, I'll tell him it wasn't your fault.'

He sounded so sweetly earnest, Nerissa couldn't help reaching out to touch his cheek. 'No, you're all right.' She made a big show of glancing at the dog, then leaned close to whisper in Max's ear. 'We'll tell him it was Toby's fault.'

'Okay,' Max whispered back, and then they were both laughing. 'Should I take them off now, do you think?' he said a few moments later, lifting one leg to display a soggy foot.

'Bit late now, and it'll be hard work getting back over the pebbles in your bare feet. We'll head for the surgery and you can dry off a bit. If your dad's still busy with Doc and Keith we can chuck your trainers in the tumble dryer for a few minutes.' Nerissa checked behind them and was relieved to see Emily making her way towards them. 'Here's your sister, now.' She raised her voice to include the approaching girl. 'I've got some ice cream in the freezer if you fancy a scoop?'

Emily looked a little wan as she drew up beside them, but her lips lifted in a small smile. 'That sounds nice.' She took in the state of her brother. 'Max! What happened to you?'

With a cheeky grin that would get him out of trouble – and into a lot more of it in a few years' time if Nerissa had any money on it – Max held a finger to his lips. 'Shh, it was Toby's fault,' he whispered. 'But we don't want to upset him.'

Nerissa couldn't hold in a burst of laughter. Honestly, this boy was clearly too clever for his own good, but so cute with it she could see him getting away with murder if left unchecked. 'You get an extra scoop, Emily, because you managed to keep your feet dry.'

'Hey, no fair!' Max protested as Emily gave him an evil grin.

'Come on, you two.' Nerissa ushered them up the beach towards the other set of steps nearest the surgery. Toby, full of excitement at having made a new friend, darted in circles around them, tail wagging and uncaring of the salt already drying in his thick coat. He'd need another bath, but not tonight. Tonight he could have an extra towel in his bed and make do – a soggy dog was a problem best tackled in the morning.

* * *

She got the children settled at the scrubbed pine kitchen table with a bowl of mint choc chip each and Max's trainers bumping around inside the dryer, then slipped through the connecting door into the surgery. The corridor was dark, but light was spilling out from the open door of the room they used for minor injuries, and she could hear the low murmur of masculine voices. Pausing in the corridor, she rapped her knuckles on the door frame, keeping her back to the open door in case Keith was in a state of undress. She heard the snap of surgical gloves being removed, but it was Tom, not Doc who came out to speak to her.

'Everything okay?' He glanced over her shoulder as though expecting her to have brought the children in with her.

'Everything's fine. They're in the kitchen.' She pointed towards the door that led to the accommodation part of the building, light visible through its frosted pane of glass. 'I've given them a bit of ice cream, I hope you don't mind.'

Tom laughed, a deep, rich sound that made something long dormant inside her stir in lazy interest. 'They'll love you forever. We're nearly done here.' He nodded his head towards the surgery door. 'Just as well Keith spoke to Malcolm when he did because another day and he might not have been so lucky.'

'What happened?' Nerissa asked. When Tom frowned as if she had no business asking, she rolled her eyes a little. 'I'll see it in the morning when I update his records on the computer. I just meant, is he all right?'

'Oh, of course you will, sorry. Nasty gash on his leg that's got infected. We've cleaned it out and given him a few stitches. Malcolm just needs to give him an antibiotic injection while I finish dressing it.'

Nerissa peeked inside to see Doc and Keith chatting away. Crooking a finger, she indicated to Tom to lean closer – he was at least as tall as her brother, though of slimmer build, and she didn't want Keith to overhear what she had to say next. 'You'll have to hold his hand,' she murmured.

'Malcolm or Keith's?'

The teasing question caught her off guard and Nerissa found herself staring a little too closely into a pair of warm hazel eyes edged with smile lines. If he leaned any further down, or she rose up a fraction on her tiptoes they'd be close enough to... 'Oh.' She stepped back before the rest of that dangerous and highly inappropriate thought could crystallise. 'Um...' God, what had they been talking about? Keith! 'Keith!' she said, a little too loudly.

'Yes?' Keith's voice came from inside the treatment room.

Oh, bloody hell! 'I was just wondering if you wanted a cup of tea? While Doc finishes up, I mean.' She didn't dare look up at Tom for fear she'd catch him laughing at her awkwardness.

'That'd be grand. You're a good girl, Nerissa. She's a good girl, your Nerissa,' he echoed himself, the point clearly aimed at Doc.

'She is,' Doc agreed, appearing in the doorway. 'The surgery would be lost without you. I bet you'd give your hind leg for someone like Nerissa to help you out, wouldn't you, Tom?'

What? Why on earth was he dragging Tom into this

impromptu love-fest? Cheeks flaming, Nerissa gave Doc a quick smile as she backed away. 'Yes, well, I'll get those teas, shall I?' she stammered out before spinning on her heel and not quite running away, her hand unconsciously seeking the comfort of the ring dangling on her necklace.

9

Waking the next morning, it took Tom several seconds to orientate himself. The ceiling above him was wrong – a sea of creamy Artex dimples instead of the brilliant white smoothness he was used to. It was normally only his heart that ached in these moments between sleep and full consciousness before his brain once more processed the absence of Anna, but this morning his left hip was screaming at him to move. Stretching his leg, Tom immediately forgot the pain in his hip as his toes connected with a solid footboard. He reared back, only to bang his head. 'Jesus Christ!'

'Dad?' The sleepy voice of his son scattered the last of Tom's confusion, setting him firmly in the present and the second bedroom of the little cottage in the heart of the village of Mermaids Point.

'I'm fine.' He checked his watch – not even six. 'Go back to sleep, Maxy.'

'Mkay.' The muffled reply came from the depths of the quilt.

When they'd returned from the surgery the previous night, it hadn't felt like a hardship to offer the main bedroom with its

double bed to Emily. She was of an age where privacy was important, and Max had been delighted at the idea of he and Tom
bunking down together in the pair of single beds set against
opposite walls in the smaller room. It hadn't occurred to Tom to
check the measurement of the beds until he'd climbed in last
night and realised they were a good half a foot lacking for a frame
as tall as his. It wouldn't have been so bad without the head and
footboards. Tom resolved to check the kitchen drawers for some
tools after breakfast. With any luck, he'd be able to unbolt them
and give himself a bit more space.

Sunlight beamed through the window above Max's bed –
likely what had woken Tom in the first place. He glanced once
more at the lumpen shape in the opposite bed and contemplated
curling up and tugging his own quilt over his head. The twinge in
his hip warned him to not even think about it, followed swiftly by
his bladder waking up and making its own needs felt.

Taking care to avoid the open suitcases spilling their contents
into the middle of the floor, Tom tiptoed across the room to tug
the curtains closed, then made his way towards the door. With
unerring accuracy, he managed to locate every squeaking floor-
board, but Max didn't so much as stir – not even when the old-
fashioned latch clunked as Tom pressed it.

Leaving his son to sleep, Tom used the bathroom and cleaned
his teeth. He considered a shower but decided it was too bloody
early to squeeze his body under the showerhead which was set
halfway up the wall. Wondering if everything in the cottage had
been fitted to Lilliputian dimensions, he made his way down the
short hallway to check on Emily. Her door was open a fraction
and as he pushed it open, he heard a soft voice he didn't recognise. 'Em?'

'Hey, Dad.'

Taking that as an invitation, he pushed the door wide and

found her sitting cross-legged on the bed, the contents of her rucksack scattered across the sheet beside her. A sketchpad was balanced across her knees, and he caught a glimpse of the shadows of a pencil drawing darkening its white surface before she lowered a protective hand to cover it. Tom swallowed a sigh at the way she felt the need to hide things from him. 'Everything all right?'

Shoving a handful of tangled hair off her face, she nodded. 'I woke up and couldn't get back to sleep, so I thought I'd listen to my book.' Her gaze moved to the phone on the pillow next to her, the source of the voice he'd heard. 'I didn't wake you, did I?'

'Not at all,' Tom reassured her. 'I'm a bit stiff this morning – too many hours in the car and sleeping in a sm— different bed.' He corrected himself just in time. It had been his choice to offer Emily this room and he wouldn't make her feel guilty and start the week off on a bad note. She had a tendency to take even the most innocuous things to heart. 'I'm going to make a cup of coffee. Do you want anything?' The owners of the cottage had left a welcome pack of basic staples, but he'd have to sort out some food shopping today.

'I'll have some juice.' There'd been a carton of long-life orange juice on the counter next to one of milk and he'd put them both in the fridge last night. She folded the sketchpad closed. 'I'll come down for it.'

'You look so settled there. I can bring it up,' Tom protested, then wished he'd kept his big mouth shut when her face fell. 'Though I'd love the company, if you don't mind – you can help me make a plan for the week, if you'd like?'

Emily brightened. 'Sounds good. I'll make a list.' She fished out a notebook from the pile of things on the bed and scrambled to her feet.

Tom waited while she tugged on a cardigan over the vest and

leggings she'd worn as pyjamas, then led the way down the steep, narrow stairs, ducking just in time to avoid whacking his forehead on a support beam. 'This cottage was built for midgets,' he grumbled, hunching his shoulders in exaggeration.

'You're just too tall,' his daughter countered, not trying to hide a smug grin when he glanced over his shoulder to see her raise her hands over her head to pat the beam as she passed easily under it.

'Somehow, I knew it would be my fault.'

'Embrace the reality of your life, it'll make things simpler.'

She had more cheek than the final scene in *The Full Monty*, but he just laughed, delighted she was bantering with him. 'Alas, I think you're right.'

While she settled at the kitchen table and opened a fresh page in her notebook, Tom pottered around filling the kettle and fetching the milk and juice from the fridge. There was a coffee machine in the corner, the cord wrapped around it in a way that said it wasn't used much. He tugged open a couple of drawers and cupboards but couldn't find any pods for it. It wasn't the same make as the one they had at home, but he might have a look in the supermarket – once he'd located the supermarket – and see if they had any of the right brand.

Drinks made, he took the seat opposite Emily and worked his way through the mental list he'd been putting together. 'Food shop. Proper look around the village. Tourist information?' He phrased the last as a question, unsure if somewhere as small as Mermaids Point would have such a thing.

'There was a rack with leaflets in it on the wall in the pub,' Emily said. 'I saw it as we were leaving with Nerissa.'

Nerissa. The one thing Tom had been trying desperately to keep off his mental list, because if he let his mind go there, he was transported instantly to that awkward moment in the darkened corridor. Awkward because she'd stepped into his personal space without him even noticing, and what made it worse was it'd felt like she was supposed to be there. For the past three years he'd worn his grief for Anna like a shield – like some kind of messed-up Ready Brek forcefield that kept everyone else away from the space beside him that had belonged to Anna since the day they'd met. He didn't want anyone else filling that gap. Or more truthfully perhaps, he didn't *want* to want anyone filling it because that would mean he was ready to close the door on Anna. And that felt like a betrayal.

'Dad?'

The uncertainty in Emily's voice dragged Tom from the precipice of yet another pity spiral. He thrust his hands into his hair, willing the dark thoughts away and forced a smile he didn't feel to tilt the corners of his lips. 'Sorry, I was thinking about what to do about breakfast.'

The lie landed between them, so obvious and heavy it did everything but thud on the table. She watched him for a long, silent moment before shaking her head in what looked unpleasantly like defeat and lowering her eyes to the notepad. Maybe he should be more open with her, but it was so hard to put his burdens on her slender shoulders. Emily shouldn't have to carry a single speck of his grief. He was the adult. He was the parent. It was his job to suck it up and cope with the shitty hand life had dealt them. He'd wait until that evening and the kids were in bed and give Alex a call. Misery loved a bit of company, and the only person with a more tragic personal life than Tom might just be his little brother. Tragic because, although the woman he'd loved beyond distraction was still alive, she was as out of reach as Anna was to Tom.

When Emily finally spoke, there was no inflection in her

voice. 'There's a café on the seafront. We could go there for breakfast.'

Knowing he'd hurt her, but not knowing how to avoid it without hurting her even more, Tom ignored the ache in his chest and stretched his smile wider. 'Is there? We should look up the opening times.' He reached for his phone. 'Any idea what it's called?'

She shook her head. 'Nerissa mentioned it. Someone in her family owns it, I think she said. Just search for cafés, there can't be that many in a place as small as this.'

'Good point.' Tom scanned the results generated by his maps app. A couple of cafés were flagged, but only one on the seafront. He clicked through to the information page. 'Looks like it opens at 8 a.m.' Placing his phone flat on the table, he slid it across to show Emily the pictures that had come up. 'It looks nice.'

'Laurie's Place,' Emily nodded. 'That must be it – I'm sure that's what Nerissa said her niece was called.' She scrolled through the photos, pausing on one showing a display case filled with tempting cakes and biscuits. 'Wow, look at those! Can we have cake for breakfast?'

She'd asked with a smile that said she was half-teasing, but Tom decided to run with it. 'We're on our holidays, sweetheart, you can have whatever you want.'

A pleased little glow lit her face. 'Do you really mean it?'

Tom nodded. 'Just don't make yourself sick.' He took the phone back and studied the photo. 'Those cakes do look incredible. I might have one as well. Maybe two, even.' He patted his stomach as it gave a little grumble of appreciation.

'I'd better wake Max. We can show you the beach before we eat – you haven't had a chance to see it yet.'

Emily was halfway out of her seat when Tom reached out and caught her hand. 'Hold on a minute.' His original plan had been to wait until the end of the week before broaching the subject of him taking over from Malcolm, but the children deserved the chance to explore the village and its surrounding area with the full facts before them. 'There's something I'd like to discuss with you first.'

Emily dropped back into her seat, her previous excitement replaced by a look of worry. 'Is something wrong?'

'No, nothing like that.' He reassured her. 'I... I've been thinking that things need to change. I need to change, I *want* to change, but it's not something I can do on my own. There are some big decisions to be made, and you and Max need to be included in making them.'

'Okay.' Emily hooked her hair over one shoulder and started playing with the strands – something she did when she was nervous or worried. 'Like what?'

'Nothing bad, I promise,' he replied, hurriedly. Tom wanted to kick himself for not thinking things through before speaking to her. Having suffered more than any child her age could be expected to cope with, she tended to fear the worst. 'First, I want to spend more time with you both. I've been spending too much time at work and I need that to change.'

Her gaze dropped to her lap. 'Is this because of, you know, what happened?'

'A bit.' When her head snapped up, Tom held up his hand. 'But only because I realised I didn't have any idea what was going on with you guys.' He swallowed, knowing he couldn't dance around the subject. 'I know it was easier for you to talk to your mum about stuff, but I want you to feel like you can come to me – and that's not possible if I'm never around.'

Emily swallowed. 'It would be nice if you were home a bit earlier.'

God, this was hard, Tom thought, as a jab of guilt shoved into his conscience. But he had no one to blame but himself. He'd seized this nettle and he was just going to have to let it sting until he'd said everything he needed to. 'And how do you feel about home? Our home, I mean. Do you like it there, or do you think you might like to try somewhere new?'

'You want to sell the house?' Emily's voice was fraught with anxiety.

'No! Not if you don't want me to. I just thought it might be a bit easier if we were somewhere else for a bit – somewhere we don't feel quite so sad all the time.' It was Tom's turn to swallow around the lump in his throat. 'If we had a little break away from the house, then when we went back we might remember more of the happy times there.'

'You want us to forget about Mum?' She said it in such a small voice it reminded him of the little girl who'd only need a kiss and a hug from her daddy to make everything better.

Tom shoved out of his chair so fast it clattered on the floor behind him as he rushed around to crouch at Emily's side. 'No, sweetheart. Never in a million years would I want you to do that – me either. I want us to be able to remember everything about her, and not just the fact that she's not here any more.'

Emily twisted on her chair until they were facing each other. 'But where would we go?'

'Anywhere you like. We've already talked about you taking a year out and Maxy's got another year before he has to think about his GCSE options so a change of school wouldn't be the end of the world for him.' Tom settled back on his heels. 'One of the reasons I brought you here to Mermaids Point is because Malcolm, the doctor I helped last night, is ready to retire and wants someone to take over his practice.'

'You... you want to move here?' Emily tucked her heel on the seat and propped her chin on her knee. 'Why here?'

Tom shrugged. 'Why not? Imagine waking up every morning with the sea right on your doorstep? Wouldn't that be more fun than the noise and fumes of the traffic in London? We'd live at the surgery, so I'd be right there whenever you need me.' He reached for her hand, stroking the delicate fingers so fine and fragile compared to his own. 'It's not a done deal, Em. It's not even halfway to being a deal, it's just something we could think about and that's why I wanted to be honest with you now, so you have some time to think about it while we get to know the place a bit better.'

'And if I didn't want to move here?' She sounded more curious than defensive, and Tom felt a flutter of pride in how well she was taking on board the possibility of such a big change.

'Then we don't do it. Same with Max. Moving to Mermaids Point – or anywhere else – has to be a unanimous decision between the three of us. No one gets a deciding vote – we're either all in or we're all out. That's why I wanted to talk to you while it's just the two of us. If you think it's a terrible idea, then we'll drop the whole thing and just enjoy ourselves for the week, but if you think it's something you might consider, then I'll have a chat with Max later and see how he feels about it.'

'What about our house in London?' A hint of worry had crept back into her tone.

Tom rubbed the bridge of his nose as he considered the best way to respond. 'That depends on how things work out. If we did decide to give Mermaids Point a go, we could give ourselves a trial run until next summer, say. We could rent the house out. I think we'd know well before then how we feel and if we don't want to stay, then I'd just have to look for someone to replace me as the doctor here.' It would be a bit more complicated than that, but those were things he'd address as and when they came to them. He wanted Emily and Max to have as much freedom to choose without feeling any burden or responsibility over those choices. He squeezed Emily's hand, then let it go. 'What does your gut say?'

She rested her chin on her knees as she pondered the question. 'That I'd like to think about it.'

Tom patted her leg as he rose, groaning when his left knee creaked in protest at him squatting for too long. 'When did I become an old man?'

Emily laughed. 'Ages ago.'

'Gee thanks, mate!' Tom hobbled around to his side of the table, making a show of it because he knew it would make her laugh again and there was no greater joy than hearing the carefree sound. When he'd sat down and taken a sip of his coffee, he settled back to regard his daughter. 'Do you want me to talk to Max about it, or wait for a bit to give you some time?'

She frowned for a long moment and he had to hide a smile at the intensity of the look. 'You can speak to him. Like you said, he has as much right to decide as we do.'

'Great, and thanks, Em, for being brave enough to even think about it. You've been through so much, the last thing I want is to stress you out.'

'You're my dad, it's what you do,' she said, but with enough of a smile he knew it was a continuation of their teasing and not a criticism.

'I try.' Tom toasted her with his mug when another thought came to him. He'd been trying hard to avoid thinking about Nerissa, but this was something that needed to be addressed head on. Hoping his voice wouldn't betray any of the unsettling feelings his close encounter with her had stirred up, he said, 'Hey, there's something else we have to consider in all this. Nerissa is Malcolm's housekeeper as well as working in the surgery. If we did decide to move here, then we have to think about her too. She might not want to take us all on if she's used to a quiet life, but we'd have to give her the option to stay – at least for a trial period. It wouldn't be fair to ask her to move out of her home straight away.'

'Oh, I hadn't thought about that.' That funny little frown creased Emily's brow once more and Tom wished again he was better at reading her.

'If I had to go out on call when someone was sick, it wouldn't mean leaving you alone in the house, if she was there.' When Emily's lips twisted in a mutinous expression, Tom raised a hand. 'I know you're more than capable of looking after both yourself and Max when I'm not around, but the point is you shouldn't have to. I've put too much expectation on you, Em, and that's not fair. If you want to go out with your friends, then you shouldn't have to babysit Max, for example.'

'I'd need some friends, first.' Her hands were back in her hair, fiddling and stroking the strands.

'That's something else we need to look into while we are here this week. I don't want you guys stuck here with no one your own age to get to know. We can ask around about clubs and activities – find out if there are other families around with teenagers.'

'Nerissa might know. She said she's lived here all her life. And she'd know everyone anyway if she works at the surgery.'

There was something in the way Emily kept mentioning Nerissa so easily that gave Tom some hope. 'You like her.'

Emily shrugged. 'I don't know her, but she was nice to me last night.' Tom waited while she wove her hair into a scruffy plait and shoved it out of the way. 'I liked talking to her,' she added quietly.

A pang of something tweaked his gut. He should be the one Emily found it easy to talk to, not some stranger she'd barely met. He shoved the petty thought away. Emily's needs were more important than his own hurt feelings. All he could do was keep encouraging her to reach out, even if it wasn't to him for now.

'Maybe we can set up a visit for you to go to the surgery on your own? Nerissa could show you around and you can ask her whatever you want.'

Emily's smile lit up her whole face. 'I'd like that.'

10

'Tom's a nice chap, don't you think?' Doc's question came from the other side of his newspaper. It would be easy to take it on face value – a reasonable observation about someone who just happened to be at the right place at the right time. A fellow doctor who'd stepped in to help out, with only the welfare of an injured man in mind. But Nerissa hadn't spent the past dozen or more years in the almost constant company of the wily old man across from her without growing wise to his tricks. She knew his traps and there was no way she was putting her foot in this one. He was up to something and until she figured out exactly what it was, she would hold her peace about the events of the previous evening.

Her mind flickered back to that moment in the corridor, the firework flash of awareness between her and Tom that had taken her so completely by surprise. With the kind of clarity only morning could bring, she knew the false sense of intimacy had been created by the lack of light and their unintentional proximity. Unfortunately, her mind had lacked anything close to rationality long into the wee small hours of the night as she'd tossed and turned and replayed the moment over and again. As a result, she'd woken grumpy and not a little embarrassed with her behaviour. Goodness knows what he must have thought as she all but ran away from him. The last thing she wanted was to be drawn into a conversation about him now, especially when she was sure Doc had an ulterior motive. Her hand rose to toy with Gareth's ring only to find nothing there. For the first time she'd forgotten to put her necklace on after her morning shower. *I must be more tired than I thought.* Unwilling to contemplate any other possible reason for forgetting it, she turned her attention back to Doc.

'Your breakfast is getting cold.' That had been the first clue that something was up because Doc preferred his food only a couple of degrees below nuclear hot. He also had a terrible poker face, which was no doubt why he was lurking behind his daily copy of *The Times.*

'Goodness me, I was so absorbed in this article I quite forgot my breakfast!' Doc folded the paper shut and dropped it on the table next to his plate. Picking up his knife and fork, he brandished them with a hearty smile that didn't quite reach his eyes. 'Well, this looks delicious.' The fried eggs he'd insisted on against her offer to poach or scramble them were beginning to congeal, little pools of grease sitting on the top of the yolks in a most unappetising fashion.

Nerissa watched his knife hover for a moment before sinking into one of the eggs. Doc placed the square of egg and toast in his mouth, the skin around the corners of his eyes tightening a fraction as the lukewarm food hit his tastebuds.

Serves him right.

It was an uncharitable thought, and any other morning she would've offered to make him a fresh meal, but she was tired of Doc and his games.

'Your first patient is due in less than twenty minutes so I'd better head next door and get everything ready.' She stood and gathered her empty plate, scraping the crumbs from her toast into the food caddy on the windowsill a little harder than was necessary.

When she turned back to Doc, he was washing another mouthful of cold eggs down with a swallow of tea and a grimace. A pang of guilt hit and she was on the verge of removing his plate when he spoke again. 'Now, as I was saying, I like the cut of Tom's jib, don't you? The way he stepped in like that to help Keith.'

Ha! He'd have to catch her with better bait than that, even after a bad night's sleep. And he could kiss goodbye to any thoughts of a fresh breakfast.

Circling the table, she swept the lightweight cardigan from where she'd hung it on the back of her chair and headed towards the surgery door. As she pulled it open, she glanced back at Doc over her shoulder. 'How fortunate for everyone he just happened to be in the pub at the time.'

In a flash, she was in the corridor with the door shut firmly on any follow-up Doc might have made. She spent the next few minutes tidying up the treatment room and making sure all the surfaces were clean. They had a brilliant cleaner who came in each evening, but she wanted to make sure everything was hygienic after Keith's unexpected visit. Bas was just about to embark on his second year of A levels and wanted to earn some extra cash to support his mum and younger sister. They'd been using a contract agency before he'd dropped into the surgery and asked if there was any work going. He'd been up and down the main street, but most of the jobs available were weekend or daytime hours. Impressed with his enthusiasm, Nerissa had had a chat with Doc, and they'd given him a trial run which had soon become permanent. After a week or two's supervision, it was clear he could be trusted, so they just left the door to the kitchen open, and he popped his head around to say hello and goodbye. He'd stuck diligently to his work throughout the summer holidays, when she was sure he'd rather be hanging out on the beach with his mates. He had high hopes of winning a university place, and though he still had another year with them, Nerissa knew they'd miss his cheerful presence around the place when he did leave.

With the treatment room surfaces disinfected, Nerissa moved on to check Doc's surgery. Not too much to do, not that there ever was because he was pretty neat and tidy, just a journal and the top sheet of his jotter to remove because he liked to start the day with a fresh page. She removed the sheet carefully before folding it small enough to tuck in her pocket. When she had a few spare minutes later, she'd check it over in case there was anything he'd noted down that needed to go on the system. Tucking the journal under one arm, she was just turning away when she noticed the box of disposable gloves on the corner of the desk was almost empty. She reached for it, forgetting the magazine under her arm, and it spilled onto the floor. 'Damn.' How was it possible to forget something she'd done literally seconds before?

Crouching down to retrieve the journal, she froze, one hand grasping at the arm of Doc's chair for balance. Staring back at her from a creased page of the journal was a picture of the surgery she'd taken herself earlier in the year when the hanging baskets had been in full bloom. Her gaze shifted to the text beneath, and she slipped from her haunches to her bottom as the significance of what she was reading sank in. Doc really was ready to retire at last. She stared, unseeing, at the journal as she wrestled with duelling emotions. Relief, more for him than herself, because even though she was irritated with him, she'd not missed how tired he looked. Out-of-hours work was getting harder for him to shake off, especially after a full day in the surgery like the one they'd had yesterday. Worry about what it would mean for her own future was followed by a swift blast of anger at him for not bothering to even talk to her about the advert he'd placed.

She checked it again, the sneaky thing had put his mobile number down rather than the main number for the surgery. She didn't know how long she sat there trying to process the implications of his actions before the sound of Doc's whistling came echoing down the corridor. Nerissa scrambled to her feet, closed and replaced the journal on his desk just in time.

Doc's whistling cut short as he spotted her beside his desk. 'Everything all right?'

'Yes. Fine.' She hesitated, knowing she needed to tell him she'd seen the advert, but not sure where to start that didn't involve kicking off a row between them.

The ring of the doorbell signalled their first patient, giving her the perfect excuse to escape.

She grabbed for the almost empty box of gloves and held it up. 'I'll get you a fresh box of these, and then I think you'll be all set.' She didn't look him in the eye as he stepped aside to let her through the door, afraid he'd see more than she was ready to admit to.

The morning was busy enough that Nerissa was able to fend off Doc's repeated attempts at friendly conversation without being rude. Not that she owed him any politeness after he'd gone behind her back like this. The first rush of anger had quickly faded. Doc was Doc and he'd always do things his own way. Even though she didn't like the way he'd gone about things, it was a positive step in so far as he seemed more interested in passing on the surgery to another doctor rather than let Michael sell it off to a developer.

She might have given him more of a chance to explain himself, but each gambit was yet another attempt to sing Tom's praises. Oh, she had more than a sneaking suspicion of why another doctor just happened to have shown up in the village, but until Doc got to the point, she wasn't going to fall in line. Maybe he was trying to soften the blow by presenting his replacement to her as a fait accompli, but she was not some child or witless ninny that needed to be managed like that. He owed her honesty, and it was disappointing to think he'd exclude her like this after all the years they'd been together.

Besides, it mattered not one whit what she thought about Tom; if he was going to come in and take over, then her feelings about the man were immaterial. There was no guarantee he, or anyone else, would be interested in maintaining the cosy little set-up she and Doc had made for themselves. She didn't think keeping her job would be a problem, but the odds on her keeping the lovely little flat tucked away under the eaves of the sprawling building she'd called home for more than a decade? Sadly, those were likely to be a lot longer.

As she turned the lock on the front door after seeing their final patient of the morning out, Nerissa decided she couldn't face smiling politely at Doc across the kitchen table over lunch. Toby wouldn't mind an extra walk and a bit of fresh air might help clear the muddle in her mind. She locked her computer and stuck her head around the door of Doc's office. 'There's a pork pie in the fridge, and plenty of salad too. I'm going to take Toby out, I'll be back by two.' And with that she turned on her heel and headed out.

The gorgeous hot spell they'd been enjoying was still in full force, drawing crowds to the beach. Keeping Toby on his lead,

Nerissa jogged down the steps and turned left, away from the busy area between the two sets of steps. There were too many rocks at this end for people to spread out their towels, chairs and other paraphernalia, though she spotted a couple of families rock pooling with their little ones. Once they were well clear of everyone, she unclipped Toby's lead and he dashed away to explore. Watching him bounce around, eyes bright and tail waving, never failed to lift her spirits usually, but even his unfettered joy couldn't chase off the black cloud hanging over her today.

Toby was Doc's dog in theory, and getting him had been another thing he'd done without speaking to her first. Doc liked the idea of a dog more than dealing with the practicalities of actually having one, especially one as energetic and full of personality as Toby. As a result, it had fallen to Nerissa to do the bulk of the work taking care of him – not that it was any hardship because she adored having him around, but what would happen if – *when* – Doc retired? Would he want to take Toby with him wherever he was thinking of moving to? And where was he thinking of moving to? Or was he planning on staying on in the accommodation and just passing on the practice to Tom or whoever else took over from him? So many unanswered questions, it was enough to make her want to scream!

With her mother's long ago advice ringing in her ears, Nerissa jogged to the edge of the water line, opened her mouth wide and let forth a long howl of frustration until she'd emptied every bit of air from her lungs.

Though he was a fair distance away, Toby rushed straight towards her, barking frantically until he reached her side and she bent to curl her arms around him. 'I'm okay, boy. I didn't mean to worry you.' He whined and stuck his cold nose into her neck, a reprimand and a demand for more attention. 'Did I scare you? Poor Toby, I'm sorry.' She scrubbed her hand through the thick fur around his neck. The dog rewarded her with a slobbery lick on her cheek. 'Gee, thanks,' Nerissa said, fumbling in her jeans pocket for a tissue. As she wiped the doggy kiss away, Toby prompted her to glance around, his attention caught by something behind her.

Nerissa froze, mortified to see Tom not five feet away. How long had he been standing there? Not long enough to have heard her, surely?

Straightening from her crouch, she decided to brazen it out. 'Oh, hi!'

'Hi.' He raised his hand in an awkward half-wave before letting it drop back to his side. 'I... We called to you, but I think you were too far away to hear us.'

At his use of the word we, Nerissa glanced past him to see Emily and Max waiting a little further away. Neither one was smiling. *Oh dear God.*

'There's not usually anyone down this end of the beach,' she offered lamely, wishing a sinkhole would open and swallow her up, because the way the three of them were staring at her made it clear they'd heard her screaming like a banshee at the sea.

'It's a good spot for a scream,' Tom said, a grin suddenly spreading across his face. 'I might try it some time.'

'I can highly recommend it.' Nerissa tried but failed to hide her own grin, hoping her face wasn't as red as she feared.

'Is there any special technique you would recommend? Do you count down, or just go for it?'

She laughed because it was impossible to stay embarrassed when he was being so sweet. 'Just go for it, that's what works for me anyway.' The next thing she knew he sprinted down to the edge of the water, paused and cast her a knowing grin. What was he doing? She hadn't expected him to take her words as an instruction!

Throwing his arms wide, Tom turned to face the sea and yelled at the top of his voice. Nerissa couldn't help but giggle, wondering if she'd looked half as ridiculous.

'Oh my God, Dad!' Emily's horrified voice only made Nerissa giggle harder.

Tom turned to his daughter, hands raised in a what's-the-problem gesture. 'Don't knock what you haven't tried. I feel amazing.' That was more than enough of an invitation for Max, who ran to join his dad, hollering at the top of his voice. 'Nice!' Tom said with an approving nod, but you really need to throw yourself into it. Like this.' He thrust his chest out and let forth another bellow.

'I think I've got it.' Max nodded before puffing out his own chest and trying again. Unable to cope with missing out, Toby ran to join them, splashing into the shallow waves barking all the while. 'Yes, Toby!' Max thrust a triumphant fist into the air, then started shouting again.

'I'm so sorry about my family,' Emily said, shaking her head as she approached Nerissa. 'They're quite mad.'

Nerissa laughed. 'Not going to join them, then?'

'God, no! They don't need any more encouragement to embarrass me.' She was laughing, too, though.

Nerissa watched for a few more minutes as the shouting session turned into a game of tug of war when Tom picked up a stick and the dog made a grab for it. He wrestled it away, then threw it. Toby set off after it, sending a spray of salt water flying in his wake, which Tom ducked a fraction too late. With another whoop, Max set off after Toby, uncaring of his trainers as he too sent a splash of water flying. Thinking she'd need to offer the use of their tumble dryer again, Nerissa shook her head as she turned to Emily. 'Your dad said something about you guys calling to me?'

'Oh, we saw you coming down the steps and wondered if

perhaps you wanted to join us for lunch? We were heading towards the café when we spotted you. You didn't hear us, I guess.' Emily made an awkward gesture towards the water.

'I had a lot on my mind, I didn't mean to be rude and have you guys end up chasing me.' She offered an apologetic smile.

'Did the scream help?' Emily cocked her head, inquisitive hazel eyes fixed on Nerissa.

'It did, actually. I used to have a bit of a hot temper when I was your age, and as I told you yesterday, my mum used to send me down here to let out my frustrations. Not that I'm down here screaming like a loon every day,' she hurried on, making Emily grin.

'You'd get a reputation,' she giggled. 'Never mind all that fuss over the mermaid, come and see the Mermaids Point Banshee!'

'Oh, can you imagine?' Nerissa covered her face with her hands for a second. 'At least it would be something new to lure the tourists with.' She shook her head. 'No, don't give me any ideas!'

'Ideas about what?' Tom asked, strolling over to join them.

'Nerissa's going to be the new tourist attraction – the screaming Banshee of Mermaids Point,' Emily told him between giggles.

'Sounds like the perfect job.'

11

The moment the words left his mouth, Tom knew he'd put his foot in it. The amusement dancing in Nerissa's lovely brown eyes fled as her arms came around her body as though shielding herself.

'Yes, well, we'll have to see about that, won't we?' The words were said in a tone as brittle as her smile.

Stupid. Stupid! Malcolm retiring was bound to be unsettling for her, and him blundering around the place couldn't be helpful. He wondered what, if anything, Malcolm had said to her in advance of his visit. She'd certainly reacted without recognition of who he was when they'd been briefly introduced in the pub.

'That's actually something we wanted to talk to you about,' he said, putting an arm around Emily's shoulders to draw her into the conversation. 'I guess you know I came here to talk to Malcolm about possibly taking over the surgery?'

'I figured it out, yes.'

The ice in her tone made him want to wince. Bloody hell, what was Malcolm playing at?

Deciding it was best to plough forwards, Tom offered her an

apologetic smile. 'Anyway, I've told Em and Max that I'll only consider it seriously if they are fully on board, and we thought it was something we should talk to you about as well.'

'Me?'

'Of course. You're probably used to a quiet life with only Malcolm around.' When Nerissa made a rude noise, he decided best to ignore it. 'It would be a big change for you to suddenly have the three of us to deal with.'

'I'm a dream to be around,' Emily chipped in with a cheeky grin. 'But I can't say the same for the other two.'

Tom could've kissed her, his sweet, empathetic girl, because she must've sensed Nerissa's unease and was trying to alleviate it. 'Yes, yes, we're dreadful, smelly boys who make your life a misery.' He turned back to Nerissa. 'So we'd understand if you didn't want to keep the same arrangement you have with Malcolm – if we do decide to move here, that is.'

'If you don't want me to stay on, I completely understand,' Nerissa said, glancing around as though looking for an escape route.

Max and Toby were quite a long way down the beach, so she'd have to wait for them to come back before she could leave. Further away than Tom liked, actually. 'Hold on,' he said to Nerissa, then cupped his hands to his mouth and yelled his son's name. When he looked up, Tom waved. Only once Max had started to jog back in their direction did he look back at Nerissa. She'd caught her bottom lip under her teeth and was worrying at the same spot over and over. A strange urge to press his thumb to her mouth and soothe the little hurt rose out of nowhere and he hurriedly shoved his hands in the front pockets of his jeans. 'Sorry, where were we?'

'You were making a hash of things,' Emily said with an aggrieved sigh. 'What he meant to say was that if we do decide to move here, then we hope you'd stay on as the housekeeper as well as working in the surgery, at least for a trial run.'

'But we'd also understand if you didn't want to,' Tom added, not wanting Nerissa to feel pressured into a situation she wasn't prepared to take on.

'That's an awful lot of ifs,' Nerissa said, still not looking convinced.

'Yes, absolutely. But we had a chat this morning over breakfast and we wanted you to have a say as well. Over your future, that is.' God, why was this so difficult? 'Whatever you choose to do would be fine by us, is what I mean.'

'*If* you decide to move here.' She gave him a hint of a smile, just enough to let him know she'd let him off the conversational hook he'd well and truly hung himself on.

'Like you said, it's a lot of ifs.'

Max barged into the space between them and dropped to the sand, panting for breath almost as hard as Toby, who flung himself down next to Max. 'Is it lunchtime? I'm starving!' Max declared.

Nerissa checked her watch. 'I'd better get back.'

'Oh.' Tom was surprised at how disappointed he was. 'We were hoping you might join us for lunch and help answer a few questions the kids have about the village.'

'I'd really like to, but I have to check on Doc and get everything ready for afternoon surgery.'

Damn, they'd taken up what little bit of lunch break she had. 'Of course. We'll leave you in peace. Come on, kids.' He reached down, hauled Max to his feet and took in the state of him. Not only were his T-shirt and jeans covered in sand, but his trainers were soaking wet again. 'Lunch will have to wait until we take a detour via the cottage and get you changed, young man.'

'It's not that bad,' Max protested, brushing his hands over the front of his top and depositing yet more sand.

Nerissa laughed. 'Good luck with that. Come on, Toby.' When the dog responded to her call, she bent to clip on his lead, sending waves of black curls cascading over her shoulder. It had been her hair Tom had spotted as she was walking down the steps, wild and blowing in the breeze. Straightening up, she tossed the wayward strands back and gave him a smile that sent something fluttering inside him. 'I really must get back, but why don't the three of you come to dinner tonight? I can show you around the place and you can ask as many questions as you like.'

'Oh, can we, Dad?' Emily grabbed his arm. 'You did say we should have a proper tour of the surgery.'

'Yes, sure. As long as we're not imposing?'

'Not at all. I've got a chicken I can roast, and tons of salad and some new potatoes.'

'Sounds perfect. What do you reckon, Max?' Chicken was his son's favourite, although he tended to prefer it coated in thick breadcrumbs and deep fried.

'Yes, please! Can I play with Toby, later, as well?'

'Not if you're going to get in this state again.' Tom shook his head. 'Let's get you sorted out.' He gave Max a nudge in the direction of the steps that would lead them off the beach and held out an arm towards Emily. When she tucked herself into his side, he couldn't help a little sigh of contentment. Though things had been a bit strained between them earlier, fulfilling his promise of cake for breakfast had been something of a breakthrough and she'd been holding his hand or happy to walk tucked under his arm as they'd wandered the length of the beach all morning. It was a blessing to be counted as he wasn't sure how long it would last.

'There's a garden behind the surgery,' Nerissa said as she fell into step beside them. 'I'm sure Max can throw the ball for Toby without getting in too much trouble.'

'Can I, Dad?' Max bounced in front of them, as eager as a puppy himself.

'If Nerissa says it's okay, then why not?' They reached the bottom of the steps, and Tom paused to let her go ahead of them. 'What time tonight?'

She shrugged. 'Whatever suits you? Doc doesn't like to eat too late, so shall we say six for six-thirty?'

'Will that give you time to do everything?' Tom asked, conscious she'd offered to cook dinner for five on top of a full afternoon's work. 'Is there anything we can do to help?'

'Why don't you pick something up for dessert? Other than that, I'll be fine,' she said with an assured wave of her hand. 'One of the joys of living and working in the same place is I can pop between the two anytime.' She started up the steps with a wave, got halfway and turned to smile down at them. 'Make sure you bring a list of questions, I'll be happy to answer them all.'

As Tom watched her trim figure negotiate the rest of the steps, he decided he had one serious question that he'd need to answer above all the others. Would living and working under the same roof as attractive Nerissa Morgan really be a good idea?

* * *

He was still pondering the question when he ushered the children up the front steps of the surgery at six o'clock on the dot. He hated being late for anything, to the point he was almost always too early, and they'd taken a very slow walk along the row of shops on the seafront to make sure they didn't spoil their welcome by catching Nerissa unprepared.

It was several minutes before she pulled open the door,

looking flustered and distracted, and Tom feared he'd screwed up. Her hair was pushed back from her face with some kind of thick cloth band and something didn't look quite right about her. It took him a moment or two to register she'd only got make-up on one eye – as though she'd been in the middle of the task when they'd rung the bell and caught her off guard. Maybe she'd said six-thirty for seven and he'd got it wrong.

He was about to reach for the children and steer them away from the door with an apology, but Max stepped forward a fraction too quickly for Tom to grab his shoulder. 'We got you these!' Max thrust the bunch of flowers they'd picked up on a whim as they'd been hanging around outside the grocer's watching him pack up the crates of fruit and vegetables that covered the table beneath the shop's awning. Tom had spotted a couple of buckets holding pretty bunches of mixed stems beside the table and the grocer had been only too pleased to sell him one. He'd offered a discount, but Tom had declined – taking cut-price flowers as a gift seemed a bit cheap, and besides they'd looked fresh and bright enough they'd have a good few days in them.

'Oh.' Nerissa seemed to gather herself and force a smile to her lips. 'They're beautiful, thank you.'

'We're too early,' Tom said, quickly. 'Come on, guys, let's go for a walk and leave Nerissa to get ready.'

'No! No, please don't go, I need your help. It's Doc.'

Tom took one look at the fear in her eyes and thrust the cake box he'd been holding into Emily's hands. 'Wait here and keep your brother out the way.' Not stopping, because he knew Em was responsible enough to do as she was told, Tom brushed past Nerissa and was three strides down the corridor. 'Where is he?'

'In the kitchen, the open door,' she said, already on his heels by the time he turned off the corridor.

The delicious scent of roast chicken hit him the moment he

walked into the room. Somewhere in the back of his brain he registered the familiar strains of Aurora Storm's summer hit song blaring from a digital radio on the windowsill, but Tom's focus was all on the man slumped at the table. There was a grey sweatiness to Malcolm's skin, and his body heaved as he struggled for breath. Toby sat vigil beside the man, whining his concern.

'It's all right, Malcolm, I'm here,' Tom said, keeping his voice calm as he knelt before the older man. The retriever nudged Tom's arm with his nose and whined again. 'Shh, Toby.' He eased the big dog aside as gently as he could with his shoulder and was relieved when he settled on the floor beside Tom, nose buried between his two paws. Tom placed a hand on Malcolm's knee. 'Can you speak? Where's your bag?'

Malcolm nodded. 'Spray,' he gasped between shuddering attempts to breathe. 'Bedside drawer.'

'I'll get it.'

He was aware of Nerissa passing close behind him, but Tom kept his attention focused on Malcolm. 'Angina?' He hazarded his best guess at the symptoms presenting and Malcolm's reference to a spray.

Malcolm nodded, pressing a hand to his chest as though that would somehow compel his unruly heart to comply.

'Is it just the pain and trouble breathing? Do you feel sick at all?'

The older man nodded at the first question, shook his head at the second.

'All right.' Tom patted his knee. 'Hold on and we'll have you sorted in no time.' A bit of calm reassurance was often a doctor's greatest tool during high-stress situations.

Nerissa returned moments later, a bit out of breath herself from dashing up and down the stairs. She handed a small canister to Tom, then hooked a hand in Toby's collar and led him away to his basket in the corner. Though he continued to whine, the dog stayed put.

Tom checked to make sure she'd grabbed the right thing, and was relieved when he recognised the brand name of the GTN spray he prescribed himself to patients. 'That's the one,' he said, giving her a quick reassuring smile.

He took a few vital moments checking the expiry date and sending a puff of its contents into the air to be sure it was dispensing correctly. Satisfied, he turned back to Malcolm, who already had his mouth stretched wide and his tongue lifted.

'An old pro, I see.' Tom pumped the spray once underneath Malcolm's tongue. 'Close. Breathe through your nose.' He ignored the look of disdain in the old man's eyes and checked the time on his watch before straightening to his full height. Bloody doctors were always the worst patients.

Out of habit, he crossed to the window and began to wash his hands thoroughly with soap and hot water. Hopefully the medicine would do its job, but he wanted to be ready in case Malcolm needed further assistance.

'That's it?' Nerissa murmured to him as she came to stand beside him, her back to the worktop and her eyes locked on Malcolm.

'Hopefully. We'll give it five minutes, and if he needs another dose, he can take one. If that doesn't look like it's going to do the trick, then we might have to call an ambulance.' He paused, wondering how long it might take for an emergency response to reach a little village like this. 'How far is it to the nearest hospital? Do you have a car?'

'Stop your bloody fussing.' Malcolm's grumbled complaint settled the adrenaline still surging in Tom's veins. 'I'm not damn well dying – not today, anyway.'

'I'll be the judge of that,' Tom said, voice sharper than he'd intended when he glanced behind him to see Malcolm already trying to get to his feet. 'Sit still and behave yourself or I will call that ambulance and get you admitted for observations.'

Malcolm snorted, muttering something Tom was sure was less than complimentary under his breath, but he did as he was told.

'Who's his usual GP?' he asked Nerissa. It would be worth having a quick chat with them and getting some background on Malcolm's condition before he decided on his next actions. When she shook her head at him, Tom thought his brain might pop from the sudden burst of anger. Only an absolute idiot, or a stubborn old coot in this case, thought they could treat themselves. 'Right then.' He accepted the towel Nerissa offered and dried his hands more thoroughly than needed, while he forced himself to calm down. He could only address the situation in front of him, not what it should be. 'Where's your bag, Malcolm?'

'I'm right as rain now, don't fuss, boy.' Malcolm scowled at him.

Feeling something inside him snap, Tom crouched very low and whispered in the older man's ear. 'If you don't shut up and let me treat you properly, the next call I make will be to the GM-bloody-C about getting your licence reviewed.' He sat back on his heels so he could meet the other man's shocked gaze. 'Are we clear?'

'Y... yes. My bag is locked away in my office. Nerissa, would you be a dear?'

With a nod, she headed for a set of hooks on the wall and removed a ring of keys. Tom listened to her jangling them all the way down the corridor, a clear sign of her unspoken irritation. Her obvious panic over Malcolm's condition made Tom suspect she knew nothing about it.

Pulling out the chair next to Malcolm he sat down and folded his arms. 'How long have you been hiding this?'

Malcolm opened his mouth as though he'd protest, closed it again and shook his head. 'About six months,' he admitted at last.

Christ. 'And it's too much to hope you've spoken to a specialist about it?'

'It's just a touch of angina. I'm not as young as I used to be.'

'And the prescription for the GTN? How are you getting around that?'

Malcolm winced. 'It's from the stock I allocate to my emergency bag.'

Of course it was. Tom rubbed at the sudden ache between his eyes. The angina might not kill the stubborn old fool today, but Tom couldn't say the same about himself. 'Who's your locum service?' When Malcolm bristled, Tom leaned forward. 'I'm going to check you over, and only if I am satisfied will I let you stay here rather than going to the hospital tonight. Tomorrow you are going to take a rest, and you and I are going to sort out an appointment with a cardiac specialist. Are we clear on this?'

Malcolm hesitated, then nodded. 'Perhaps I have been overdoing it a bit.'

When Nerissa returned and placed a large brown leather bag on the table, Tom smiled at her in thanks. 'I'll see Malcolm upstairs and get him settled, could you call whoever you use as an emergency cover and see if you can get someone in for tomorrow – maybe see if they'll do until the end of the week so Malcolm can split the load a bit?'

'Yes, of course.' With a horrified look, she clapped a hand over her mouth. 'The children! We left them outside.'

Tom hadn't forgotten about them, but he trusted them both to say with confidence, 'I'm sure they're fine.'

She pursed her lips as though not sure she agreed. 'I'll check on them first, then I'll make that call.'

'Thanks. You're a lifesaver.'

He only realised what he'd said when she laughed, the sound a combination of relief and black humour. 'That's you, not me, *Dr* Nelson.'

Tom grinned. 'We make a great team.'

12

We make a great team. Those words came back to Nerissa time and again over the next couple of days as she handled the fallout of Doc's angina attack.

Angina! Every time she so much as thought the word, it sent her temper spiralling. How on earth had Doc kept something that important hidden from her? But even in the depths of her anger, she knew. He had already been finding it hard to acknowledge the reality of things, how much more difficult must it have been for a man as proud as Doc to come face-to-face with the frailties of his body?

It didn't excuse it, any more than she was ready to excuse him for putting that ad in the journal without talking to her about it first, but she understood. Imagine if Michael had got wind of Doc's health condition? The nasty little creep would've swooped down on them like a vulture spying juicy carrion. They couldn't keep it hidden from him forever, though. Secrets never lasted long in the Point, but she hoped they'd at least be able to get Doc properly assessed and a treatment plan in place before he descended on them again.

After a day in bed, he'd been itching to get back to work, and though she'd kept a close eye on him, he didn't seem to be suffering any after-effects from his angina attack. Dr May from the locum service had offered to take a couple of half-day shifts until the end of the month. She was also covering their out-of-hours and weekend emergency callouts so Doc had the weekend to put his feet up.

Nerissa paused in her task of washing up the pans she'd used to make breakfast, and glanced over her shoulder to where Doc was relaxing with a stack of Saturday's newspapers and a fresh pot of tea. Would it be too much to hope he had also resolved the issue of his successor?

Though he'd not said anything either way, Nerissa had the impression Tom was leaning towards the idea. The children certainly seemed enamoured with the place. Emily had popped in the day before with a tape measure and asked if she could look again at the room she'd earmarked for herself as a possible bedroom, and Max had asked her what times she normally walked Toby. The fact he'd shown up on the beach at 6 a.m. the past couple of mornings showed his adoration for his new best friend. Which reminded her, she and Doc still hadn't talked about his plans for where he intended to live.

Setting the last pan on the draining rack, she dried her hands on a tea towel, then resumed her usual seat. 'Doc?'

'Hmm?' He half-lowered the paper and peered at her over the rims of his glasses. 'Everything all right, my dear?'

She smiled. 'Yes, fine, I was just wondering about something...' She hesitated, considering whether she was as bad as Michael for trying to control Doc's future. She shook the thought away, though Doc's plans would have a big impact on her life, she needed to be sure he would have someone looking out for him if it wasn't going to be her every day. 'I was wondering what your plans are for after you retire – where you intend to live, that sort of thing.'

Doc closed his paper and removed his glasses, laying them both aside. 'Want to be sure you're rid of me, is that it?'

Nerissa's stomach lurched. 'What? No, of course not!' A hot flush of guilt crept up her neck, because she had indeed voiced that very thought to Sylvia and Laurie on more than one occasion over the past few months. 'I just wanted to know if there's anything I can do to help you, that's all.'

Doc reached across the table to pat her hand. 'There, there, I'm only teasing. I know what a pain in the backside I can be, my dear. You've been a saint to put up with me all these years.' He withdrew his hand and folded his arms across his chest with a sigh. 'And I can see now that I've gone about all this in the wrong way. I thought I was being so clever, that I could handle everything without having you worry about your future.' He shook his head. 'Barbara told me I was being foolish, but I was so sure I could handle it on my own.'

The only Barbara either of them knew was Mrs Mitchell who was part of the local knitting circle. Her husband had suffered terrible injuries in a trawling accident a few years ago and Doc had spent a lot of time helping Will to be as comfortable as possible before he'd finally passed away about eighteen months ago. 'What's Barbara got to do with any of this?'

Doc's face turned a shade of red she'd only ever seen on him when he'd fallen asleep in the garden and caught too much sun. 'Well...' He picked up his glasses, unfolded the arms as though he meant to put them on, folded them again and set them back on top of the paper. 'She and I are friends.'

Oh. Nerissa bit her lip to stop a smile at his obvious discomfort. 'That's nice. She's been very lonely since Will passed.'

'Yes, yes she has.' He stared down at his hands. 'We've been friends for a long time, and I've always held her in great affection.' The way he said it made Nerissa wonder if there was more to this than a recent connection, but she held her peace and waited for him to continue. 'She invited me to move in with her, and, well, I've accepted.'

'That's lovely,' Nerissa said, because it really was. For all his foibles, Doc was a kind-hearted soul and Barbara deserved a second chance at happiness after everything she'd been through. If they'd found comfort in each other's company, then she wished them both nothing but joy. 'I won't say anything until the two of you are ready to share your news, of course.'

'Thank you, my dear.' Doc sounded relieved. 'I've been wanting to say something for ages, but Barbara preferred to keep things between the two of us until we were both sure. You know how tongues wag around here!'

She certainly did, and given that much of the gossip spread outwards from the knitting circle, it was close on a miracle that Barbara had been able to keep her and Doc's little romance hidden from her pals.

'You'll be moving into her place, then?' Barbara lived in one of the old fishermen's cottages in the heart of the village, just a few doors along from the one Linda was renting. It was one of the few remaining in original hands and had been in Will's family since the community had formed a mutual society and built homes for each other. Nerissa pictured the postcard-sized yard behind Linda's cottage where there wasn't room for much more than a table, a couple of chairs and a washing line. 'There won't be much space for Toby.'

'That's true,' Doc said, like it had occurred to him for the first time. 'And I'm not sure how well he and Carlotta will get along.' Carlotta was Barbara's enormous tabby cat who spent the day lounging on the front windowsill and hissing at passers-by. 'I don't suppose there's any chance of him staying on here? He is rather more your dog than mine, these days.'

And whose fault was that? Nerissa shook her head. 'If it was down to me, then of course he could stay – but it's not, is it?'

'Tom's boy seems very keen on him.'

'Doc!' Nerissa scolded. 'You can't expect Tom to solve all your problems.'

He laughed, not sounding the least bit repentant. 'Why not, when he's so good at it?'

'Honestly, what am I going to do with you?' Nerissa couldn't help but laugh as well. 'He still hasn't made up his mind, you know.'

'Ah, but I heard he's having lunch with a very pretty, very charming woman today. I'm sure that'll tip the balance.'

She would let Doc get away with a lot, but not with that. Rounding on him, she wagged a finger across the table. 'Stop it! I'm meeting Tom *and the children* for lunch to answer any last-minute questions they might have before they head home tomorrow. He's a nice man and I'll be happy to work for him if he decides to move here – but THAT. IS. ALL.' She crossed her arms and glared at him. 'Weren't you the one complaining about village gossip not five minutes ago, and now you're trying to put me in the middle of something!'

Doc held up his hands. 'I'm sorry, I'm sorry, my dear. I was just teasing. I didn't think for a moment there was anything between you.'

'Well,' Nerissa shoved a hand through her hair, feeling all hot and bothered about how much she'd overreacted. 'Just make sure you keep it that way.'

'Whatever you say.' Doc reached for his glasses, popped them on the end of his nose and studied her over the top of them.

'That's a very pretty blouse. Is it the one Sylvia bought you for your birthday?'

She stared down at herself. The peach coloured top she'd taken from the wardrobe that morning was one of her favourites. It had two layers: a plain opaque wide-shouldered vest, with a floaty sheer square-necked upper the same shade and covered in white cherry blossoms. It was perfect for a summer's day and could be dressed up or down depending on the occasion. She'd teamed it with a pair of white denim cropped jeans and white deck shoes. Was it a bit too much for a casual lunch? She'd thought only about how cool and comfortable it was on a day as hot as today was promising to be, but what if Tom thought she was dressing up for him?

'I've got a few things to sort out upstairs,' she muttered to Doc, who was already back behind his paper, then rushed from the room and up the stairs to get changed.

With her pretty top back on the hanger and replaced by a baggy white T-shirt with embroidered sunflowers around the neckline and hem, Nerissa bound back her thick hair with a white cotton scarf and gave herself one final check in the mirror. She'd applied a touch of make-up – a tinted moisturiser with a high SPF factor and just a dash of eyeliner and lipstick – the same as she would normally wear.

She checked her watch and decided to head to the café early. Hopefully it wouldn't be too busy, and she could catch up with Laurie for a chat between customers.

* * *

Nerissa took one look at the packed tables and headed straight behind the counter and into the kitchen to wash her hands and pull on a spare apron. Though her hair was loose at the back, the scarf was wide enough to keep it well away from her face. If Laurie needed a hand with any food prep, she could tie it back more securely, but it would do for taking orders and waiting on tables.

She grabbed a spare notepad from the pile beneath the counter and glanced around the room. A cross-looking woman sitting at one of the smaller tables by the window caught her eye and immediately raised her hand. Deciding it was easier to tackle someone who was already looking frustrated, rather than worrying about if she was next or not, Nerissa fixed a broad smile to her face and hurried over.

'Hello, so sorry if you've been kept waiting. What can I get you?'

'A large cappuccino, a small latte and is there any chance you can warm this up for us?' The woman reached into a huge bag on her lap and drew out a bottle of milk. The initial wave of conversation had hidden the sounds of the very fractious baby being jiggled by the man occupying the other seat at the table.

'Yes, of course. I'll do that straight away and then I'll sort out your coffees, okay?'

'Please,' the woman's expression melted into a grateful smile and Nerissa realised she hadn't been cross at all, just likely stressed about having a crying baby bothering other customers.

'I'll be right back.' Nerissa took the bottle and hurried back towards the kitchen. She squeezed her way between Laurie, who was now manning the coffee machine, and Sylvia, who was lifting an enormous Victoria sponge cake out of the display cabinet. 'Morning both!' She blew them a kiss.

'Oh, Nerissa, thank goodness! Katie called in sick this morning and it's been an absolute zoo since I opened for breakfast.' Laurie banged the milk jug a little harder than necessary to settle the foam.

Nerissa popped the bottle in the warmer in the kitchen and left it to heat up. Laurie got enough families in that it had seemed a sensible investment, much easier than heating a pan of water or risking an accident in the microwave. She leaned against the door frame, where she'd be able to keep an eye on the warmer and still speak to Laurie. 'You should've called me.'

Laurie topped off a couple of wide-rimmed cups with the milk, creating a perfect swirl of foam and coffee. 'I literally haven't had a chance. Poor Mum came in to get her and Dad a brew and that was forty-five minutes ago.'

'Don't fuss about me, darling, and your dad won't die if he has to wait a bit for his morning break.' Sylvia slid thick slices of sponge cake onto two plates. 'These for table six?'

'Yes, please, and these coffees as well.'

'I'll take those.' Nerissa pushed away from her spot and reached for the cups Laurie had just added a dusting of chocolate to. 'Can you do me a large cappuccino and a small latte?'

'Of course.'

Within a couple of minutes, the family by the window had their coffees and a nice warm bottle of milk, which the baby grabbed at with both hands, her whimpers settling the moment her father popped the bottle in her mouth. Nerissa had no time for more than a smile at the sweet little thing before she was called away by another customer.

Twenty minutes of madness later, Sylvia was back in The Mermaids Cave next door with a couple of carry mugs full of coffee and a slice of Andrew's favourite millionaire's shortbread which Laurie had insisted she take for her dad. 'I've sent Jake a message and he's on his way to help me with lunch,' Laurie said as she joined Nerissa behind the counter. She surveyed the decimated remains of the display cabinet. 'I'd better top this up.'

Nerissa stilled her hand as she was reaching inside. 'Leave it for five minutes, you look shattered already.' When Laurie gave a weary nod, Nerissa fetched a bottle of sparkling water from the fridge and split it between two glasses. 'Drink,' she ordered, pushing one of the glasses towards Laurie.

'Yes, ma'am.' Laurie grinned before gulping down the icy cold liquid. 'Oh, I needed that. What brings you here, anyway? Not that I'm not grateful you showed up when you did!'

'I'm meeting To— the Nelsons for lunch. They're heading home tomorrow, so I said I'd help with any last-minute questions they might have.'

Nerissa picked up a cloth and wiped down the already clean counter, hoping her niece hadn't noticed her slip over Tom's name. Ever since Doc made that stupid joke, she'd been having second thoughts about the meet-up. Dinner at the surgery had been a surprisingly relaxed affair given the panic over Doc's angina attack, but they were all such easy company it hadn't taken long for her to put aside her worries and enjoy the evening. What if they'd rather have spent their last day relaxing but were too polite to refuse her invitation? She thought she was being helpful, but maybe it was a bit too pushy. They were supposed to be on holiday after all.

'What's going on in that head of yours?' Laurie nudged her hip. 'I can practically see the cogs whirring.'

Nerissa folded the cloth into a neat square and dropped it in the sink with a sigh. 'I don't know. Nothing, everything.' She pressed a hand to her forehead, wishing she had an on/off switch for her brain. 'Doc made this stupid joke about how me being an attractive woman would help persuade Tom to take over the practice, and now I can't stop thinking about it.'

Laurie rolled her eyes. 'Nice one, Doc.' She nudged Nerissa's hip again. 'He's got a point, though, you are very attractive – and I'm not just saying that because family loyalty obliges me to.'

Nerissa laughed. 'That's why you're my favourite niece.' Laurie was her only niece, but it was something she'd started saying when Laurie was an adorable toddler and it had stuck. 'But, seriously, if he does decide to move here, I don't want the gossips putting two and two together and making five.'

'Putting one and one together, you mean,' Laurie said with a knowing grin.

'Yes, exactly that.' When Laurie continued to smile like the Cheshire Cat, Nerissa swatted her arm lightly. 'Stop it! Oh God, if you're thinking it, then everyone else is bound to as well.' She picked up the cloth and started folding and refolding it again. 'I don't want people talking about me.'

Laurie snatched away the cloth, tossed it in the sink, then took both of Nerissa's hands in hers. 'This is the Point. People are always talking about someone.' She said it with some feeling, having been the target of some malicious gossip when she'd been younger, and recently a more benign topic of interest when she and Jake had started seeing each other. 'This week's news is next week's chip wrapping. The best thing to do is ignore it and it'll blow over. Besides, you don't even know if Tom's going to move here, so you're borrowing trouble that might never come to pass.'

'You're right. I know you're right, and it's not me I'm worried about so much as him. Having lost his wife, the last thing he'll want is anyone speculating about his love life. Not that there will be any love life to speak of,' she added in a rush. 'Not with me, at least.'

Laurie squeezed her hands. 'Like I said, it'll be something and nothing.' The bell over the front door jangled, signalling the arrival of yet more customers. 'Right, I'd better see if I can squeeze them in somewhere. Do you think you could do a quick walk round, clear a few empties and perhaps see if you can clear out those who have finished – politely, of course!'

'No problem.' Nerissa knew the drill. Asking customers if they were finished or if they wanted anything else often prompted them to ask for their bill.

'Thanks.' Laurie stepped away, paused and glanced back at Nerissa. 'Word to the wise. Don't cling to preconceived ideas of what can and can't happen and risk cutting yourself off from something wonderful. Look at me and Jake, if I'd stuck to my silly rule about not dating visitors I might have let the best thing that's ever happened to me slip right through my hands.'

Nerissa shook her head, amused and frustrated in equal measures. 'You're worse than your mum.' She adored her sister-in-law to bits, but Sylvia was never shy about interfering if she thought someone she loved needed a push in the right direction.

That unrepentant grin was back on Laurie's face. 'That doesn't mean I'm wrong, though. Besides, you have to admit Tom's hot for an old guy.' And with that she swanned off across the café, leaving Nerissa wishing she'd kept her big mouth shut. She wanted no assistance from the Morgan Matchmaking Service, thank you very much. Tom Nelson might be decent-looking – okay, *hotter than the surface of the sun* – but the only relationship he and Nerissa might ever share would be a professional one.

13

A few minutes before their prearranged meeting time, Nerissa hung up her apron, washed her hands and grabbed the last free table. It was near the back of the room and a bit too close to where a couple of the knitting circle ladies were lingering over a pot of tea and a pair of crumb-covered plates. Though Kitty was an absolute sweetheart, Bev had a bit of a sharp tongue and Nerissa tended to avoid her whenever possible.

She cast a final hopeful scan over the rest of the room, but everyone looked settled in, so she had no option other than to sit down. Pulling her chair a little to the left away from them, she acknowledged their smiles of greeting. 'Hi ladies. Busy today.'

'I was just saying the same thing,' Kitty said with a nod. 'We'd better finish up, Bev, let someone else have our table soon. Laurie will be wanting room for her lunchtime customers.'

'We've as much right as anyone to sit here as long as we like,' Bev retorted. 'She'll be glad enough of our money when the visitors pack up and go home at the end of the season.'

Nerissa closed her eyes on a brief prayer for patience. 'You know how much Laurie values you. Take all the time you need.'

'I was going to, but thank you so much for the permission,' Bev snapped before turning back to Kitty. 'As I was saying, it's been over a month since Michelle picked up the phone to me, and I know they're not busy because the kids are at *her* mother's.'

'Why don't you call her then if you're worried? That's the wonderful thing about phones, Bev, they work both ways.'

Nerissa bit her lip to hide a smile at Kitty's soft but deadly rebuke, before she tuned the conversation out. If she wasn't careful she'd be drawn into their circle and then Tom and the children would have to contend with Bev's scrutiny. And if anyone was likely to put them off moving to the Point it would be her.

The familiar jangle of the bell above the door drew her attention and she spotted Tom enter the café and hesitate at the sight of the packed tables. She stood and gave him a little wave, which he returned with a relieved smile as he began to weave his way towards her. It was only as he reached her table that she realised the children weren't with him.

'Is this seat taken?' he asked, grasping the back of the chair opposite her.

'Help yourself.' She waited until he was settled before asking. 'No kids?'

Tom shook his head. 'I left them on the beach. They wanted to make the most of their last day before the dreaded drive home in the morning.'

Nerissa felt her stomach lurch. It was as she'd suspected and she was encroaching on their time when she'd only meant to be helpful. 'We don't have to do this.' She waved a hand between them. 'I'm sure you'd rather be enjoying the sunshine.'

'No, it's fine.' He glanced around, then leant forward like he was sharing a secret. 'You've done me a favour, actually. I hate sitting around at the best of times, and hate it even more when it's this hot.' He straightened up and gave her a smile that she tried to pretend didn't make her tingle all the way to her toes. 'We can lunch in peace and then I'll grab some takeout for them. After nearly a whole week with me, they were very insistent about how happy they would be to hang out on their own.' His smile turned rueful.

'Well, as long as you're sure.' Pointedly ignoring the interested looks she could feel emanating from the table next to them, Nerissa turned the menu around and pushed it towards him. 'Here you go.'

'Don't you want to look first?'

She shook her head. 'I know it off by heart. I help out here sometimes when Laurie is stuck. If you'd come in about ten minutes earlier you would've caught me in my apron.'

It was Tom's turn to frown. 'Does she still need your help? I must admit this is the busiest I've seen it in here all week.'

'The sunshine has brought an influx of day trippers, most likely, and Jake came to help out.' She pointed across the room to the man who made her niece light up like a Christmas tree. Jake's pen was flying across the notepad in his hand as he took an order from a large group who'd pushed two of the tables together. 'He's her boyfriend, they've just moved in together in a cottage up near the top of the Point.'

'How is it possible for anyone to write that fast? My handwriting is illegible at the best of times,' Tom said as they both watched Jake scribble something, point his pen at the next person at the table, nod, scribble, repeat until he'd covered everyone in the group in no time at all.

'That old doctor cliché?' Nerissa asked with a laugh as they turned back to face each other.

'Sorry?'

'You know, the bad handwriting thing.' When Tom continued

to frown at her, she hurried on because the joke had fallen flatter than a pancake. 'Never mind. I think Jake was using shorthand so that's why he's so fast. He's a journalist by trade. He came here to investigate the mermaid sightings and ended up staying.' Realising she was babbling, Nerissa forced herself to stop.

An awkward silence stretched between them as Tom studied the menu and she looked everywhere but at him or at the table next to them, which had fallen suspiciously silent. When he pushed the menu back towards her and said, 'I'll have a cheese and ham panini and an iced coffee,' she felt a wave of relief that he'd broken the silence.

'That sounds good.'

She was about to go and fetch their order when Jake approached. 'What can I get you?'

'Oh, I can sort it out,' Nerissa protested.

Jake pointed the end of his pen at her. 'I am under strict instructions from the boss to let you have your lunch in peace, and I'm not arguing with her.' He softened his declaration with a grin towards Tom. 'Hello, I don't think we've met.'

They introduced each other, Tom half-rising from his chair to shake Jake's hand. 'I hear you're a journalist. Is this an undercover assignment?'

Jake and Nerissa exchanged a look. 'Strictly above board. No more sneaking around for me.' When he'd first arrived in the Point, he'd posed as a writer on a research trip, which had led to some problems between him and Laurie, but they seemed to have settled everything between them, much to Nerissa's relief. Jake turned his attention back to Tom. 'I hear you're checking out the village. What do you think so far?'

'It's a great place, and the kids love it here.'

'Yeah, it has its attractions, all right.' Jake smiled the smile of a man in love. 'Right, what can I get you?'

They placed their order and once Jake had headed back towards the kitchen, Tom leaned across the table once more. 'Sorry for being a bit weird, just now. It was the handwriting thing, it struck a nerve.'

'Oh, I'm sorry. I just meant it as a joke because, you know, doctors' writing being illegible and all that.' Nerissa grimaced.

Tom placed his hand over hers, sending a jolt of warmth up her arm. 'It's not your fault.'

Nerissa nodded, unable to take her eyes off the back of his hand. The heat from his palm soaked into her skin, increasing her awareness of just how very long it had been since a man she wasn't related to had touched her. Doc didn't count – he was practically a part of the family. If Tom did decide to take over from him, then they were bound to come into contact with each other, something else she hadn't really considered.

When he still didn't withdraw his hand, she forced herself to meet his eyes. 'It's fine. I didn't take any offence.'

'That's a relief.' Tom patted her hand once, then lifted his away like it was nothing, while she sat there, frozen, willing her stupid heart to stop pounding. 'When I was growing up, I was naturally left-handed. My dad didn't approve, so every time I picked something up with my left hand, he took it from me and put it in my right hand.'

'That's a very old-fashioned attitude,' Nerissa said, glad for the distraction, even if the topic was a difficult one. 'I remember when my brother and sister-in-law realised Laurie was left-handed. It came as a bit of a surprise as none of the rest of us are and Mum got in a proper tangle trying to teach her to knit when she was little, but other than that it just wasn't a thing.'

'My father has very set ideas about things, unfortunately. And it got worse when I started trying to write. He tied my left hand behind my back so I had no choice but to use my right.' He lifted one shoulder like it was no big deal, but she could tell it had left a scar – and like a lot of the ones on the inside, it still hadn't quite healed. 'I got used to it in the end, but my writing's always been atrocious.' He smiled at her. 'Like you said, perfect for a doctor.'

'I'm really sorry I stirred up what must be a very difficult memory.'

He did that one-shoulder-shrug thing again. 'Honestly, I haven't given it a second thought in years. I was a bit anxious about it when the children were little, but they're both right-handed, like their mum. Crazy how these things from the past can blindside us when we least expect it.'

Jake arrived at that moment bearing plates and drinks and Nerissa let the conversation drop. They focused on their food for a few moments, the silence between them much easier this time. Nerissa cut her panini in several pieces and spread them out on her plate to cool a little. She'd had too many encounters with hot melted cheese and the tender skin on the roof of her mouth. It was hard to resist taking just a nibble though when the bread had that perfect crunch as her knife sliced through it. She pinched off the corner nearest her and blew on it a couple of times before popping it into her mouth.

Tom, by contrast, was already halfway through one half of his. When he paused to take a long sip of his iced coffee, she decided it was time to turn the conversation towards the original point of their meeting.

'So, did you have any last-minute questions for me?'

He shook his head. 'Nothing that comes to mind – I mean, I'm sure that things will come up over the next couple of weeks, but we had a good chat about everything last night and we're going to give Mermaids Point a go.'

'Oh! Well, that's wonderful news.' Nerissa picked up her own drink and clinked it against the side of Tom's glass. 'Congratulations.'

'Thanks.' He surveyed the contents of his glass. 'Not exactly champagne, is it?'

She laughed. 'There'll be plenty of time to celebrate properly once everything is finalised and the move completed.'

Tom's face grew serious. 'This is probably a weird thing to ask because we don't really know each other that well, but do you think I'm doing the right thing? For the children, I mean.'

'It's very hard for me to say.' While it was true that they didn't know each other well, she felt comfortable enough to be honest with him about what she'd observed over the past few days. 'They seem to like it here – Max, especially, and Emily was certainly talking with enthusiasm about her room the other day. We had a good chat about how she might decorate it and she was bookmarking colour charts on her phone to look at later.'

Tom grinned. 'Yeah, that was part of the chat last night. I've vetoed black walls for both of them, but other than that I've decided they can do what they want.' He picked up the remains of his panini. 'A decision I will no doubt live to regret.'

Nerissa laughed, recalling similar battles Andrew and Sylvia had fought when Laurie and Nick were growing up. 'If there's any preparation you want me to do, just say the word.'

Tom chewed, his expression thoughtful. 'Do you know what Doc's plans are for his furniture?'

She hesitated, conscious of being overheard. 'I'll ask him and then let you know, if that's all right?'

'Yeah, no rush. It was just something that occurred to me. I think I'll rent our place in London for the time being, give us more flexibility for the future. It'd be handy to know at some point so I can decide what we need to bring and what we might leave as part-furnishing. There's a few things we'd definitely want to hang on to, but I can't get sentimental over Ikea bookcases, you know?'

Nerissa nodded. 'I'll talk to Doc and put together a room-by-room inventory for you, how about that?'

'Brilliant.' Tom finished his meal and pushed his plate to one side so he could rest his folded arms on the table. 'Honestly, just knowing you're here makes the prospect of this so much less daunting.'

'I'm happy to help,' she said, meaning every word. With Tom taking over from Doc, she at least knew her future was secure for a while. 'And you must treat the surgery as your place to do with as you wish. Ideally, I'd like to keep my nook up in the attic, but I'm prepared to be flexible to ensure the house works for your needs.'

'Oh no, you must keep that,' Tom protested. 'I wouldn't dream of encroaching on your personal space. You've got a nice little set-up there, and we're already going to be disrupting your routine.'

It was her turn to shrug. 'Maybe a bit of disruption is what I need to shake things up. I've got very set in my ways with it just being me and Doc.' When she saw Tom's gaze lower she realised she was toying with Gareth's ring at her throat and she quickly dropped her hand. 'It'll be nice to have some noise and energy around the place.'

'I'll remind you that you said that when Max is murdering zombies on his PlayStation at full volume and Emily's playing the latest Harry Styles song on permanent loop.'

'I won't be able to hear it when I've got Absolute 80s blaring on the radio,' she said with a cheeky grin. Once the kitchen was a Doc-free zone, she'd never have to listen to Radio Four again.

Tom covered his face with his hands. 'And I thought you would be on my side.'

'I'm not taking sides in any of it. Consider me Switzerland.'

When he dropped his hands and gave her a quizzical look, she continued, 'Neutral territory.'

'Oh, right.' He laughed. 'I thought for a minute you were offering to be a permanent source of cheese and chocolate.'

'Well, that too.'

Nerissa picked up a piece of her forgotten panini and ate it, barely registering how cold the filling was. She felt happy – happier than she had been in ages. Hopeful too. After months of uncertainty, she was starting to believe there were brighter days ahead. Yes, it would take some adjusting to, having Tom and the children around, but it was a challenge she was looking forward to. He seemed like a decent guy, and his desire to do right by Emily and Max had been paramount in all their interactions this week. And yes, it was time to admit to herself how attractive she found him. It wasn't a sin, and it wasn't as if she was dead from the neck down. Pretending she didn't feel drawn to him was getting her nowhere – besides, no one else needed to know about what was nothing more than a silly crush. She just needed to keep her guard up and her mouth shut. Once she became more accustomed to being around him, she was sure it would fade into friendship.

14

'Good God, Tom, how did you manage to accumulate so much crap?' Alex moaned as he heaved himself out of the passenger seat of Tom's people carrier and pulled on a pair of heavy-duty gloves. This was their third – and hopefully final – trip to the local recycling centre in the past couple of hours, and they were both knackered and filthy.

'Last push and then you can have a hot shower and a cold beer, I promise,' Tom said as he opened the boot of his car and surveyed the mishmash of broken toys, boxes of unwanted crockery and bags of clothes the children had cleared out of their wardrobes and drawers.

'I'll hold you to that.' Alex heaved a box of mismatched plates and bowls into his arms and called out to one of the high-vis-clad men supervising the various containers. 'Where do you want these?'

'In with the soil and rubble, mate.' The man pointed down the row.

'Really? I thought you had a place where people can help themselves to stuff that's still useful.'

The man laughed. 'Unless you've got a full dinner service, it'll sit on the shelves for weeks and then I'll have to lug it over here myself.'

'Fair point,' Alex conceded and headed off in the direction he'd been sent.

Ten minutes later and the car finally unloaded of everything, Tom steered his way through the mass of parked cars, barely managing to miss a woman who stepped out in front of him, both hands full of black bin bags. Thankful he'd obeyed the council's five-mile-an-hour speed limit, Tom gritted his teeth in a fake smile as the woman paused to glare at him before marching across the road towards the opposite row of containers to where she was parked. 'Perhaps coming on a Saturday wasn't the best idea.'

'Ya think?' Alex tugged off his gloves and chucked them on the floor beside his feet. 'I swear people lose their minds in places like this.' As though to prove his point, two men started arguing about one being parked too close to the other.

'Let's get out of here before they start trading punches,' Tom said, easing his foot off the brake and inching forward, everything on high alert in case someone else with a death wish jumped out in front of them.

'But what if they need medical assistance?'

Tom didn't need to glance at his brother to see the obnoxious grin – he could hear it in his voice. 'Then they can call nine-nine-bloody-nine because I am off duty for the next week.'

A week didn't seem like long enough to oversee the removals at both ends, unpack and get the children settled in, but it was all he could afford to take. His partners in London hadn't been happy about his decision to quit, which had made his last few weeks quite an awkward experience. Feeling guilty, Tom had stayed on longer than he'd intended to ensure a smooth transition for his replacement, which is why he was stuck doing everything at the last minute and had roped Alex in to help out.

At least one thing had gone in Tom's favour. Fraser, the incoming partner, was new to the area and had decided to rent Tom's house for an initial three-month period, with an option to extend month-by-month while he and his husband went hunting for somewhere to buy. Relieved to avoid agents' fees, Tom had agreed a rental price that cleared the monthly mortgage payments and not much more. It had seemed like a good deal for the peace of mind of knowing whoever was living there would take care of the place. It had also put the pressure on to get the house sorted and in a liveable state for them to come into.

Fraser and his husband had furniture they wanted to bring from their current rental so, with the exception of the white goods, Tom was taking everything from the house down to Mermaids Point. He'd had a good look through the inventory Nerissa had kindly put together, but most of what Doc didn't want was old-fashioned without being antique, so Tom had declined to keep much of it. A house-clearance firm was due this weekend, so it would be empty in time for Tom's movers to unload on arrival. Though he'd worried about the inconvenience, Nerissa had assured him she could cope quite happily with a couple of days' disruption. Her flat would be untouched and the kitchen basics were staying put, so she wouldn't be completely stranded. Still, Tom would owe her a bottle of her favourite wine by way of thanks – probably a dozen bottles by the time the move was over and done with.

He was still musing over what kind of wine she liked when he pulled into the driveway and stopped with a groan at the sight of a large racing-green Jaguar blocking his path. 'What the hell is Dad doing here?' he asked. One look at Alex's face was enough to provide him with an answer. 'Bloody hell, Ally. What did you say to him?'

Alex sighed. 'I didn't say anything to *him*, exactly. Mum asked if I was going over for lunch tomorrow and when I told her I was busy, it kind of slipped out.'

Unlike the golden child sitting next to him, Tom saw as little of their father as possible. They'd never really got along. Growing up, nothing Tom did had ever been quite good enough in Archie Nelson's eyes. It'd been a relief when he'd upped and left Tom's mother for his very pregnant personal assistant – a scandal which had forced him to step down from his chairmanship of one of London's leading stock brokerages. Instead of taking the considerable settlement they'd given him to go quietly and starting up his own business as most people had expected, Archie had seized the second chance at fatherhood with both hands and taken early retirement. He doted on his new son, adored his second wife, Philippa, and had become a cheerful fixture at the local golf club. Tom's mother had been dignity personified, quietly taking her half of the divorce proceeds and encouraging Tom to maintain a bond with his father, though she'd stopped pushing that when he'd turned sixteen and been deemed old enough to decide for himself. Once he'd struck out on his own to go to university, she'd sold up and moved to a gorgeous villa in Portugal, where she spent her days painting and her nights in the company of her long-term partner, Eduardo.

If it hadn't been for Alex, Tom might well have cut ties with Archie altogether, but he'd adored Ally from the moment he'd first been allowed to hold him, so he'd kept in contact. When Anna had died, he'd been glad he'd stayed in touch because as much as Archie rubbed him up the wrong way, there was no doubting his love for his grandchildren. He and Philippa had been a godsend in the early days when things had got too much and Tom needed a break. With a sigh, Tom did his best to park the people carrier without blocking the pavement behind him, and climbed out. 'Best see what chaos he's brought down upon us.'

Before he'd even unlocked the front door, Tom could hear the boom of explosions and shouting coming from the lounge. *What the hell?*

Letting himself and Alex in, he called a greeting, but the only response was his father shouting, 'Trebuchet! Fire the damn trebuchet, they're attacking from all sides!'

Tom tossed his keys on the side table and exchanged a glance with Alex.

'I'm going to grab that shower,' his brother said, making his way towards the foot of the stairs.

'Coward,' Tom taunted him, but with a smile.

Alex held his hands up. 'Guilty as charged. No way am I getting between you and him.'

Schooling himself to patience, Tom turned left towards the lounge and waited on the threshold until grandfather and grandson finally noticed his presence over the sound and fury of one of Max's PlayStation games.

'Hey Dad!' Max raised a hand, eyes still glued on the TV screen.

'Hey, yourself. Where's your sister?'

'Dunno. Upstairs,' Max replied without looking up.

Given how loud the TV was, Tom couldn't blame Emily for seeking sanctuary in her bedroom. It really was deafening. 'How about we don't make enemies of the neighbours?' Walking across to the sofa, Tom picked up the remote resting on the arm and turned the volume down from forty – *forty!* – to around half that.

'Spoilsport,' Archie said, poking his tongue out as though he were the child. 'Who gives a stuff what the neighbours think when you won't be here much longer – or so the grapevine tells me.' The last words were as barbed as if coated with thorns.

'I was going to let you know; things have been a bit upside down here.' Tom tried and failed not to sound like a sulky teenager. He hated the way he regressed to that disappointed boy he'd been when Archie had walked out. It had been what? Thirty years ago, for God's sake. More than enough time to get over it. Giving himself a mental kick in the arse, Tom smiled at Archie. 'It's good to see you, Pop.'

Archie raised an eyebrow as though he could see straight through Tom's effort at civility, before turning his attention back to the game. 'Come on, Max, my boy, we're nearly at the next level.'

Deciding to leave them to it, Tom bent to clear away the jumble of empty cups and plates littering the coffee table and took them into the kitchen. The breakfast things he'd asked the children to put in the dishwasher earlier had been stacked instead on the kitchen worktop above it. 'Give me strength.' He opened his mouth to yell for Max, then decided it just wasn't worth the hassle. Archie would only stick his oar in and moan at him for being too hard on the boy – which was a bit bloody rich all things considered.

By the time he'd tidied the kitchen, he heard the thump of the hot water shutting down, signalling Alex was finished in the shower. Tom cast an eye over his grubby clothes and decided to follow suit before facing their father again and headed for the stairs.

Clean and dressed in a fresh T-shirt and jeans, Tom emerged from his bedroom about the same time as Alex appeared from the doorway of the guestroom opposite. 'How is he?' Alex asked.

'His usual charming self,' Tom retorted, then stopped himself. 'Sorry. He's fine, and Max seems delighted to see him, so I'll make an effort. Just let me check on Em and I'll be down.'

'I'll get those beers, eh?' Alex placed a hand on his shoulder. 'I know it's not easy for you, Tom, and I'm sorry I said anything in front of him.'

Tom shook his head. 'It's really fine, and my fault for not speaking to him earlier.'

Alex gave his shoulder a final quick squeeze, then padded away on bare feet towards the stairs.

Resolving to not let his complicated feelings about Archie spoil what might be the last time the kids saw him for a while, Tom knocked on Emily's door. 'Hey, sweetheart. Do you need anything?' When she didn't answer, Tom knocked again. 'Em?' Still nothing. Deciding she probably had her earphones in to try and block out the racket from downstairs – it hadn't escaped Tom's attention that the game's volume had snuck back up while he'd been in the shower – he turned the handle and opened her bedroom door, knocking again as he did so. Expecting to find her in her favourite position, lying on her back with her feet propped up on the wall over her headboard, Tom was surprised to see her bed was empty – the quilt as neat and smooth as when she'd made it that morning. He stepped inside to find her perched on the deep windowsill of her bay window, arms curled around her bent knees, Anna's old blanket draped over her shoulders. 'Em?'

Refusing to look at him, she shook her head. 'Go away.'

Now what? The last thing either of them needed was a confrontation ahead of what would be a very stressful few days, so Tom opted for something neutral and stuck to his original reason for knocking on her door. 'I just wanted to let you know I'm back and to see if you wanted a drink.' She shook her head again. 'Okay, well, we'll be downstairs when you're ready to come down.'

Feeling like he'd failed her yet again, Tom was almost out the room when she spoke.

'It's that easy for you, is it?' Her words were full of venom and accusation and froze him to the spot.

'What on earth are you talking about?'

Half-turning on the windowsill, Emily waved her arms in an all-encompassing gesture. 'This! Leaving this house, leaving Mum behind.'

Oh, shit. The kids had seemed to be coping so well, fired up and excited for the move to Mermaids Point, so he'd thought it best not to raise the subject of Anna and what they'd be leaving behind. He'd had some second – and even third – thoughts about the wisdom of taking them away from everything that was familiar, but Max especially had been excited about the prospect of starting at a new school, and had already begun making a playlist on his phone for the daily bus ride. 'No, sweetheart. Nothing about this is easy.' Crossing the room, he settled on the floor beneath where she was perched. 'Your mum and I spent almost every day of our married life in this house, of course it's breaking my heart to leave.'

'Then why are you making us go?' She started crying then. The sobs ripped through Tom like the blade of a knife.

'I... I thought it would make it easier for all of us, you and Max especially, not to be surrounded by all the sad memories. I thought if we were in a new place we'd find it easier to remember the happy times we all shared.'

'You want us to forget about her – don't lie to me! I'm not a child,' Emily said, sounding exactly that. 'Pop said so!'

Fucking hell. What had his dad said now?

Reaching up, Tom grasped Emily's hand, clinging on when she tried to shake him off. 'Look at me.' He tightened his grip, tugging on her hand to be sure he had her full attention. When she turned sullen, accusatory eyes on him, he lessened his hold and stroked the back of her hand with his thumb. 'I loved your mother more than it should be possible to love another person. I still love her, still think about her, and miss her every second of every day. Wherever we go, wherever we live, I will carry her and my love for her in my heart. Always. So will you. So will Max. She's what made us, *us*, sweetheart. She's the jam and cream and we're the sponge cake. She filled us up and made life sweet and special and perfect.'

'Then why don't you ever talk about her?' Emily sobbed. 'You never say anything!'

'Because it's too bloody hard.' Tom hung his head, fighting back tears of his own. 'I look at you and I see her in the curve of your cheek, the way your hair shines like spun gold in the sunlight. I hear her in Max's laugh. She's in every breath I take until sometimes it's too hard to breathe. And I'm sorry. I'm sorry she's gone and you are stuck with me and I'm so useless and I can't find the right words to help you through this because I'm still struggling to navigate it myself. I'm so sad, Em, all the damn time and it's exhausting. I just wanted us all to feel a bit less sad, and I thought moving away might help us to do that.'

Still crying, Emily slid from the windowsill and down into his lap, a tangle of arms and legs and cornfield gold hair. 'You should've told me. You should've said something, I would've helped you.'

'It's not your job, sweetheart.' Tom held her close, pressing kisses to the top of her head, his own eyes swimming with tears. 'Shh. Shh. Don't cry, sweet Em, I can't bear it.' He rocked her in his arms the way he used to when she was tiny.

'I'm sorry,' he murmured when her sobs quietened.

Nodding, she pulled back a little to dig in her pocket for a tissue. 'It's okay.'

'No. It's not. I thought I was protecting you, but I've been protecting myself instead. I promise I'll try harder to be more open with you. You're growing up before my eyes, sweetheart, give an old man a chance to catch up with that fact.'

She smiled – a bit wobbly around the edges, but a proper smile. 'You are a bit slow on the uptake, sometimes.'

'Cheeky.' He kissed her temple. 'Look, Em, none of this is too late to stop, you know? Just say the word and we'll forget about the whole thing. I know things were difficult at school, but now everyone's had a chance to calm down over the summer break it'll be a different atmosphere next term.' He touched her cheek. 'You didn't do anything wrong so don't feel like your friends won't still be your friends over one silly thing.'

She fiddled with the balled-up tissue in her hand before lifting her eyes to meet his. 'What if I still want to go? Does that make me a bad person for wanting to get away from everything too?'

'No.' Tom gathered her close, something settling inside as he realised some of the accusations she'd thrown at him might be her trying to deal with her own guilt about wanting to move on. 'Like I said, Mum will be with us wherever we go. We'll keep her safe in our hearts.'

Emily sat up once more and placed a hand on his cheek. 'I don't want you to be sad all the time, Daddy.'

Leaning forward he pressed a quick kiss to her forehead. 'I don't want you to be sad all the time either.'

'Then we'll both have to try,' she said, leaning in to rest her head against his shoulder.

Out of the mouths of babes, he thought. 'Yes. Yes, we will.'

* * *

It took a couple of hours, but he finally persuaded his father they still had work to do and the kids, particularly Max who was hyper after playing his game, needed a bit of time to relax. He escorted Archie to his car, placing a hand against the door when his father would've pulled it open. 'What did you say to Emily earlier, Pop? She was really upset.'

Archie pulled at the cuffs of his shirt, not meeting Tom's eyes as he said, 'Nothing.' When Tom turned to lean his weight against the car, his father sighed. 'All I said was it'd do you good to forget about everything and move on with your life.'

Tom had honestly thought Emily had misheard, or at least misinterpreted, what he'd said, but it looked like he owed her a mental apology. 'What were you thinking?'

Archie fiddled with his keys before shoving them in his pocket. 'What? It's true. I'm sick of the sight of you moping around the place, and it's not good for the children to see you making such a meal of it. Anna's gone, boy.'

'You think I don't know that!' Tom snapped. He cast a quick glance to where he'd left the front door ajar, then forced himself to lower his voice. 'Not all of us can walk away without a backward glance and start a new life.'

'Is that what you think happened?' Archie reached for the handle and pulled against Tom's weight trying to open his door. 'All these years and you still haven't got a bloody clue what the truth is. Poor Tom, always the victim, always the one who suffers.' He yanked again on the door, clearly furious, though Tom had no idea how on earth he thought he could be in the right about any of this.

Still, he yielded his spot and let Archie get into the car before he responded in a hoarse voice. 'I know what happened Pop, I was there.'

'You only *think* you know what happened because you still see everything through the eyes of the child you were at the time. I thought things would change over the years, particularly once you were married yourself, but no. You had the perfect mother and then the perfect wife and the perfect marriage with two perfect kids and so you never took off those rose-tinted spectacles. Now, move your car, I'm going home!' Archie slammed the car door closed, almost catching Tom's fingers.

He jumped back out of the way, absolutely floored by the litany of accusations spilling from Archie's mouth. The car engine started, and Archie glared at him through the closed window. Not knowing what else to do, Tom fished his keys out of his pocket and quickly backed his car out of the way so Archie could reverse out. As soon as the driveway was clear, he pulled back in and parked, only realising Archie's big Jaguar was stationary in the road once he'd got back out. The car window slid down and he met his dad's gaze. The anger was gone and for the first time Tom realised how old he looked. 'Pop, come back inside so we can sort this out.'

Archie shook his head. 'I need to get home. Philippa and I have a dinner reservation at the club.' He stared at Tom for a long moment before his shoulders heaved up and down under the weight of a sigh. 'You always were one for dwelling on the past, Tom. You've got so much life left to live, but if you're not careful you'll waste it obsessing over what should have been instead of embracing what might yet be.'

15

Three days later and Tom was regretting ever hearing the words Mermaids and Point. He'd never liked chaos and disorganisation, and at the moment that was what every waking moment consisted of. He'd even suffered his first anxiety dream since those early awful weeks after losing Anna, managing to wake Alex, who'd been snoring away in the second double bed of the chain motel they'd booked into, to break their journey from London. As a result, they were both even more tired and grumpy with each other than the already stressful moving process warranted.

'No, no, turn it the other way,' Tom snapped as Alex all but crushed him against the wall.

'I can't turn it the other way,' Alex said through gritted teeth. 'There's no bloody room because *you* insisted we move the chest of drawers first.'

He had a point, but Tom was damned if he would admit it. 'Put your end down then and we'll try and pivot it from this side.'

'Pivot it how?'

'I'll pivot you in a minute. Stop asking stupid questions and get round here.'

'Tom?' Nerissa's voice echoed up the stairs, interrupting what threatened to be all-out war between them.

God, if one more person asked him one more bloody question, he was going to throw himself into the sea. Taking a deep breath, he ignored the evil glare Alex was sending him from the other side of the bed they were wrestling with and called out, 'In Emily's room.'

They'd just about manoeuvred the heavy frame to the correct spot beneath the window when Nerissa appeared in the doorway, a little out of breath from running up the stairs. 'There you are! Sorry, the removal guys want to know where you want the sofa and armchairs putting.'

It was on the tip of his tongue to say he didn't care, but given they'd already had to rearrange most of Emily's furniture not ten minutes after the movers had humped it up the stairs, he quickly decided that wasn't true. 'Thanks, I'll be right down.'

She nodded, sending the ends of the scarf she'd tied around her hair floating about her neck. It was a red one today, with big white polka dots, and matched the red T-shirt she was wearing. There was a smudge of dirt on her left cheek and her faded jeans had dark stains down the front as though she'd wiped her hands on them. She looked as tired as he felt, but still found a smile as she said, 'Hang in there, they're nearly done.'

It was true. The van was well over three-quarters empty. Funny considering how long it had taken them to load it up. He'd heard them talking over a cigarette break about staying in the local pub, so perhaps the thought of a pint or two had given them added impetus.

'And then all we'll have to do is unpack all the boxes,' Alex said with forced merriment. 'What fun!'

Nerissa grinned. 'I can tell which one of you is the joker of the family. I'm going to make a cup of tea if anyone wants one?'

Alex fell to his knees at her feet. 'You are truly a goddess made flesh. I'll have a coffee, black, three sugars and in return I pledge you my undying devotion.'

'Idiot.' She was laughing now. 'Cup of tea, Tom?'

He wanted to blow her a kiss at the prospect of a piping hot cuppa to chase away the dusty, dry feeling in his mouth and throat but settled for a nod, worried she might take it the wrong way. 'Please.' He waited until she'd left the room before nudging Alex none-to-gently with his foot. 'You shouldn't flirt with her.'

Alex sat back on his haunches, an unrepentant grin on his face. 'Why? She's gorgeous, sexy and single – just like me.' He pushed to his feet, stepping a little closer into Tom's space. 'Or is she the real reason you've been so gung-ho about moving here?'

'Nerissa is an employee – nothing more,' Tom snapped.

Rolling his eyes, Alex held up his hands. 'Christ, Tom, it was a joke. We all know you're never going to get over Anna. I'll go and help Nerissa with the drinks.'

Tom stared in disbelief at his brother's retreating back, wondering what the hell was wrong with everyone. First his dad, and now Alex all but accusing him of – what? Spending too much time grieving for his wife? Was there a prescribed timetable for these things, because if so, no one had bothered to tell him about it.

'Can someone tell us where this sofa is going?' The impatient shout from downstairs told him he didn't have time to dwell on it now. He'd catch up with Alex later, once things had calmed down, and find out what was going on.

* * *

Having sorted out the layout of the lounge – subject to change once the kids started moaning about not being able to see the TV properly from their favourite seats – Tom directed the movers to dump the last few boxes in one of the two empty surgery rooms. The practice had clearly been designed for several doctors to share, but from the looks of it, neither of them had ever been used.

Satisfied they were happy to be left to get on with it, Tom headed into the kitchen to find not only his, but the rest of Nerissa's family crowded into the room, half a dozen different conversations on the go at once. Alex was leaning against the wall near the back door, his shoulder a little too close to Nerissa's for Tom's liking. He'd been serious when he told Alex not to flirt with her. Since his break-up with Jo, Alex had lurched from one bed to another, which was his own business as far as Tom was concerned, but there was no way he was going to treat Nerissa like that.

'Here he is! Shove over, lad, and let Tom get at his tea,' Andrew Morgan boomed from next to the kettle, where he was overseeing the filling of an array of mismatched mugs, none of which Tom recognised. He'd met the big, burly man in passing on his visit to the Point, but the way Andrew was beaming at him now, it was like they'd been friends for years.

Accepting the mug Andrew offered him, Tom read the slogan on its side – 'It takes work to be this pretty' – and grinned. 'I'll take that as a compliment.'

'What's that?' Andrew caught sight of the mug he'd given him and laughed. 'That's one of Nick's. Laurie bought it for him for his birthday years back. We thought the last thing you'd want was a mountain of washing up, so we brought enough for everyone. We'll take them all home afterwards.'

'Thanks.' Tom found space to prop himself against the wall

and watched Andrew and the young man he assumed to be Nick make short work of dishing out the drinks. He certainly had the family look about him, with the same dark curls they all sported, apart from Sylvia whose poker-straight red hair was cut into a neat bob.

Once everyone had a mug in their hands, Andrew came to stand next to Tom. 'Hope you don't mind us descending on you like this. Thought you might need a hand with the unpacking and what-have-you.'

'It's great,' Tom said before taking a cautious sip of his tea. He was absolutely parched, and the almost too-hot liquid soothed his throat and lifted his spirits nearly as much as their surprise guests. 'The more the merrier.'

'That's what Sylvia thought.' Andrew nodded to where his wife was sitting at the kitchen table, Emily and Max on either side of her. She was telling them a story, if her expansive hand gestures and their rapt expressions were anything to go by. 'We've got the barbecue and a cold box full of food in the car. Didn't think you'd feel like trying to cook tonight, and it promises to be a lovely evening, too nice to be cooped up inside. Oh, and some beer,' he added with a grin.

'And I thought this cup of tea was good.' Tom laughed. 'Honestly, it's so kind of you, I can't tell you how much I appreciate it.' And he really did. Though he understood their familial connection to Nerissa, there weren't many who'd put themselves out for a stranger to this extent.

'Well, we appreciate you for giving Nerissa a bit of stability.' Andrew cast a fond look across the room at his younger sister. 'She's never complained, of course, but Doc's given her the runaround for a while now.'

'Can't be easy on him, giving up after all these years.' Though Tom had been frustrated with Malcolm for letting things slide for too long – especially the issue of his own health – he liked what he knew of the man and he'd served his community well for many years.

'True that.' Andrew clicked his mug against Tom's like he'd made a toast. 'None of us is getting any younger.' He took a sip, then grinned at Tom over the rim. 'He's set all the tongues about town wagging, shacking up with Barbara Mitchell the way he has. Sly old dog.' Andrew said the last with great admiration.

'If he's found someone that makes him happy, then good on him.'

'Quite right, too. Man wasn't made to be alone. I'd be lost without my Sylvia.'

Tom didn't like the stab of what felt too much like jealousy at the tenderness he heard in Andrew's voice and he was sure that if he looked up, he'd see him gazing devotedly across the room at his wife. But he didn't look up, keeping his eyes on the remains of his tea as he pushed down hard on the ugly feeling trying to creep through him. He couldn't allow what had happened to him to taint his outlook.

A long silence hung between them before Andrew murmured, 'Sorry, that was thoughtless of me.'

'No, you're fine.' He looked up to meet Andrew's concerned gaze, placed a hand on his arm and said again, 'It's fine, really. There's no use dancing around my situation and I know you didn't mean anything by it.' He tapped his mug against Andrew's. 'Cheers to your Sylvia.'

'I'll drink to that.' Andrew beamed, then took a long draught of his tea. 'Right, let's get this lot moving so we can toast her again with something a bit more refreshing.'

'Now that sounds like a very good idea,' Tom replied, relieved they'd negotiated their way around the awkwardness. He instinctively liked this man, and it would be good to make a few friends for himself – people who would take him as he chose to present himself, not look at him and see only what wasn't there any more.

They split up – Sylvia and Laurie going upstairs to focus on unpacking the children's bedrooms, while Tom stayed downstairs with the rest of the men to try to clear the boxes in the lounge and kitchen where Nerissa had stationed herself to put away things to her liking. Tom didn't much care which cupboard the pans or crockery went in, and she could sort out any duplicates and decide what to keep and what could be sent to the thrift shop. The only thing he felt like he should hang onto was the dining service Anna's parents had given them as a wedding present. They'd used it for all their family celebrations over the years, and he hoped Emily might like it when she was ready to set up her own home in the future. He surveyed the pile of boxes with a sigh – that's if he ever managed to locate it in all the chaos.

'What's the plan, then?' Andrew asked, hands on hips as he too surveyed the box mountain.

'Pick one and empty it, I reckon,' Alex offered. 'They'll all have to be opened at some point and I've got a fairly good idea where stuff belongs too, so between Tom and I we can answer any questions.'

'Works for me,' Tom agreed. 'Why don't you and Jake tackle the kitchen boxes, though? If all five of us try to work in here, we'll be falling all over each other.'

They made good progress for the next forty minutes, though it soon became clear the movers had been somewhat liberal with their labelling of the contents of the boxes, and a steady pile of items that belonged elsewhere grew in the hallway.

'These are all DVDs,' Nick said, holding up a handful to show Tom. 'I didn't realise people still had them.'

'Shove them to one side and I'll look at them later. Most of them can probably go to the charity shop because we stream pretty much everything these days.' He should've gone through them before they were packed, but they held a lot of memories – particularly the old Disney ones they'd watched first with Emily and later with Max. Tom had worried he'd get bogged down trying to decide what to keep and what to get rid of, so he'd decided to just bring them with him. He tried not to think what else he'd put off as he folded down the box of cushions he'd just emptied and added it to the stack propped against the back wall.

Before he knew it, the lounge looked more or less straight. Nick was sprawled in front of the TV and other electronics connecting everything up and making sure it all worked, and Tom was happy to leave him to it. With Andrew's help he ferried the pile of empty boxes out through the back door to add to the ones Alex and Jake had cleared from the kitchen.

'Working hard, I see.' Tom nudged Alex as he passed where he was sitting at the table next to Jake, the pair of them unrepentant as they sipped beer from a couple of bottles.

'Hey, if you were as efficient as us, you'd be able to relax too.'

Nerissa turned from where she was rinsing something under the tap and raised a brow. 'Says the man who sat down not thirty seconds ago.'

Tom laughed. 'We're about done too. I'm not bothered about the stuff stacked in the surgery – it's mostly things from my office and I can work my way through that myself. I'll just nip upstairs and see how they're getting on.'

'I'll fire up the barbecue then, shall I?' Andrew asked. When Tom nodded, he laid a hand on Jake's shoulder. 'Want to give me a hand, son?'

'Sure.' Jake rose, picked up his beer and followed Andrew out towards the garden.

'They get on well,' Tom said to Nerissa.

She nodded. 'Thick as thieves, those two – three if you count Nick.'

'Count me in what?' Nick appeared as though mention of his name had summoned him. 'You've started on the beer without me?' He clutched his chest and staggered back. 'How could you?'

Laughing, Alex crossed to the fridge and opened it, displaying shelves packed with fresh meat, salads and lots of beer and wine. He retrieved a couple of bottles and popped the tops off before handing one to Nick and the other to Tom. 'Now are you sure you aren't having a drink, Nerissa?'

She shook her head. 'I'll wait for the others to come down.'

'I'm just going to see how they're getting on,' Tom said.

Nerissa tugged off the bright yellow rubber gloves she'd been using to protect her hands and hung them over the tap. 'I'll come with you, see if they need a hand with anything.'

They were about halfway up the stairs when the sound of raised voices reached them and a flustered-looking Laurie appeared on the landing. 'Oh, there you are, I was just coming to find you.'

'What's going on?' Tom took the last few steps two at a time, realising it was Emily he could hear. She sounded distressed.

'I don't know.' Laurie shook her head. 'Something about a blanket?'

Tom brushed past her, knowing instantly what was wrong as he rushed towards his daughter's room.

Laurie followed on his heels. 'We've emptied all the boxes, but there wasn't a blanket in any of them.'

When he entered Emily's room, Tom registered for a moment how pretty it looked. As well as unpacking everything, Laurie and Sylvia had strung some fairy lights over the bed and added a vase of pink roses to the dressing table. He noted these thoughtful additions in passing as he moved to where Sylvia was trying to calm Emily, who was red-faced and crying. 'It's all right,' he said to the older woman, touching her arm. She looked visibly upset as she stepped back to give him room, and he wondered what Emily might have said to her. He'd deal with that later; first, he had to stop her working herself up into any more of a state. 'Em?' He reached for her arms to steady her, but she thrashed away.

'Where is it?' The last word reached a high, hysterical note.

'Shh, it's all right, calm down.' Tom put his arms around her, letting her push against him for a few moments before she threw her arms around his waist and started crying for real.

'It's gone! What if it went in one of the recycling boxes? I need it, Daddy, you have to find it!'

'Emily!' He almost never raised his voice to her and it stopped her instantly in her tracks. When she tried to pull free, he let her step back, holding her shocked gaze. 'Calm. Down. Okay?'

She paused, then nodded, her chest heaving in little gasps as she tried to catch her breath.

When he was sure she was calm enough to pay attention, he led her over to the side of her bed and sat down. 'We checked every single one of the boxes before we took them to the recycling centre, remember?' Both she and Max had been worried about accidentally getting rid of something they wanted to keep so he'd let them double-check everything before it went in the car. He waited until Emily nodded, then continued. 'We've found all sorts of stuff jumbled up in the wrong boxes downstairs. I'm sure it's been packed away with something else. Can you remember when you last had it?'

She shook her head, sinking down onto the bed next to him. 'No, I don't remember packing it.' A panicked look crossed her eyes and Tom squeezed her hand quickly before she could get herself worked up again.

'We'll find it, okay?' He turned to meet the concerned expressions of the women gathered by the door. 'The blanket is the one Anna used when she nursed the kids.'

'Ah.' Nerissa nodded in understanding, while Sylvia approached them, pulling a folded tissue from her pocket.

'Don't fret, darling.' She handed Emily the tissue before stroking a hand over her hair. 'We'll find it for you.' She glanced at Tom over his daughter's head. 'We'll be fine, you go on.'

Tom left the pair to it and followed Nerissa and Laurie out of the room to where a wide-eyed Max was waiting anxiously on the landing. 'What's wrong?'

'Nothing. We've misplaced Mummy's blanket somewhere and Em's a bit worried that we've lost it.'

Max frowned. 'I haven't got it. I just came to say the last of my boxes is done.'

'Good lad. Do you want to show me your room?' Though the matter of the blanket was pressing, he needed to make sure Max didn't get lost in everything. He was such an easy-going kid it was easy to forget how difficult all the change must be for him too. Five minutes wouldn't make much difference.

Max grinned and dashed down the hallway. 'I can see the sea from my window, come and look!'

Tom let Max guide him around the room, hiding a smile as he pulled open the doors to his wardrobe like he was performing a magic trick to reveal the neatly hanging row of clothes. 'And you're going to keep it like this, right?'

Max gave him a sheepish grin. 'I'll try,' he promised, though they both knew it was a lie. Max was chronically untidy – always had been. Half his baby pictures were of him covered from head to toe in whatever he was supposed to be eating. As he'd grown, the food had been replaced by mud, grass stains and blood from whatever latest scrape or fall he'd got himself into.

'Come on, let's find that blanket and then we can eat. Mr

Morgan is doing a barbecue for us and we're going to have a bit of a moving-in party in the garden.'

Max whooped. 'Can I have a beer?'

Tom laughed. 'No, but nice try.'

A quick check with the others confirmed none of them had seen a crocheted blanket when they'd been unpacking, and everyone abandoned what they were doing to take up the search. With most of the boxes unpacked, there weren't many places left to look, and Tom did his best to quell his worry that perhaps the blanket had indeed made its way into one of the recycling boxes by mistake. While he and Andrew unstacked the boxes piled into the spare room in the surgery so they could be quickly opened and searched, Nerissa stayed in the main house to do a sweep of the rest of the rooms. They'd slit open about half the remaining cartons when she appeared in the corridor holding up a cream-coloured bundle. 'Is this it?'

'Oh, thank God!' Tom abandoned the box he was checking and hurried over to her. 'You bloody miracle worker. Where did you find it?'

'It was folded up in the bottom of a box full of DVDs in the lounge.'

Those bloody DVDs. Tom heaved a sigh of relief. 'Will you take it upstairs for me while we sort out this mess?'

She nodded. 'Of course.'

'Never mind the mess,' Andrew said, clapping him on the shoulder. 'Go and see to your girl and we'll get these put away.' He nodded encouragingly when Tom hesitated. 'Go on. By the time you come down it'll all be straight, and we can get on with what we should be doing – celebrating your arrival!'

16

'I can't possibly eat another thing,' Nerissa said as she put her plate on the table next to her and settled back in one of the fold-out beach chairs her brother had brought with him – along with half the contents of both their fridge and freezer given the amazing spread he and Sylvia had laid on.

'Those might be the best burgers I've ever eaten in my life.' Linda cast a longing glance towards where Andrew still manned the barbecue, as he grilled yet another round of sausages, burgers and home-made chicken and vegetable kebabs.

'Give it a few minutes and you might find room for another,' Nerissa said with a grin.

'Oh, I couldn't possibly.' Linda pressed a hand to her stomach as though she had something to hide, when in Nerissa's opinion she was still a few pounds shy of being a healthy weight. Her skin had lost that awful grey pallor from when Jake had brought her to stay in the Point at least, and her hair shone with vibrant health. She cast another look at the barbecue. 'Well maybe half a one.'

'That's the spirit.'

Nerissa surveyed the happy chaos of the garden. Nick, Jake

and Alex had found a football from somewhere and were playing some kind of improvised game with Max and the dog which seemed to involve knocking each other over as much as trying to actually score a goal between the two cushions, which had been spaced apart at the far end of the garden. Plates and half-empty glasses were strewn across the grass, tucked under chairs and stacked on the table, where the remains of the salad accompaniments were congealing in the sun.

A large wasp buzzed past her ear and started hovering around the table, prompting her into action. The last thing she wanted to do was move, but if they didn't clear up a bit, then they'd be inundated with, not just wasps, but all sorts of other insects attracted by the smell.

'Oh, here, let me help.' Linda rose a few seconds after her. 'It was so nice of you to let me gate-crash the party, it's the least I can do to help out.'

'You're not gate-crashing, Linda, you're part of the family.' Nerissa knew it would take time for the other woman to really believe that she was welcome within the ever-expanding family group.

'Jake said the same thing when he phoned me.' Linda's voice was soft, her tone holding a hesitant longing.

'He was the one who asked me about inviting you,' Nerissa said, giving Linda a smile of thanks as she lifted a stack of dirty plates from the table. Knowing her son actively wanted her to be part of things lit Linda's answering smile – as Nerissa had hoped it would.

'That's nice.' She looked across at the raucous game, laughing when she saw Jake stiff-arm Alex so Max could duck between them and steal the ball, which he carried over the goal line with a cheer of triumph. 'He's the happiest I've ever seen him.'

Nerissa gathered as many glasses as she could between her

fingers and led the way into the kitchen. She'd already removed everything from the table in anticipation of the clear-up operation. 'Put the plates on there for now.' She nodded towards it as she stacked the glasses on the worktop beside the sink. 'Let's get everything in first, and then we can sort it out from there.'

At that moment, Tom appeared in the doorway, a pile of serving bowls in his hands. 'Where do you want these?'

'On the table, please.' Nerissa came over to join him. 'You didn't have to do that.' She was supposed to be looking after things, and it was her family who'd turned up and made all the mess.

Ignoring her comment, Tom studied the half-empty dishes. 'I reckon anything without mayonnaise looks fine, don't you? Someone with more sense than me has already put the lids back on the olives and stuff from the deli, so I think most of it can go back in the fridge.' When Nerissa turned for the door to fetch another load, he stopped her with a gentle hand on her arm. 'Leave it. Linda and I can bring in the rest while you carry on in here.'

She hesitated. 'Well. If you don't mind?'

'Of course I don't.' He gave her a frown. 'We need to make time to sit down tomorrow and work out exactly what your duties are going to be. I'm very grateful to have your help, but I'm not expecting you to do everything. The kids have always had chores and that's going to continue – and I'll pitch in as well. I'm not Malcolm, expecting you to do everything for me.'

Nerissa didn't get a chance to reply as the kitchen was suddenly full of willing helpers laden with various bits and pieces from the garden, and all her attention was on marshalling them into some sort of order. Mindful of what Tom had said about wanting the children to do their bit, she put Emily in charge of rinsing the plates and stacking the dishwasher, while Laurie sorted out some clean plates just in case anyone else wanted a last burger or kebab. Sylvia took over the task of salvaging what would do for another day and between her and Linda they soon had the table cleared and the food caddy full of the waste. Rather than wait for the dishwasher to run through its cycle, Nerissa washed the glasses by hand, while Tom dried them and set them back on the now-clean table ready for people to help themselves if they wanted another drink.

With perfect timing, the boys appeared at the door, sweaty and unkempt from their exertions. 'Anything we can do?' The cherubic grin on Nick's face said he knew full well they'd waited until everything was finished.

Biting her lip so as not to smile, but goodness it was hard to resist when he was so cheeky and charming, Nerissa tugged off her rubber gloves before turning to face them properly. 'I was just saying to Tom, we might as well get the rest of those boxes emptied while everyone is here. You three can make a start on those while we finish up in here.' She tilted her head towards the door leading to the surgery and the room still stacked with the rest of Tom's things.

Three matching expressions of dismay stared back at her. 'I... I thought we'd agreed to leave those for another day,' Alex said, looking not at her but towards Tom.

'I know we did, but honestly Nerissa's right, it'd be great to get everything sorted tonight.' Tom had a much better poker face than she did and Nerissa had to turn back towards the sink to hide her laughter.

'But we've just eaten,' Nick protested, like he hadn't been rolling around on the grass two minutes earlier with Jake in a headlock. 'It's not good to exert ourselves on a full stomach.'

'Chop chop!' Sylvia clapped her hands together, never one to

be excluded from a joke. 'It shouldn't take you more than an hour
– two at most.'

When Tom started moving towards the surgery door, the
three of them trooped into the kitchen in various stages of
disgruntled acceptance.

Nerissa held her silence, wondering how far he'd take it – or if
in fact he'd decided it would be a good idea to tackle the boxes
after all. Only at the last minute did Tom stop by the fridge and
yank the door open. Reaching in, he pulled out a couple of
bottles of beers and shoved them towards Alex and Jake, while
Nerissa, Sylvia and Linda burst out laughing.

'You—' Alex appeared to remember the presence of his niece
at the last minute and cut off whatever rude word was obviously
on the tip of his tongue, while a grinning Tom handed him
another couple of beers, then retrieved a bottle of wine from the
shelf in the door.

'The look on your face,' Tom spluttered. 'It was almost worth
going through with it just to see if you'd actually start unpacking
again.'

'The next time you want help from me, you can swing for it,'
Alex muttered darkly, before he too started laughing. 'I can't
believe you got me like that.'

Tom pointed at Nerissa with the hand still holding the wine
bottle. 'She started it, not me.'

'Hey!' Nerissa protested. 'Talk about throwing me under the
bus.' She eyed the bottle in his hand, good sense warring with the
desire to make the evening last. 'Perhaps I should put the
kettle on.'

Sylvia looked at her watch. 'It's not even half-past seven. We
could have another little drinky first.'

'Half a glass, then,' Nerissa agreed, demonstrating an embarrassing lack of willpower. 'But I'll need something stronger than a

cup of tea if we do, so just as well Tom bought that fancy coffee maker with him.'

With the coffee machine set up and brewing away, and everyone shooed back out into the garden, Nerissa gave the clean work surfaces one more wipe down for good luck before resuming her seat next to Linda. The game of football had been abandoned for a much more leisurely, though no less boisterous, card game which reminded Nerissa of the Top Trumps games Andrew had loved when they were children. Deciding it was too complicated, she, Linda and Sylvia had opted out, but everyone else was sprawled on the grass in a big circle, each clutching a handful of colourful cards. From the amount of laughter and vociferous accusations flying around, it was clear that at least some of the group had taken a flexible approach to the rules.

'What are you up to next weekend?' Linda asked, nibbling on the half a burger she and Sylvia had split, even after both protested they really shouldn't.

'I haven't even thought that far ahead,' Nerissa admitted. 'Tom starts seeing patients on Thursday, once he's got Max started at school. There's bound to be a few teething problems while we get used to his way of doing things. I'll probably spend it changing things around to suit him.'

'But you can't work all weekend,' Sylvia protested.

'I probably won't, but I wanted to keep things free to give me the option to do that if I need to.' Nerissa took a sip of wine, then tilted her head back to watch the last of the fluffy clouds float away across the deepening sky. It was that lovely point of the evening, just on the cusp of twilight, when the breeze off the sea had chased away the worst of the day's heat and it was the perfect temperature. The noise and laughter washed over her and she closed her eyes briefly to allow the joy and contentment of the moment to soak in. When she opened them again, Sylvia and

Linda had their heads together giggling over something on Linda's phone. 'What are you looking at?' She leaned closer to see.

Linda turned the phone and showed her a selfie she'd taken while wearing a wetsuit. 'Look at the state of it! I finally got the courage to try it on last night and, my God, it was a full-body workout just getting in and out of it.'

'You look great.' It was the truth. Even red-faced and with her hair dishevelled from her exertions, there was a hint of pride in Linda's expression. 'When's the first session?'

'Saturday afternoon.' Linda pulled her phone back and tucked it in her pocket. 'That's one of the reasons why I was wondering what you were doing next weekend.'

'Oh.' Nerissa forced herself to keep her expression neutral. Though they'd chatted about Linda joining the local open water swimming group, Nerissa was pretty sure she hadn't said anything to indicate she planned on joining in as well.

'I thought you might come with me if you were free. A bit of moral support.' Linda shrugged it off with a smile. 'But, of course, you are busy. Don't worry it was just an idea.'

'I'd come and cheer you on,' Sylvia said, giving Linda a pat on the leg. 'But it's coming towards the end of the season so we'll be making the most of it in the shop. I can meet you for a coffee afterwards, though, and you can tell me and Laurie all about it.'

Nerissa couldn't help the twinge of guilt as the other two continued to make plans for Saturday. Linda was trying so hard since coming to the Point, and it couldn't be easy to keep stepping outside her comfort zone and push herself into meeting new people and trying new things. Nerissa had always loved playing in the water since she was old enough to splash around in the shallows and was a strong swimmer. It had just never occurred to her to get involved with it as an organised activity. Hadn't she decided that she needed to change things around, though? Stuff like salsa dancing really didn't appeal, but she needed to take a leaf out of Linda's book and try a few new activities for herself. She'd always blamed Doc for taking up too much of her time, but maybe it'd also been a convenient excuse to hide behind. Though she and Tom hadn't agreed her exact hours and responsibilities yet, it'd been clear from their brief conversation in the kitchen that he didn't want or expect her to run around after them in the same way she had with Doc. If she didn't like it, she didn't have to do it again, and it sounded like Linda was feeling a bit nervous about it. 'All right,' she found herself saying. 'I'll give it a go.'

Linda turned to stare at her. 'Give it a go? You mean you're going to swim as well? I only meant it would be good to have a bit of company when I headed down there, and I thought it would be easier as you'll probably know most if not everyone already.'

'Oh, but I thought, well, I mean, of course, I'd be happy to offer moral support and introduce you...' Nerissa trailed off from her attempted backtracking as Linda's expression dimmed a little. 'What the heck! I've said I'll do it, so I'll do it.'

A beaming smile lit Linda's face. 'Oh, fantastic! I'll WhatsApp you the details of where I hired the wetsuit from. I'm sure they'll have something in your size. And if you hate it, you only have to do it once.' She laughed. 'I'll probably only get in as far as my knees and change my mind anyway!'

Nerissa ignored the amused expression on her sister-in-law's face as they both listened to Linda chatter on about what she thought it might be like. Like Linda said, she only had to try it once – and what was the worst that could happen?

* * *

To her relief, Nerissa and Linda weren't the only people trying open water swimming for the first time. The group gathered on a secluded part of the beach and received a full safety briefing from a local volunteer from the RNLI on potential dangers and what to do if they got into any difficulties. They were then each handed a bright pink swimming cap to ensure they would be visible at all times, before being paired off with a buddy who was a more experienced member of the group.

She'd felt a bit awkward about taking off her padded winter coat – they'd all been advised to have something warm they could put on when they got out – but when everyone else started stripping down to their wetsuits, she took a deep breath and did the same. It had taken a lot of baby powder and muttered swearing to wriggle her way into the thing, but at least the zip up the back had a long enough tag attached that she'd been able to do it up without any problems.

There were people of all shapes, sizes and ages in amongst the group and they were so friendly and matter-of-fact about piling their things up above the waterline, telling Nerissa, Linda and the other newbies hilarious horror stories about coats and towels getting washed out to sea when people had forgotten about the incoming tide.

Getting her mass of curls into the swimming cap was almost more difficult than her struggles with the wetsuit, and by the time Nerissa and Paul – her buddy for the session – had managed to tug it on tight enough it wouldn't pop off her head like a cork leaving a bottle, they were both laughing so hard she forgot any lingering anxiety over how much of her shape the figure-hugging wetsuit revealed.

She knew Paul in passing – he and his wife, Victoria, had retired to a town house a few doors down from where Andrew and Sylvia lived about five years previously, and though they were registered at the surgery, she never saw much of either of them. As he helped Nerissa over the pebbles and onto the sand near the waterline, he smiled at her. 'Vicki and I first started open water swimming at a local reservoir before we moved here. It was wonderful, but nothing like being in the ocean.'

'It seems silly not to have tried it before when I've lived here all my life. I mean, I swam all the time in the summer growing up, but I haven't been in for more than a paddle for years now,' Nerissa admitted as they took a couple of steps into the shallows and he halted her with a hand held in front of her.

'Well, hopefully this taster session will change all that.' Paul bent over and began splashing water up his chest and over his arms. 'Even though the temperature isn't too bad now because of the consistently hot weather over the summer, it's still vital to give your body a chance to adjust.'

The lifeguard had said as much, Nerissa remembered as she copied Paul and tried not to wince at the shock of the cold even through the wetsuit. Her feet were already tingling from being in the water, and she swished them around to keep her circulation going.

Over the course of the next ten minutes, they eased their way gradually deeper until the waves were finally lapping well up her chest with each gentle surge towards the shore. With Paul at her side, keeping himself between her and the open water, they began a leisurely breaststroke parallel with the shore. All around her, pink hats bobbed and dipped in the water like shiny beacons as the group made their way to the agreed turning point.

It was harder than she expected, and by the time they reached that halfway mark, some fifteen minutes later, Nerissa felt a little breathless.

'Do you want to take a break?' Paul asked, treading water beside her.

'I think I should,' Nerissa nodded, forgetting for a moment where she was and ending up with a face full of water as a wave washed into her. Spluttering, she turned for the shore and was grateful when Paul touched her shoulder and said it was shallow enough to find her footing. As they waded in, she was relieved to notice she wasn't the only beginner who was heading for the beach. 'I'm sorry to drag you out so quickly,' she apologised to Paul as they walked briskly towards the pile of coats. The sun overhead was still warm, but her face, hands and feet tingled from prolonged contact with the cold water and she knew it wouldn't be long before the rest of her body caught up.

'Don't you worry about it,' Paul assured her as he handed her the big, hooded parka, pausing to zip up the front when her fingers were a bit clumsy. He shrugged into his own coat, then tugged gloves and thick socks out of the pockets and sat in the sand to pull them on. Nerissa had brought a pair of old sheepskin boots which she used mostly for dog-walking and she wiggled her toes into their cosy depths with a sigh of relief.

Nerissa looked around the people sprawled on the sand nearby, but she couldn't see Linda amongst them. Hoping she was all right, she raised a hand against the bright reflection of the sun on the water and felt herself relax as she recognised Linda and petite Victoria wading into the shallows a short distance down the beach.

'So, what did you think?' Paul nudged her elbow, drawing her attention to the plastic mug of tea he'd poured from a flask.

'I'm thinking I didn't come half as well prepared as you!' Nerissa grinned as she accepted the tea with thanks, wrapping her hands around it to soak heat into her chilly fingers.

'You'll have more of an idea of what you need to bring next time.' He tilted his head to one side and gave her a speculative look. 'Assuming there's going to be a next time.'

'I'll think about it.' And she would. Though she was feeling the after-effects now, it had been exhilarating while she'd been in the water. The lack of time she'd been able to spend in there also said something about how much she'd neglected her fitness. Her daily dog walks with Toby were all well and good, but it'd been a long time since she'd done anything to get her heart racing. She turned her attention to Linda, who was approaching them with a huge grin on her face. 'How was it?'

'Wonderful!' Linda plopped down onto the sand beside her, grimacing as she tugged the tight swim cap off her head. 'Exhilarating and a tiny bit terrifying too.' She smiled in thanks as Victoria handed her the towel and coat she'd brought with her. 'I don't think I would've enjoyed it half so much without your help, though.' She blotted the worst of the water off, then wrestled her way into her coat – with a bit of assistance from Nerissa when her damp arm got snagged in one of her sleeves. 'Thanks. So, did you enjoy it?'

Nerissa considered for a moment. 'I think so.' She laughed. 'Gosh, that sounds so wishy-washy. Yes. I did enjoy it, but it was also a lot harder than I thought it was going to be.'

'It's not like doing a few lengths in the pool on holiday, is it?' Linda agreed. 'I want to give it a few more goes before I really make up my mind.'

'That's a good idea,' Paul chipped in. 'And this is the best time of year to get accustomed to it before the weather turns. This is about the warmest the sea will be all year, so if you find it too cold now, then you really won't enjoy it once we get a bit later in the year.'

'You won't swim all year round, surely?' Nerissa asked. The storms they got in the winter could be brutal and the tidal surge treacherous.

'No, definitely not. Depends on how lucky we are with the

conditions.' He held his crossed fingers up to the sky. 'If this good weather continues, then I reckon we'll go for another six, maybe eight weeks. After that it's a case of watching and waiting. We'll get the odd calm patch which goes on until the spring when we'll start organised sessions like this again.' He glanced up at his wife, who had put her own coat on and was draining the last of the tea she'd poured for herself. 'You fit, my love?'

Victoria nodded. 'I am.' She smiled at Linda and Nerissa. 'It was so lovely to spend some time with you both and I really hope we'll see you again next weekend. We have to dash as our daughter and her husband are coming for lunch.'

Nerissa handed back her mug, then pushed herself to her feet. 'Thank you for giving us so much help.' She hesitated for a moment, and then decided what the hell. 'If Linda is up for it, then I'll definitely give it another go next week.'

'I'm game if you are.' Linda tried to push herself up from the sand, then shook her head and held out a hand to Nerissa. 'I definitely need to work on my fitness!' she said with a laugh as Nerissa helped her stand. They said their goodbyes to Paul and Victoria, and waved to the other members of the group who were starting to gather their things and move away.

'Right, let's get going, shall we?' Nerissa wrapped her arms around herself to ward off a shiver. 'I need a hot shower and something to eat.'

They began to trudge across the pebbles towards the steps that would take them to the main road.

'Is there an indoor pool anywhere nearby?' Linda asked. 'Even if I don't stick with this during the colder months, it would be nice to get into swimming regularly – that way I'll be in better shape for when the season starts again next year.'

Nerissa wondered if the other woman was even conscious of the way she was talking like she would be a permanent fixture in the Point, but decided not to mention it. It was hugely encouraging if Linda was starting to feel like she could make a home for herself here – it would certainly make Jake's life easier if she was nearby. If Sylvia was here, she'd likely jump on it. Her sister-in-law had very fixed ideas about what was best for the people in her life and Nerissa didn't think Linda was quite strong enough to stand up for herself. It wouldn't help her or Jake if Linda was persuaded into something she might later regret by too much well-meant interference. 'There's a sports centre next to the high school in Yardston,' she said, referencing the nearest big town. 'I'm sure it's open to the public, but we'd have to check the website for the times.'

'We can have a look over lunch, maybe?' A hint of shyness had crept into Linda's voice, like she was worried she might be taking up too much of Nerissa's time.

'I'm definitely up for it. I've agreed with Tom and the children that they'll fend for themselves at the weekends apart from an evening meal, so I have the rest of the day to myself.' They reached the top of the steps where they would part company, Linda's cottage being in the opposite direction to the surgery. 'I'll see you in Laurie's when you're ready. No rush.'

Linda shifted her weight and for a moment Nerissa thought she was going to hug her, but she settled for a gentle touch to her arm. 'Lovely. And thanks for coming with me today. I don't think I would've done it without you.'

'That's what friends are for.'

17

Tom ripped the tape off the last of the boxes he'd emptied, balled it up and tossed it in the bin, then unfolded the box and propped it against the wall with a sigh of satisfaction. His office looked like a small bomb had gone off, but he reckoned another couple of hours after lunch and he'd have everything squared away. He'd originally planned to use one of the spare rooms in the living quarters as an office, but decided having the flexibility of a second guestroom would be better. Alex had headed back to London that morning, but he'd left most of the things he'd brought with him in the main spare room, saying he'd be back again in a couple of weekends time. If he was going to lay claim to that space, they might as well keep the second one for things like the children's birthdays and the Christmas holidays when his dad and Philippa might want to visit as well. He'd hung onto one of the old bedframes Malcolm hadn't wanted to take with him, so all it would need was a new mattress and a few soft furnishings – something even Tom could manage to sort out. Besides, he mused as he wandered back down the corridor towards the connecting door to the house, one of the reasons he'd moved here was to get a better work-life balance. Keeping everything to do with the surgery behind this door would be a good start.

The kitchen was empty, as was the lounge when he poked his head around the door. Max had gone to a new friend's for the morning but was supposed to be home for lunch. The plan was to make a start on a project they'd been assigned at school, but Tom secretly hoped they were working on their budding friendship more than worrying about schoolwork. His mobile started to ring at that very moment, an unknown number. 'Hello, Tom Nelson.'

'Dr Nelson, hi, it's Miranda, Ben's mum.'

'Hi Miranda, please call me Tom. Is everything okay?' He perched on the arm of the sofa and hoped Max hadn't got into any mischief in the couple of hours he'd been gone.

'Oh, yes, Tom.' She gave that embarrassed half-laugh new people often used when he encouraged them not to use his title. His was one of those jobs some folks found hard to look beyond. 'Everything is fine. That's why I'm calling, actually. The boys are having a blast together, so I thought I might keep Max here for lunch, if that's all right with you?'

Tom sighed in relief. 'That's great, really kind of you, thanks. I appreciate the invitation in the first place.'

'Well, we were all new at some point, weren't we?' She laughed. 'Well, not us because I was born and bred in the Point and so was Freddie, but you know what I mean.' Tom nodded, though of course she couldn't see that through the phone. 'Ben was a bit anxious about going up to the high school, so I was glad when he mentioned he and Max were sitting next to each other on the bus. He has his friends from the village school of course, but he said he didn't want Max not to have anyone to sit with.'

'That was very kind of him. I'll be happy to have him over anytime. I'm keen for Max to settle in as quickly as possible.'

'That would be great. And we'd like to have you over for

supper one evening soon as well. We'll invite some other friends so you can get to know a few people. Nothing fancy.'

Tom's gut sank like he'd swallowed a rock because he'd learned the hard way what those words often meant from well-meaning friends of his and Anna. 'Thanks.' It was the most non-committal response he could manage.

The line went silent for a moment and then Miranda laughed. 'Oh God! I've just realised how that must have sounded. Don't worry, I don't have any single friends that I'm looking to hook up with the handsome new doctor.'

Tom coughed at the comment, wondering how many rumours were flying around the village about the 'handsome' new doctor, then laughed. 'Then, in that case, I'd be very happy to accept. Just text me a date and I'll make sure I'm available – emergencies aside, of course.'

'Lovely. We'll drop Max off later. Take care, Tom.'

'You too, and thanks again for the invites – plural.'

'My pleasure, bye!'

Smiling to himself at the idea that just maybe Max wasn't the only one who'd made a new friend today, Tom tucked his phone away and headed towards the stairs. He was a bit hot and sweaty from humping and dumping boxes in his office, so a quick shower before lunch would probably be a good idea.

'Em?' he called as he started up the stairs. 'I'm making some lunch in a minute if you want anything?'

He checked her room and found it empty. Pausing to fold over the rumpled quilt, he picked up a couple of items of clothing that had been chucked on the floor and laid them over the stool in front of her dressing table. The clutter of bottles, tubes and bits of make-up spilling across the top he left for her to sort out. At least she was making herself at home.

He crossed to the window but couldn't see any sign of her in the back garden. Frowning, he pulled his phone out again and was relieved to see a little red '1' on the WhatsApp icon.

Taken the dog for a walk with Bas.

Wondering who the heck Bas was, but resisting the urge to start messaging a barrage of questions, he sent a quick 'OK' back as he wandered across the hallway into his own room. He chucked his phone on the bed, then pulled his grubby T-shirt over his head as he toed off his trainers.

He'd just bent over to pull off his socks when he heard Nerissa calling. 'Hello? Emily, can you give me a hand a minute?'

'She's out walking the dog,' he called out without straightening up.

'Oh, sorry! Sorry!'

Tom peered under his arm to see a red-faced Nerissa hovering in the doorway of his room dressed in nothing more than a figure-hugging wetsuit. Her long curls hung in thick wet strands around her face. As he straightened up, she spun on her heel so her back was to him. Suppressing a grin at her display of modesty, he grabbed his T-shirt and tugged it back on, not bothering to tuck it in. 'I'm decent.'

She spun to face him once more. 'I'm so sorry to barge in on you like that.'

'No harm done. Is everything all right?'

Nerissa stared at her toes for a moment before glancing up at him through her lashes. 'I was rather hoping Emily might be around to help me.' She held up a long strip of black material, very similar to the fabric of her wetsuit. 'The tag came off.' Her cheeks reddened once more.

Confused, he looked from the strip in her hand to her wetsuit, then back again before it dawned on him. The front of her suit was completely smooth, meaning it must be one that zipped up the back. 'Are you stuck?'

She nodded, then blew out a breath. 'Completely. I've tried for about ten minutes, but I can't get hold of the end of the bloody zip now the tag's come off.'

He could picture her huffing and puffing and getting more and more stressed out as she wriggled around trying to grab it. Not hiding his grin this time, he motioned with his hand for her to turn around, which she did. As he stepped up behind her, she swept her hair away from her neck, the long, wet curls dangling from her fingers, leaving the delicate column of her neck exposed. He'd seen hundreds of necks in his time, and much more private parts of many, many people, but that was in a medical context and this suddenly felt much more intimate. There was something about the juxtaposition of her pale skin against the harsh black of the suit. The fact the rest of her body was hidden beneath the padded neoprene only emphasised the vulnerability of the exposed patch of skin.

He rubbed the pads of his fingers together, feeling suddenly awkward at the unexpected awareness that he'd not been this close to a woman who wasn't Anna for over twenty years. *Cervical spine, not her neck.* The mental correction helped him reach out and take hold of the zip. He gave it a tug with just the tips of his fingers, but it didn't budge. Damn.

'You might need to hold the material at the top to give it some tension.' Nerissa's voice was low, husky almost, and Tom found himself swallowing down a laugh because there was already enough tension to cut with a knife – at least on his part.

'Hang on a sec.' He had to pull at the tight material to get the fingers of his left hand underneath the neckline enough to grip it. A shudder rippled through her, shocking Tom out of his stupid daze. The poor woman was freezing! 'Here we go.' He tugged the zip down a couple of inches. 'How's that.'

Nerissa scooped her hair into one hand and scrabbled behind her back with the other. 'A little more?' She flashed him a quick, embarrassed smile over her shoulder. 'I must have T-Rex arms or something.'

He laughed then, the last of the tension breaking, and he tugged the zip down towards the base of her spine, revealing a column of silky skin – well, it might have been silky had it not been pebbled in goosebumps. At least the suit was tight enough that it stayed in place, because if it had started to slip he wasn't quite sure what he might have done about it. Fingers itching from the need to soothe the chill from her skin, he forced himself to take several steps back. 'There, that should do it.'

She reached behind once more to check she could manage on her own, then all but sprinted from the room. 'Thanks,' she called, her feet already pattering on the stairs leading up to her suite of rooms on the top floor.

Tom heaved a deep breath, then another, before deliberately crossing the room and closing his bedroom door. He shucked his T-shirt, jeans and underwear and strode quickly for the shower in his en suite bathroom. Setting the dial several notches cooler than he normally preferred it, he stepped under the stream before the temperature had even adjusted and recited the anatomy of the spine from the C1 Atlas vertebrae to the coccyx until he could stop thinking about the possibility Nerissa had shivered from something other than the cold.

* * *

Half an hour later, he was sitting down to enjoy a massive doorstep cheese and pickle sandwich when the kitchen door opened and in bowled Toby, all wagging tail and happy barks.

'Hello, you mad thing,' Tom said, taking one hand off his sandwich to knuckle the top of the dog's head. When Toby leaned against his thigh and gave him the most pleading expression on his face, Tom laughed as he lifted his sandwich higher out of the way. 'Not a bloody chance.' With a disappointed sigh, Toby abandoned his fleeting begging attempts and wandered over to his basket in the corner, leaving a patch of drool staining the leg of Tom's jeans as a parting gift. 'Great.'

Abandoning his food, Tom went to the sink and sponged the mark, then washed his hands again for good measure. It was only as he retook his seat that he noticed the murmur of conversation drifting in through the open door – Emily's familiar light cadence and a slightly deeper, definitely masculine responder. Curiosity piqued, Tom leaned a little closer towards the door, but he couldn't make out what they were saying. At that moment, Nerissa walked into the kitchen dressed in a pretty summer dress – one of those floaty things that always looked so cool and comfortable. Tom immediately raised a finger to his lips.

Nerissa paused, frowning for a moment until the voices drifted in once more from outside. A knowing grin spread across her lips and she pointed towards her floral tote bag which was hanging over the back of one of the kitchen chairs, before she tiptoed towards it. Carefully opening the flap, she pulled out a little notepad and scribbled something before sliding it towards him.

Going to the café for lunch, do you need anything from the shops?

Tom shook his head, then reached for the pen.

Who's Bas???

Nerissa took the pen back and wrote:

The lad who cleans for us. You met him briefly yesterday. Good boy. V smart.

Tom pictured the smiling young man he'd seen in the waiting area the previous evening as he'd come out to welcome his last appointment of the day and nodded to Nerissa to indicate he remembered.

Nerissa gathered the notepad and pen and stowed them back in her bag, before hooking it over her shoulder. 'Right,' she said in a loud, bright manner. 'I'm off to meet Linda and Sylvia for lunch. If you think of anything you need from town, just send me a message and I'll pick it up.'

The pair outside had fallen silent.

Tom grinned at Nerissa, then said in an equally loud voice, 'Thanks. Max is out at a friend's and I'm not sure what time he'll be back, and I need to finish sorting out my office, so take your time and enjoy yourself.' He spoke the next words in his normal tone, deciding Emily and her new friend had more than enough warning. 'Shall we just have something lazy for dinner?'

'Sounds good.' Nerissa crossed over to the fridge and tugged it open. 'There's plenty of salad left over from yesterday, I could pick up a couple of fresh pizzas from the deli to go with it?' She cast the question over her shoulder at Tom.

'Great. Any flavour, as long as there's no anchovies.' He gave a shudder. Horrible, hairy little things, he didn't know how anyone could eat them.

Nerissa closed the fridge and headed towards the back door. 'No anchovies. I think I can manage that.'

She was almost outside when Tom suddenly remembered he hadn't given her any money. 'Hang on.' He bolted from his seat, pulling his wallet from his back pocket to fish out a twenty-pound note. 'That reminds me,' he said, holding it out to her. 'I need to go online and sort out that housekeeping account. I'll do it this afternoon.'

Nerissa accepted the cash. 'Thank you. No rush on the account, I know you've got a lot of things still to sort out. I'm keeping a record of everything anyway.' She stepped over the threshold. 'Right, well I'll see you later.'

Tom tucked his hands in his pockets, conscious he'd all but chased her to the door. 'See you.'

He waited until she'd greeted the two lurking teenagers and moved away before poking his head around the doorframe.

'Hello, sweetheart, I didn't realise you were there.'

Emily rolled her eyes. 'Could you be any more obvious, Dad?' She turned to the dark-skinned, tall boy leaning on the wall beside her. 'Sorry. If we ignore him, he'll go away in a minute.'

He might well have done just that if she'd kept her smart mouth shut, but though he knew there was an element of bravado and showing off for her new friend, there was no way Tom was letting that pass. Instead of returning to his lunch, he stepped fully out into the garden. If she was going to accuse him of being embarrassing, then he was more than willing to deliver it up in spades. Meeting Emily's scowl with a smile that showed more teeth than a shark, Tom took up sentry opposite the pair. 'Why don't you introduce me to your new friend, poppet?' She bloody hated it when he called her that.

Seizing the initiative and winning a massive amount of respect from Tom, Bas straightened up and offered his hand.

'Sebastian Donovan, Dr Nelson. We didn't get a chance to meet properly yesterday.'

Tom shook his hand, liking the direct eye contact as much as the firmness of the boy's grip. 'Of course. Sorry, I meant to catch up with you afterwards, but I got called away to a home visit. Nerissa tells me you're a really hard worker, and I must say I've been impressed with the little bit I've seen so far.'

Bas ducked his head briefly, a smile of what Tom hoped was pride breaking out. 'Cheers, Dr Nelson.'

'You can call me Tom.'

Bas laughed. 'Not anywhere my mum can hear me I won't!' He glanced at the smart watch on his wrist. 'Speaking of which, I better be getting back to look after my sister.' He offered his hand again to Tom. 'Nice to meet you, Dr... Tom.'

'Dr Tom works for me and shouldn't get you any grief from your mum,' Tom said with a grin as he shook the boy's hand once more. 'See you soon.'

'I'll be in Monday evening,' Bas confirmed, then turned to Emily. 'Think about it and let me know, yeah?' And with that he turned on his heel and walked away in that long, loping stride of a boy-not-quite-a-man who was still growing into his final frame.

Tom watched him go for a moment before turning to face Emily. Without Bas there she'd shrunk a little in upon herself and Tom hoped she was reconsidering her earlier attitude. He didn't want to be constantly butting heads with her. 'Do you want some lunch?'

She nodded and followed him into the kitchen.

His long-abandoned sandwich had started to harden so Tom rescued the slab of cheese from inside and chucked the bread in the food caddy. He cut himself another couple of thick slices from the fresh baked loaf and a pair of thinner ones for Emily. 'Nerissa's going to grab some pizza for dinner, if that's all right with you?' he asked his daughter, who was stretching up to lift a glass down from one of the cupboards.

'Fine with me.'

He watched her silently add a dash of squash to the glass before filling it with water, but that was all he was getting, apparently.

Swallowing a sigh of frustration, he opened the fridge and perused the shelf. 'Cheese, ham or there's some tuna mayo already mixed?'

'Tuna's fine.'

Fine. He might have to ban the bloody word.

Tom spread the filling on the bread, slapped the two slices together and tossed the sandwich on a plate. He set it down on the table in front of Emily with perhaps a little more force than was required, then took his own seat opposite. They ate in silence. No sign of the chatty, sparky girl he'd overheard speaking in the garden just a few minutes earlier.

He knew better than to pry but the protective urge got a bit too much to resist sometimes. Bas seemed like a decent young man, but Em was still so vulnerable. Doing his best to sound casual, he asked 'So, what was Bas talking about when he left?'

Her shoulder lifted, her gaze remaining fixed on her plate. 'Nothing, really.'

'*Em.*'

She sighed. 'Look, I didn't want to tell you because you'll just make a big deal out of it.'

Well that didn't sound great. 'And if I promise to just listen?'

She laughed. 'As if.'

He waited, all but grinding his teeth against the need to fill the silence. He'd promised to listen, so that's what he'd do.

'It's not that big a deal,' she said, finally, using her finger to press up the crumbs on her plate. 'Bas starts back at college on

Monday, and he said the student advisory team there is really cool. I thought I might go in and have a chat with them. See what my options are, you know, with resits and whatever.'

She'd been devastated when her exam results came through and she'd missed the predicted scores on a couple of key subjects. Tom had been worried as hell about it, but he'd promised her she could take a gap year, and though it'd gone against his every instinct, he'd stuck to his word. Just the idea she might be ready to think about going back to her studies was enough to make him want to jump for joy. Just as well Bas had gone home or he might have kissed the poor lad. 'And is that something you're happy to do on your own?'

That shoulder shrug again. 'There's a bus that goes from the high street and stops almost opposite the college. I can go in with Bas and there's a couple of other people he's promised to introduce me to.'

Though he was excited at the prospect of her making new contacts that would hopefully grow into friendships he knew better than to push. 'If that's what you want, then I think it's sensible to get some advice.' When she didn't look up, he reached across and gently pushed her plate out of reach of her fiddling. She cast him a look from under her overgrown fringe and he gave her what he hoped would be an encouraging smile. 'I'll support whatever you choose to do.'

Her eyes narrowed a touch. 'But you think I should go back.'

'I think...' he cut himself off and really thought for a moment about what he wanted to say. 'I think you are old enough to recognise the importance of good results in ensuring you have the widest possible options open to you for your future. But I also said you could take a year off and I will one hundred per cent stick to that promise if that's what you decide to do.' He nudged his own plate aside and rested his folded arms on the table.

'Look, Em. I'm going to need you to tell me if you want my help with any of this. I'm a bloody awful mind-reader so I can't tell when you want me to back off and when you want me to wade in. It's hard work this dad stuff, you know?'

She smiled then. 'This daughter stuff isn't exactly easy.' She heaved a sigh. 'I'll go in on Monday and talk to them, and then maybe we can talk it over afterwards?'

Tom nodded. 'You've got yourself a deal. Now, do you want anything else to eat?'

Shaking her head, Emily pushed back her chair and rose. 'I'm going to go upstairs for a bit, if that's all right?'

'Sure. I've got to finish sorting my office out anyway.' He let her get almost to the door before he called her name. When she looked back at him, he held out his hand, palm flat. 'Forgetting something?' He might not have made a big deal about the way she'd spoken to him earlier, but she must think he was born yesterday if she imagined she'd get away with it scot-free. She knew the rules, and regardless of whatever else was going on between them, actions had consequences.

She rolled her eyes, but still tugged her phone out of her pocket and slouched back to the table to put it in his hand. 'When can I have it back?'

'After dinner. Go on, now.' She flounced from the room and there was a moment when he thought she might slam the door, but instead she closed it very slowly and deliberately. 'That's my girl,' he murmured to himself as he shoved her phone in his pocket and began clearing away the plates.

18

'And then what happened?' Sylvia leaned so far forward she all but tumbled off her chair.

'Nothing! I got out of there as quickly as possible before I made an even bigger fool of myself.' When both Linda and Sylvia responded to that with sighs of what could only be described as disappointment, Nerissa scowled at them. 'He's my boss,' she hissed.

'He's six foot something of exactly what you need,' Sylvia countered, making Linda all but snort coffee out of her nose.

'Stop it!' God, why did her sister-in-law have to be so indiscreet? Nerissa glanced nervously around the busy café, worried about who might be listening. Her hand fluttered towards her neck before she forced it back into her lap. She'd taken Gareth's ring off before she'd gone swimming and after her reaction towards Tom touching her – as innocent as it may have been – she'd felt awkward about putting it on after her shower so had left it resting in the little glass dish on her bedside cabinet.

'Everything all right?' Laurie paused beside their table, a pair of dirty mugs hanging off one hand, a small stack of plates balanced on the other.

'Your aunt's been getting up close and personal with sexy Dr Tom,' Sylvia said, eyes flashing in amusement.

'Whaaattttttt?' Laurie's eyes grew round as saucers as she slid into the spare chair at their table and dumped the dirty dishes in front of her. 'Tell me more!'

'I hate you,' Nerissa mouthed across the table as Sylvia launched into an altogether more lurid recounting of the unfortunate incident with the wetsuit, as those few humiliating moments would forever be known in her head.

'And when he touched her neck as he was unzipping it, she went all goosebumpy,' Sylvia was saying to Laurie with far too much relish.

'It was cold!' Nerissa interjected.

'Funny how that didn't come up when you were describing it to us,' Linda said, mildly.

'I thought you were my friend,' Nerissa huffed.

As the three of them cackled like hens, she folded her arms and sat back in her chair. Honest to God, she should've never said anything in the first place. She'd meant it to be a humorous anecdote, a joke they'd laugh at together that she could then dismiss from her mind. Only, it hadn't quite come out the way she'd intended and now she'd never hear the end of it.

Groaning, she covered her face in her hands. 'I never should've said anything.'

'Oh, come on, Nerissa, it's all right.' Laurie gently tugged her hands away and gave her a sympathetic smile. 'We're just pulling your leg, that's all.'

'Speak for yourself,' Sylvia countered. 'I think this is the best thing that's happened in years. I must admit I had high hopes of something happening between the two of you, but I didn't think the sparks would be flying this quickly.'

'Mum!' Laurie glared at her mother before turning back to Nerissa. 'Ignore her, she's just winding you up. I'm sure he'll think it was something and nothing, don't even worry about it.'

'I hope so.' Nerissa took a sip of her now-cold tea and shoved the cup back onto the saucer with a grimace. 'I don't want him getting the wrong idea about me.'

'The right idea, you mean.' When both her daughter and Nerissa turned on her, Sylvia held her hands up in surrender. 'All right, all right. If you don't want to take advantage of living under the same roof as the village's most eligible bachelor, I won't say another word on the matter.' She zipped her fingers across her lips.

Nerissa wanted to believe that was indeed the last she would hear on the matter, but she knew Sylvia a lot better than that. Once she got fixated on an idea it was almost impossible to get her off it. 'Give it a rest, will you? He's not for me.'

Sylvia snorted. 'No one will ever be for you unless you let them in. At least you've had the good sense to take that ring off. There's a point when a memory becomes a millstone, you know.'

Nerissa's hand flew protectively to the bare space at her throat. 'That's not fair.' They'd had this argument too many times before. 'I'm not against the idea of falling in love again – I've just never met the right man.' When her sister-in-law opened her mouth to speak, Nerissa held up a hand. 'Don't. Just don't.'

'I only want what's best for you.'

Nerissa leaned forward, deciding it was time to try a different approach. 'The man has lost his wife. He and I work together. He has two children he needs to take care of. What about any of that makes you think he would be remotely interested in me?'

'He's got eyes. And a pulse.'

Frustrated beyond words at that flippant response, Nerissa started to lean back. There was just no point in talking to her when she got like this.

Sylvia laid a hand over her own, holding her still. 'You weren't made to be alone, Nerissa. You and your brother are peas in a pod. All that love inside you – you need to find someone to give it to. Someone who will treasure it and give it back to you tenfold.'

Nerissa swallowed down the lump forming in her throat. 'I had that once.'

'And what? You think you can't have it again?' It was Sylvia's turn to sound frustrated. 'There's no such thing as soulmates. There's no *one* person who is our perfect match. Save that nonsense for the romance books. What there is are people who come into our lives and make the risk worth the reward. It's messy and difficult and wonderful, but never perfect. If you wait for perfection, you'll end up with nothing. Am I right?' she addressed the last words to Linda. 'Tell her that I'm right.'

Linda held up her hands. 'Don't drag me into this.'

'There, see! Now you've upset Linda,' Nerissa snapped. 'This was supposed to be a nice lunch with friends, can we please get back to that?'

'Oh, I'm not upset,' Linda said, her tone matter-of-fact. 'I'm just the last person in the world to give romantic advice, based on my track record.'

Nerissa cringed and even Sylvia had the good grace to blush. 'Sorry. That was tactless of me.'

Linda shrugged. 'It's the truth.' She turned towards Nerissa. 'Look, I'm a long way from even thinking about another relationship, but I will agree with one thing Sylvia said. I'd hate to think that Nigel was my one shot at a happy relationship, because if he was, then life owes me a damn refund.'

'Exactly my point!' Sylvia folded her arms and gave Nerissa a smug smile. 'I'm not saying you should throw yourself at Tom – though you never know, he might like it.'

'Sylvia!' Nerissa half-laughed, half-despaired.

'Just be open to the possibility, that's all I'm saying. Give it time and see what develops naturally.'

'Naturally? Nothing is going to develop between us naturally. We're co-workers.'

'But you could be friends given time, and the right circumstances. He just needs to see you in a different light, that's all. A non-work environment. You should both come to Sunday dinner tomorrow – and the children, of course. Your brother always cooks enough to feed the five thousand. Linda's coming, aren't you?'

Linda jolted from what Nerissa suspected was a kick under the table. 'What? Oh, umm, yes. Sunday lunch, lovely. The more the merrier.' She gave Nerissa a helpless look of apology.

'No.'

'No?' Sylvia widened her eyes in mock-surprise and Nerissa wished she was close enough because she'd be giving *her* a kick under the table – and not a gentle one. 'Well, perhaps another time.'

Perhaps when the ocean froze over. Or mermaids really did start showing up in the bay – and not ones who were pop stars staging a publicity stunt, but the proper, mythical ones Nerissa and Laurie had both been named after. 'Perhaps,' Nerissa said in the same tone with which said 'no'.

Whether she'd decided she'd made her point or as a gesture of peace, Sylvia reached for one of the menus Laurie had laid on their table earlier. 'Right then, what shall we have for lunch? I quite fancy a slice of quiche.'

* * *

Thankfully, the rest of their lunch passed smoothly, and by the time Nerissa let herself back into the surgery, it was after half-past two. The kitchen was empty, but she followed the sounds of revving engines to the lounge to find Max sitting cross-legged on the sofa, a game controller in his hand and what looked like a Formula One type racing game on the screen. From somewhere overhead, she could hear the thump-thump of music and deduced from that Emily was up in her bedroom.

'I'm back,' Nerissa announced to Max, before noticing the empty glass on the coffee table. Moving to pick it up, she waved it towards him. 'Need a refill?'

'No thanks.' Eyes glued to the screen, he still managed a smile.

'I'll leave you to it, then. I'm going to make a start on tomorrow's lunch.' If she got the prep done now, she could leave the meat to cook and have a couple of hours to herself before she needed to finish everything off.

She'd only had time to tie her hair up out the way, wash her hands and slip an apron on to protect her dress when Max appeared. 'What are you making?'

'I got some nice steak from the butcher yesterday, so I thought I'd make a pie.'

'Make it?' He pulled a chair out from the table and plonked down on it. 'Can't you just buy one?'

Nerissa smiled. 'I could do, but home-made is always nicer. Besides, it doesn't take very long.' She opened the cupboard she stored all her baking things in and pulled out the large earthenware mixing bowl that had belonged to her mum, followed by a deep, ceramic pie dish. She placed them both on the table, then rummaged in a drawer for her rolling pin, pastry brush and a fork to crimp the edges of the crust.

'What's this for?' Max picked up the pastry brush and started playing with it.

'Wash your hands, please, if you're going to help me.' She hadn't meant to suggest it, it was just something her mum had always said to her and Andrew when they were kids messing about in her kitchen.

Max looked up at her. 'Can I help you?'

He sounded surprisingly eager, so she nodded. 'If you want to. There's a spare apron hanging on the back of the door.' When he turned his nose up at the idea, she folded her arms. 'My kitchen, my rules, and as I'll be the one trying to get bits of stuck-on pastry out of your clothes later, rule one is you have to wear an apron.'

He grumbled a little but did as he was told.

When he'd washed his hands, she asked him to show her and she lifted first one hand, then the other to study his nails for any dirt. 'You'll do,' she said, with a wink. 'Now, have you done any baking before?'

Max hesitated. 'I made some fairy cakes with my mum, but that was a long time ago.'

Her heart ached at the forlorn expression on his face, and she couldn't fight the urge to touch his cheek. 'We can do that another day, if you'd like? It's good to remember the fun you had together.' When he nodded, she decided to leave it at that. 'Right, let's get everything we need for today. Can you get me eggs and butter from the fridge, please?'

While he did that, she got the flour, her trusty kitchen scales and a large wooden board, which she placed on the table with a cloth beneath it to catch any stray flour. It took her probably twice as long to show Max each step in the process rather than doing it herself, but he was eager to learn and it was nice to have a bit of company. She was surprised at how well he concentrated throughout the process, having expected him to get bored, and once they wrapped the prepared pastry in cling film and set it in the fridge to rest, she expected he'd be eager to get back to his game. 'Thank you for your help.'

'Is that it?' He frowned at her.

'Well, I need to make the filling and let that cook for a couple of hours, but that's it for now so you can go back to your game if you want to.'

Max's face fell. 'Oh, okay.'

'I mean, you can stay if you want to – it won't be very exciting, chopping some mushrooms and peeling a few carrots, that sort of thing.'

'I can do that!'

The pieces of carrot were a variety of sizes and the mushrooms cut a bit too big, but Nerissa didn't care because it was worth it. She found a station on the radio that played hits from the 80s and 90s and in spite of Max's many protests about how rubbish the music was, they ended up having an impromptu disco once the meat and vegetables were simmering away in the oven.

'And now,' the DJ announced. *'Here's one I'm sure you'll all remember the moves to. Get up off your sofa and join in because here comes Los del Rio and "Macarena".'*

The pulsing beat of the music kicked in and Nerissa clapped her hands together. 'Oh, I remember this.' She started doing the hand movements automatically even though it must've been twenty-five years or more since she'd last done it. 'Come on, Max,' she called out to him as she swung her hips in a circle and did a quarter-turn jump to the right. 'It's easy.'

'What do I do?' he asked, standing next to her.

'Just follow my lead. Shoulder, shoulder, behind your ear, and again. Hip, hip, bottom, bottom, big circle, now jump!' She called out the instructions as she moved and he started to copy her and they both started laughing when he jumped the wrong way and ended up facing her.

'Like this?' He was using the opposite hands to her, but she was amazed at how quickly he picked it up.

As the 'Aiiiiieee!' end of the chorus played again, they both jumped and Nerissa found herself face-to-face with Tom, who was leaning in the doorway of the surgery corridor, a huge grin on his face. She should probably have been embarrassed, but damn it, she was having too much fun. 'Come on, Tom! I bet you know this.'

'Dad doesn't dance,' Max said before almost falling over laughing as he got his arms all tangled up and lost his place in the dance.

'Ha. Shows what you know.' Shoving up the sleeves of his rugby shirt, Tom stepped into line with them and, to Max's delighted horror, he picked up the moves at exactly the right point and performed a perfect round of them.

The song was just coming to an end when Emily came marching in from the other door. 'Can't you turn it down?' She stopped dead at the sight of them all gyrating around the table. 'Oh my God, what is this?'

'Join in, Em!' Tom wiggled his extended fingers towards her.

'You're all mad!' With a flip of her long, blonde hair and a look of absolute disgust, she turned on her heel and stomped out of the room.

Nerissa exchanged a look with Tom, and they burst out laughing.

'I think we've just been told off,' he said, holding onto the table as he pretended to be out of breath from their dancing exertions.

'Oh, you get used to it.' Max said it in such a blasé way that Nerissa couldn't help laughing all over again. As she watched Tom grab his son and the pair mock wrestle around the kitchen, her heart gave a funny little twist. She rubbed the spot with the heel of her hand, hoping to drive it away. Damn Sylvia for putting stupid ideas in her head.

19

After an initial flurry of appointments, Tom found things settling down into an easy routine at the surgery. Most of his first couple of weeks had been people wanting to check in and welcome him to the village while taking his measure. He got the feeling he was probably the talk of the place – it had certainly felt that way when he was stopped in the street every time he ventured outside the surgery walls. As they moved into October, he was recognising more faces when he was greeted by name everywhere he went, but the sense of familiarity still felt a bit strange at times.

There were several areas of improvement he'd identified already, and the most important one was around the lack of specialist women's health support. When it came to sexual and reproductive help, it seemed like Malcolm had farmed his patients out to the regional health clinic, but that was a good half an hour's drive away. He wanted the residents of the Point to be able to access as many services as possible under the one roof. They certainly had room in the surgery for regular health visitor sessions. He was already in discussions with the county's sexual health service about one of their nurses coming in for at least a couple of days a month to offer on-site appointments. In the long run, he hoped to recruit a full-time practice nurse, but he wanted to get a bit more of a feel for the needs of the community before he committed to that.

The phone on his desk buzzed and Tom shook off his wandering thoughts to answer it. 'Hi Nerissa.'

'Donald Turner's here for his ten-thirty appointment.'

Tom glanced at the clock on the wall. Like most of his recent attendees, Donald was in good time. 'Thanks, I'll be out shortly.'

He took time to read through the man's most recent history. Like a lot of men in his age group there were a few weight concerns and a blood pressure issue. He checked the latest prescription notes, frowning over the outdated medication listed. It wasn't the first time he'd come across something similar. He was trying hard not to be too much of a new broom and change everything to the way he would've done it, but Donald looked like a prime candidate for statins. As far as Tom could see, there wasn't anything in his notes to indicate so much as a discussion about it.

Locking his screen, Tom headed to the reception area. The custom in London had been for patients to be directed to the right room, but he liked adding a more personal touch to things. Now he was the boss rather than a cooperating partner, he could do what he wanted with little things like this.

Apart from a red-faced gentleman sitting awkwardly in the chair nearest the door, the waiting area was empty. There was a buggy parked in the corner where there were a few toys to keep little ones occupied and when he looked over at Nerissa it was to find her cooing at a very small child sitting in her lap.

She glanced up and raised the baby's hand to give him a wave. 'Say hello to Dr Tom.'

'I'll be right with you,' Tom said to the waiting man, then

crossed over to the desk. 'Hello,' he said, bending forward so he didn't loom over the child. 'What's your name?'

'This is Samuel.' Nerissa patted the little boy's head. 'He's not been feeling very well, have you, darling?'

'Poor thing.' Tom touched the back of his hand to the boy's forehead. He was a bit warm, but that might be because he was bundled up in about six layers. 'We'll soon have you right.' He smiled up at Nerissa and mouthed 'Donald?' with a sideways glance at the waiting man. She nodded and he returned to the waiting area, offering his hand as the man stood up. 'Sorry to keep you waiting, I'm Dr Nelson.'

The man shook his hand. 'Donald Turner. I just need a repeat on my prescription. I normally get it straight from the chemist, but I was told I had to come in for an appointment.' He sounded a bit disgruntled, as though resenting what he thought was a waste of time.

He wasn't the first reluctant patient, and he wouldn't be the last, but Tom was not prepared to dispense prescriptions without meeting the patients first. 'Well, I appreciate your time. Come on through, now.'

Having led the way into his surgery and closed the door behind them, Tom indicated the chair beside his desk while he washed his hands at the sink.

'So, how've you been?' he asked as he resumed his seat.

'Fine. Like I said, I just need a repeat prescription. I'm not a time-waster when it comes to things like seeing the doctor. Too many people rush up here at the slightest thing. We've raised a generation of malingerers.' He shook his head, the ruddy hue of his cheeks darkening several shades.

'No one who wants to speak to me is wasting my time,' Tom said in as gentle a tone as he could muster. 'Support services in small villages like this are few and far between, so I'm happy to see anyone who needs a chat – regardless of whether there's an urgent clinical need.' He unlocked his computer, then turned back to Donald. 'I'm making a point of seeing everyone as their current prescriptions come up for renewal, not just you. I want to put a face to the name, have a quick chat and give you a once-over.' He glanced back at the screen. 'It says here you haven't been in for a physical appointment for the past eighteen months.'

'Hasn't been any need,' Donald harrumphed. 'Doc sorted me out with my pills and I've been right as rain ever since.'

'I'm sure that's the case, but I'd still like to run a few basic checks. If you can take your jacket off and roll up your sleeve, please.'

With a near constant grumbling from Donald, Tom managed to run through the basics with a blood pressure check, weight, eyes, et cetera. He was just about to roll down his sleeve when Tom caught sight of an angry patch of reddened skin on Donald's elbow.

'Hold on a tick, let me have a look at that.'

Donald huffed. 'It's nothing. Flares up now and then.' He stood still and allowed Tom to take a look.

'And what do you put on it?'

'Nothing. Well, a bit of Vaseline when it gets sore.' He pulled his arm away and started rolling down his sleeve. 'Doc says it's fine.'

Tom tried not to grind his teeth. 'I'm sure Malcolm gave you his best advice, but as your records say, it's been over eighteen months since you were last in the surgery.'

Donald huffed a laugh. 'I saw him the other night and he had a quick look. It's fine.' He reached for his jacket and shrugged back into it. 'Look, I've got work to be doing, can I get my prescription now?'

Tom resumed his seat as he tried to understand the implications of what Donald had just told him. 'You spoke to Malcolm and he offered you medical advice?'

'No need to make it sound so hoity-toity. I had a pint with him the other night and he took a look, that's all. Don't know why you're making such a fuss about everything.' Donald sat back in his seat, arms folded across his chest, the look on his face saying what he thought of Tom wasting his time.

Keeping his cool, Tom tapped a few notes into the computer, then clicked through to the prescribing section. He waited for the printout, checked and signed it, then slid it towards Donald, keeping his fingers pressed on the paper so the other man couldn't snatch it away. 'I want to try you on something slightly different. It should do the same job as your previous tablets, it's just a bit newer on the market.'

'Newer doesn't necessarily mean better,' Donald said sourly. 'I told you I'm fine on what I'm taking now.'

Tom retrieved a second printout. 'This is some information about your new medication, and there's results from a study on the other side which shows it's improved effectiveness.' He folded the sheet and tucked it under the prescription. 'I've also prescribed you a corticosteroid cream which should help calm that eczema down. Use it two or three times a day as per the instructions on the leaflet.'

'Steroids? Isn't that what weightlifters use? You won't be catching me down the gym anytime!' Donald laughed as he scooped up the papers and pocketed them all.

More's the pity. Tom decided that was an argument for another day. It would take time for Donald and some of the others to come around, and Tom didn't want to put him off by going in all guns blazing on their first meeting. 'I'll give you a call in a couple of weeks to see how you're getting on with the new medication. If you've got any questions or concerns, then pick up the phone anytime, or pop in the surgery.'

'All right, Doc.' Donald's tone said he wouldn't be doing either any time soon.

Holding back a sigh, Tom showed the older man out, shook hands with him and spoke to the young woman who he assumed was Samuel's mother as she was now holding the grizzling child and rubbing his back. Tom would've liked to take a bit of time to get his system ready, but she looked worried and the baby was not at all happy.

'Take him on through,' he said, giving her a reassuring smile. 'And I'll be right behind you.'

He waited until she'd steered the buggy one-handed down the corridor before leaning over the reception desk.

'What's Samuel's mother's name?' he murmured to Nerissa.

'Molly. First-time mother, bit of a worrier, but then her mum always fussed over everything.'

Tom flashed her a grin. It was very handy having her to rely on for the inside track on everyone. 'Cheers.' He turned away, then turned back. 'Do you mind keeping an eye on the kids tonight?'

Nerissa raised her brows but shook her head. 'It's fine. Have you got an out-of-hours appointment?' She turned towards the computer. 'I haven't got a note of anything.'

'No, it's more of social thing.'

'Oh, going out dancing?'

Tom's mind immediately filled with visions of her jumping around in the kitchen, her raven hair flying as she held hands with Max and spun to the music. Laughter. She'd looked like laughter, and joy, and a warmth he'd wanted to cup in his palms and protect.

'Tom?'

Realising he'd been staring at her too long, Tom took a step back. 'I'm going to the pub.' At her look of amused surprise, he shook his head. 'Not what you think, I'll explain later.'

While he sympathised if his predecessor was struggling a bit to let go of the reins, he and Malcolm needed to have a quiet little chat about boundaries. And while he was out, he'd better take some time to give himself a mental pep talk about boundaries of a different kind.

The Sailor's Rest was a lot quieter than the last time Tom had set foot in there now the summer crowds had gone and the weather had taken a turn. Seeing the array of coats hanging from the hooks just inside the door, Tom took his cue and removed his soaking-wet anorak, shaking it out of the door to remove the worst of the moisture, before finding a hook to leave it on. A dark mat he didn't remember stretched across the entrance, so he made a point of wiping his feet, too, before stepping onto the polished hardwood floor.

A couple of tables were occupied, but the majority of the clientele were stationed at various points around the square bar area which dominated the back wall of the pub. Malcolm was in what Tom guessed might be his usual spot on the right-hand side of the bar. Though it was tempting to make a beeline straight for him, Tom decided a more casual approach might be in order, so he found a space further along the bar and waited.

Pete, the landlord, caught his eye over the pump and gave him a nod to say he'd be with him, and Tom smiled in return.

'Evening, Dr Tom.'

Tom didn't recognise the man a couple of stools down from him who'd leaned forward and raised his pint in Tom's direction, but he was getting used to that now. Resting his elbow on the bar, he turned to face the man who greeted him and said, 'Evening. Filthy night out there.'

The man nodded. 'First of many before the autumn's out.' He gave Tom a bit of sly grin. 'That'll teach you to view the Point when she's wearing her summer best.'

Tom laughed. 'I think you're right there, but I've no regrets.'

'Yet.' The wry interjection came from another man sitting further along and they all laughed.

'Well, at least I know what to expect now,' Tom said just as Pete finished serving and moved towards him. He ordered a bottle of alcohol-free lager, which raised an eyebrow until Tom lifted the mobile he'd set on the bar in front of him. 'On call.'

'Then this one is on the house, Dr Tom,' Pete said as he placed the bottle in front of him.

'Oh no, I couldn't, I didn't mean... I wasn't fishing for a freebie or anything!' By the time he'd stuttered to a stop, most of the men at the bar were either grinning or outright laughing.

'Get on with yourself,' Pete said, shaking his head. 'No one thinks you were, but in a small place like this we have to look after those that look after us. Enjoy your drink.' And with that he wandered off to serve another customer.

'Come sit here, Dr Tom.' The first man who'd engaged him patted the empty stool next to him. 'Save me cricking my neck trying to talk to you.'

Tom took the stool and offered his free hand to the man. 'It's just Tom.'

The man shook his hand. 'I'm Tony and you might as well get used to being Dr Tom because that's what the village has settled on. You can't be Doc because, well, Doc is Doc'. He nodded across the bar to where Malcolm was sitting. 'But you're still *a* doc, so Dr Tom it is.'

'Fair enough.' Because, really, it sounded like he'd already lost the battle on this one. 'What do you do, Tony?'

'I run a boat tour business from the harbour.' He paused to take a sip of his drink before continuing. 'You'll have already met the rest of my mob, what with Nerissa living with you, and all.'

Tom decided he definitely didn't want to get into a conversation correcting that perception of his living arrangements because any caveat he tried to put on it would likely only stoke rumours neither one of them needed to deal with. 'You're a Morgan?' He didn't mean to sound surprised, but the man next to him looked nothing like Nerissa or Andrew, with his sandy hair turning white at the temples.

Tony laughed. 'Not exactly, Sylvia's my sister, though Andrew and I've been thick as thieves since we were lads, so might as well be considered brothers. Our Nick works for me on the boats.'

'He's a good lad,' Tom said, thinking about how much time both Nick and Jake had spent playing with Max in the garden, as well as how hard they'd worked with the unpacking.

'He has his moments.' Tony grinned around the glass he raised to his lips. 'So,' he said when he set his pint down once more. 'What brings you out on a rotten night like this?'

'I haven't had much of a chance to get out and about so I thought it'd be good to show my face.' He cast a surreptitious glance towards Malcolm, then leaned closer to Tony. 'I heard Doc might be running a bit of an impromptu clinic here.'

Tony laughed. 'He's always made himself available to people, wherever he is around the village. I guess after doing a job like that for so many years it's a struggle for him to let it all go.' He rubbed a hand across his chin, expression thoughtful. 'My dad was the same when he finally stepped down as skipper on our trawler. Used to drive me bloody crackers the way he questioned every little detail of what I was doing. He used to corner the crew and demand a full recounting of our trips, then come and bend my ear if he felt I'd made the wrong choice about something.' He shook his head. 'I miss the old goat, but bloody hell was I glad that he wasn't around by the time I decided it was time to sell up and switch to what I'm doing now.'

His expression was so bleak, Tom reached out to touch his shoulder in a gesture of comfort. 'Change is hard.'

Tony barked a laugh. 'You're not wrong there. Still, it was past time, and I think Sylvia might have done for me if I'd kept Nick out on the trawler for too much longer. I won't lie, we had a rough couple of years when we got washed out and the tourists stayed away, but thanks to the mermaid and the sunshine this has been our best summer yet.'

'She brought a lot of luck to us,' one of the other men said. 'The mermaids always come when the Point needs them the most.'

Several more raised their glasses in toast.

Bemused, but not wanting to insult anyone, Tom leaned in towards Tony once more. 'I thought the mermaid turned out to be that pop star.'

Tony grinned as he pressed a finger to his lips. 'Don't spoil the story now, Dr Tom. I expect that most legends have a much simpler explanation, but we're men of the sea and always have been. Let us have our tall tales.'

'Fair enough.' Tom tipped his bottle towards Tony's glass. 'I'll drink to that. Mind you,' he said, setting his beer down once more, 'I think half the reason I was able to persuade the kids to give it a go moving here was the prospect they might run into Aurora Storm.'

Tony shook his head. 'Been and gone, I'm afraid. Took my nephew's heart with her when she left, so maybe there's something in those mermaid myths after all.'

Nick hadn't struck Tom as being someone suffering from a broken heart, but then again he'd perfected his public mask after losing Anna. Everything was about perception, about choosing what to share and what to hide away. Tom had been a little too good at hiding his feelings away and almost cut himself off in the process. He hoped Nick wouldn't do the same.

'Anyway, enough of that. How are you and the kids settling in?'

'Good,' Tom said, before draining the last of his beer. 'Max is finding his feet at school and Emily's going to the college a couple of days a week to study for some resits.' He checked the time, then grabbed his phone and sent a quick text to Nerissa.

Everything okay?

All good. M's playing a game…

No surprise there, Tom thought.

E's in her room on a live watch party with some friends from college (whatever that is).

Nerissa added a shrugging emoji at the end of her message.

He wondered what Nerissa was doing for the evening. Was she curled up on the sofa in her little sitting room upstairs, or pottering around in the kitchen preparing things for breakfast the next morning? Whatever she was doing, it was none of his damn business, Tom reminded himself.

He tapped into the phone:

Thanks. Won't be long.

Take your time.

Clearly, she wasn't bothered about him staying out – and why on earth should she be? Irritated with himself for feeling irritated about her apparent lack of interest, he slung his phone down on the bar. Glancing up, he found Tony watching him with an expectant look. 'What?'

'Just wondered if you fancied another?' Tony pointed at his empty beer bottle.

Tom hesitated, though there seemed little point. It wasn't like anyone at home was missing him. He was enjoying the other man's company and it would be good for people to see him out and about around the Point, get to know him a bit outside the surgery. He knew it would take a long time for people to become as comfortable with him as they were with Malcolm. He glanced over to where his predecessor was taking his leave of his companions. 'I will have another,' he said to Tony. 'My shout, though. Just give me a minute.'

He caught up with Malcolm as the older man was struggling with the sleeve of his coat. Reaching out, Tom tugged the tucked-in end free, then stepped back while Malcolm finished putting it on.

'Thank you. How's things?' He gave Tom the once-over. 'You seem to be surviving.'

Tom laughed. 'Just about. Not sure I'm winning everyone over with my bedside manner.'

Malcolm chuckled. 'Ah, yes. I heard as much from Donald when he was in here earlier.'

'Checking back in with you, was he?'

When the older man flushed, Tom felt a twinge of guilt.

'Look, I don't want to fall out with you, but I can't have you contradicting my treatment of patients.'

'But it's all right for you to override every decision I've made?' Malcolm scowled as he reached for a hat hanging on one of the pegs. 'My body might've slowed down, but my mind is still sharp enough, I'll have you know.'

Tom raised his hands, palms out. 'I didn't mean to cast any kind of aspersions on your treatment of your patients, Malcolm. From what I've seen so far, you've done a remarkable job managing a patient list that size on your own. All I'm saying is we need this transition to go as smoothly as possible – for all our sakes.'

The older man bristled before lowering his shoulders and nodding in agreement. 'You're right. It's just...'

'Hard.' Tom finished for him. 'And if I was in your shoes, I'm sure I'd feel exactly the same way.' A thought occurred to him. 'Look, I'll understand if you say no, but I'm thinking about doing a bit of a push around men's health, but I'm not sure how well that would be received, particularly with the older generation.'

Malcolm turned the brim of his hat through his fingers. 'I'm listening.'

'When Donald came to see me today, it was obvious he's of that mindset where you don't bother the doctor unless it's something dire. Too many men leave things too late because they don't want to talk about stuff, or don't want to make a fuss. I'd really like that to change and I'm hoping it's something you might help me with.'

Malcolm stopped fiddling with his hat, a gleam of interest in his eyes. 'What did you have in mind?'

Tom shrugged. 'I haven't worked it all out in my head, exactly, but something along the lines of a well man clinic. Something you could take the lead on if you'd like to still be involved with things. It wouldn't take more than one or two sessions a month – maybe a couple of chats here in the pub just to float the idea, and then you could host drop-in days at the surgery – or booked appointments if you'd prefer, or a mixture of the two.'

'Hmmm. Not sure there'd be much take-up.'

It wasn't an outright refusal though, and Tom would take it. The more he thought about it, the more excited he was by the idea. He was already making progress with better preventative support for the female population of the Point, so why not the men? 'Even if one or two dropped in and we caught something early, that'd be a win in my book.'

'And this isn't just something you've made up on the fly to stop me interfering?' The look on Malcolm's face said he knew that's exactly what it was.

'Doesn't make it a bad idea, does it?' Tom countered, deciding honesty was the only way to win him over. 'Have a think about it, and if you're interested then come by the surgery and we can talk it through properly. I'd value your input because no one knows better than you what this community needs.'

'All right.' Malcolm set his hat upon his head, then turned up his collar. 'I'd better get back before Barbara comes and drags me away. Confounded woman wants to know where I am twenty-four hours in the day.' There was enough affection in that grumble to say he didn't really mind having someone keeping tabs on him.

Tom offered his hand, and they shook. 'I'll hear from you soon, hopefully.'

'We'll see.' Malcolm turned and tugged open the door, muttering to himself as he did. 'Well man clinic indeed! Who comes up with these things?'

As the door shut on the cold blast of air, Tom couldn't help smiling to himself. For all Malcolm's bluster, he'd bet it wouldn't be too long before he heard from him.

20

'I won't be long,' Nerissa called towards the open door leading from the kitchen to the lounge as she removed Toby's lead from one of the hooks on the wall. She couldn't help smiling at the full key rack as she bent to clip the lead on the retriever's collar. When it had just been her and Doc, there'd only ever been a couple of sets of keys hanging there – the spare one for his car, her backdoor key. Now it was a busy jumble of things – much like the rest of the house. Emily's keys took up the most space, thanks to the myriad keyrings hooked onto them, including a teddy bear and dangling chain festooned with stars, moons and a piece of pink quartz. Nerissa recognised it from the rack of similar trinkets her brother sold in his shop.

Next to it Max had hung both the lanyard holding the swipe card he used to pay for his lunches and his school jumper. Sighing at the hole the sharp hook had poked through the grey wool, she carefully took it down. Folding it up, she set it on the kitchen table so she'd remember to pick it up on her return and catch the damage with a couple of stitches before it got any worse. The boy was a menace. A sweet-faced, smiling menace she found it impossible to be cross with even when he did silly things like put a hole in something he'd only had for a few weeks.

She did a mental count of how many it'd been since he started school. Six weeks – that's all it had been since the Nelsons had arrived and turned everything upside down. Some days it was hard to remember what it was like before they'd arrived.

Her gaze strayed to the detritus of breakfast plates and bowls stacked on the worktop directly above the dishwasher and she tried to ignore the itch in her fingers to sort it out. Loading and unloading it was one of the chores Tom had assigned to the children. While she applauded his attempts at getting them to accept a level of responsibility for things around the house, she really, really wished he'd given them tasks outside of her beloved kitchen.

She'd just pushed to her feet when Max bounced into the room, hair sticking up every which way as though he'd rolled out of bed and headed straight for the sofa. She eyed the T-shirt and stretchy pyjama bottoms he was wearing; come to think of it he probably had. 'Are you taking Toby for a walk in this weather?' he asked with an incredulous look on his face.

'Yes, of course I am.' The glorious sunshine they'd been blessed with for most of the summer had been swept away by an endless parade of autumn storms – the kind that seemed to blow in from nowhere. The rain which had been lashing the windows since the previous evening had eased to a fine drizzle, so she was making the most of it. The thunderheads looming on the horizon promised the storm wasn't over by a long shot. 'He needs lots of exercise every day.'

'Oh.' Max seemed to think about that for a moment before nodding as though he saw the sense in it. 'Can I come?'

'I thought you had chores to do.' Nerissa cast a pointed look at the pile of dirty dishes.

'Oh, I'll do them when I get back. Just let me go and get changed.' Max turned around and all but bumped into Tom who'd followed him into the kitchen. His hair didn't look much neater than Max's, but that was down to a callout in the early hours to attend a sick baby with a high temperature. The dark circles under his eyes said he hadn't managed to get any more sleep since he'd got back.

'You'll do them now,' Tom said, taking Max firmly by the shoulders and turning his son to face the mess on the worktop. 'What have I told you about being considerate of the spaces we all have to share. Nerissa doesn't want to live in a pigsty any more than I do.'

'But she said I could go for a walk with her and Toby,' Max protested, being more than a little economical with the truth.

The rude noise Tom made said what he thought in a succinct if not exactly elegant way. 'Rubbish. She was probably hoping to escape for a bit of peace and quiet, not have you pestering her.'

'I don't mind,' Nerissa said, because she really didn't. Max might leave a little too much chaos in his wake, but she was growing increasingly fond of his boundless curiosity and the way he kept finding ways to join in with whatever she was doing. She wondered if he was subconsciously missing his mother – and the kind of things he might have done with her – so she made a point of letting him help whenever he showed an interest in things. The crust on the steak and mushroom pie they'd made for Sunday lunch the other week might have been a bit thick in places, but the laughter filling the kitchen as she'd taught him how to make the pastry had been worth it. The fairy cakes they'd baked had been more successful, and when Laurie had taken another batch to sell in the café and given him a couple of pounds in profit back, he'd been over the moon. So, no, she didn't mind gaining a little shadow at all.

She made a show of checking her watch. 'I'll give you ten minutes. That should be more than enough time to tidy up in here and get changed.' She bent to unhook Toby's lead, rubbing his head and laughing at the mournful look he gave her. 'Just a few minutes,' she promised him, as she wound the lead into a tight loop and tucked it in the voluminous pocket of her wax jacket. The dog gave her a look which on a human would be described as abject disgust and slunk over to his basket to curl up.

Max all but hurled the dishes into the machine and Nerissa forced herself to turn away from him before the urge to tell him he was putting things in the wrong place overtook her.

'How's Molly's little lad?' she asked Tom in a soft voice which wouldn't be heard over the enthusiastic crash of pans in the sink.

'Okay.' Tom heaved a tired-sounding sigh. 'I rang the hospital a few minutes ago and it looks like he picked up a nasty tummy bug. They're going to keep him in for observation and to make sure he's properly hydrated, but they don't think it's anything more serious than that, thank goodness.'

Nerissa's relief was an echo of his own. Though she tried hard to remain detached, it was always hard with the little ones, especially when she'd followed them through from the initial excited, fear-tinged moments of confirmation of the pregnancy and the prenatal appointments, to their first visits to the surgery for their checks and inoculations. Little baby Samuel was Molly's first child and Nerissa had been delighted to see their family starting to grow. She'd known Molly and her husband, Dan, since they were tiny tots themselves. A bittersweet wave swept through her as she thought about all the lives that had passed through the surgery door, each one leaving a little mark on her own life.

Perhaps something of what she was feeling had shown on her face because Tom stepped closer and touched a gentle hand to her arm. 'He's going to be fine.'

She forced a smile. Of course he would think she was worrying about Samuel. He couldn't possibly know that it was the ghosts of her own never-would-be children that haunted her in moments like this. How could he, when he had two wonderful children of his own? 'I know.' She hesitated, then confessed a tiny part of what she'd been thinking about. 'I was just remembering when Molly's mum first came in to find out she was pregnant with her. I must've been eighteen or nineteen. I was the office junior then – doing a bit of filing and typing for Doc under the eagle eye of Miss Kennett.' Gosh, she hadn't thought about Isobel Kennett in years, talk about a trip down memory lane. She might have been an old dragon at times, but she'd been nothing but kindness and compassion as Nerissa had stumbled through those first terrible months after losing Gareth.

'You've worked at the surgery for that long?'

She nodded. 'I hadn't planned on making it my life's work.' She'd taken the job as a means to earn a bit extra while Gareth was on deployment, but then he'd never come home, and somehow she'd never left. 'But my circumstances changed and...' The imprint of Gareth's ring pressed deeper into her fingers where she'd unconsciously reached for it and she let it go, but not before she caught Tom's gaze on it. She clammed up, not knowing how to explain without sharing more than she wanted to.

'Finished!' Max declared, and, grateful for the interruption, she turned her attention from father to son.

'Well done,' she said, ignoring the patch of crumbs he'd missed during his haphazard attempt to wipe off the table. 'Go and get changed, then.' She watched him race from the room before ducking her head to check the horizon through the window. 'Looks like we might get wet.'

Tom leaned forward next to her. 'I don't like the look of that sky at all. I was thinking of joining you, but I've just remembered there's a documentary I've been meaning to catch up on.'

'Chicken.'

He laughed. 'Damn right. Enjoy your walk, though! I'll think of you while I'm cosy and warm inside with a nice hot cup of coffee.' He strolled across to the kettle and flipped it on, making no attempt to hide his smug grin.

'I could go off some people, you know,' Nerissa muttered, making him laugh harder, and she smiled to see the way it took years off him. He'd gone from looking haggard and stressed to relaxed and cheerful, and a little piece of her glowed inside knowing she'd helped lift his mood.

Max was back a few minutes later, hair even more impossibly mussed from the thick jumper he'd put on. They'd both look an absolute fright once the wind got hold of them, so Nerissa just smoothed the worst of it down with a quick trace of her fingers.

She glanced down at his trainers – the same ones that he'd soaked in the sea on their first unexpected walk together. 'Have you got some wellies?'

When he shook his head, she glanced at Tom.

'It's on the list!' he declared, and she couldn't help but laugh. It'd become one of his regular sayings, usually when he thought she was going to tell him off for not doing something. Not that she would dream of telling him off, but she'd found he had a tendency to let things slide without at least one or two pointed reminders. She'd have to go over her own mental list and make sure it tallied with his. Both the children would need some sturdy footwear to see them through the coming months, and Max was already growing out of his winter coat, if the two inches of bare wrist she'd seen sticking out the end of his sleeves was any indication.

Speaking of which. 'Get your coat,' she prompted Max. 'And a hat if you've got one to hand.'

She followed him back into the hallway to retrieve a wide-brimmed, olive green waterproof hat from one of the pegs. It wouldn't win her any style prizes, but it kept her warm and dry, and the toggle beneath the chin was a godsend on windy days.

'I've got a hood.' Max popped it up and down to demonstrate.

'Looks like we're all set then.' She pulled the lead from her pocket and handed it to him. 'Do you want to do the honours?'

Tom followed them to the back door. 'Make sure you do what Nerissa tells you, okay?' he said to Max.

'I will!' He plunged out into the drizzling rain with a re-energised Toby barking excitedly at his heels.

'You're sure you don't mind him tagging along?' Tom said in a voice low enough not to carry.

'He's not a bother.' When Tom still looked a little unsure, Nerissa reached out and touched his arm. 'Really.'

She realised her mistake the moment she touched him. It was too intimate, and too damn easy to do because it was all she thought about when she was around him – this need she had to comfort him, to ease his troubles and make him laugh the way he had just a few moments ago.

She pulled her fingers away and stepped out into the rain. It might not be a cold shower, but hopefully the storm would blow these foolish thoughts out of her head because it had to stop. She had to stop wishing for something she couldn't have. She felt like she was at a crossroads: the past still called to her, but not with the same power it once had. The future thrust upon her by circumstances would just as likely lead to more heartbreak if she didn't learn to guard her emotions better.

'Nerissa.'

There was something in the way he said her name, a tone

she'd not heard before. For a second she believed it might be a quiet echo of the yearning she felt inside. She wanted to turn to him, to see what she was feeling reflected in his eyes. Or perhaps it was all in her head and she would turn and see nothing at all.

She raised her hand and waved without looking, not sure she was ready for the reality of either of those things. 'Won't be long.' She hurried down the path after Max, hoping her voice hadn't sounded as loud and forced to Tom as it had to her.

Having agreed with Max he could let Toby off the lead as long as they stayed further up the beach and well away from the water's edge, she turned her face into the combination of stinging salt spray and rain and let go of everything other than the majesty of the scene before her.

Wild, white horses rode high on the cresting waves, pounding towards the shore in a fury of foam that washed higher with each gust of the wind. It didn't take long for the sea to work its magic, the churning chaos of it making the turmoil inside her seem pathetic in comparison. *Give it to the sea.* Reaching beneath the collar of her coat, Nerissa unhooked her necklace and tucked it and the ring it held safely into her pocket. 'Goodbye, Gareth.' The wind stole the words from her lips and carried them away out over the ocean. She waited for the pain to strike but felt only peace.

Feeling more settled, she turned her back to the water and watched Max and Toby racing around in circles. Momentum had taken them further along the beach and she was happy to stroll in their wake, close enough to call a warning if they strayed too close to the sea and still be alone with her thoughts.

She'd closed off one path – the other... well, where to start? It was time to face facts. She liked Tom. Could probably stretch to more than liking him under the right circumstances, but it was too soon. And it wasn't because she was expecting perfection – whatever Sylvia might think about it – it was because she was afraid that it wasn't Tom she was falling for. It was the *idea* of him. Everything she'd always wanted had all but landed in her lap – an attractive, intelligent man and two terrific children to fill the terrible aching gap that had always been a corner of her heart. A ready-made family for her to slot into. It was all just a bit too convenient. A bit too good to be true.

And besides, they'd already had, and then lost, the perfect piece that completed their family jigsaw. No matter how hard she might want to slot herself into that empty space, her edges and corners were shaped differently. She wasn't Anna. She could never be her – never *wanted* to try to be her.

It would take some time, but she would find a way to steer the right course. If she couldn't, then perhaps she'd have to think again about her current living arrangements. She let it sit for a moment and it felt like the right thing. For everyone.

'Ready to head back?' she asked when Max and Toby came racing over to join her. The rain hadn't got any worse, but the storm wasn't going anywhere either.

'Do we have to?' He sounded so disappointed that she couldn't help but smile. There'd be plenty of nights when he'd be stuck indoors because of the weather so no harm in letting him run free while he had the chance.

'Not straight away, but we shouldn't stay out too long.' They'd already made it quite a distance along the beach, so if the weather turned now it would be a soggy trudge back to the surgery.

Delighted at the reprieve, he bounced on his heels as though he had more energy inside than his body could contain. 'Can we race to the fence then?'

Nerissa eyed the structure which had been erected a few years back to keep tourists away from the caves at the end of the beach. 'I'm not sure I can run that far,' she said, doubtfully.

'Not you, silly!' Max exclaimed. 'I meant me and Toby could have a race.'

'Oh, well, that's a relief. Off you go then, but move a bit closer to the wall and watch out for rocks.'

'I will!' The wind snatched his words away as the boy sprinted off, cutting a diagonal path up the beach at first until he was just a few feet from the wall that lined the edge of the beach where it met the base of the point of land which had given the village its name.

A sharp gust of wind tried to tug her hat from her head and Nerissa quickened her pace. By the time she reached them, Max was trying to climb up on the first rung of the fence, but he couldn't get any purchase because of the wire netting blocking the gaps.

'Why can't we go down there?' he asked when she told him to get down.

'Because it's not safe. Come on now, we'd better be heading back.'

'But I want to know what's down there,' he insisted, one hand still threaded through the loops of the netting.

'A few caves and lots of rocks.' A rattle of sleety rain came lashing in on the wind. 'Come on, Max, before we get soaked to the skin!' When she tugged his arm, he reluctantly let go and began to follow her, all but dragging his feet across the pebbles. Toby had plastered himself to her side, more than ready to be out of the rain, and Nerissa quickened her pace, hoping Max would get the message and hurry up.

By the time she reached the steps and had stopped to clip Toby's lead back on, Max had caught her up. 'Can we explore the caves, some time?'

Nerissa shook her head, giving him a little push to get him moving up the steps. 'They used to be open, but there were too many close calls, so the decision was made to fence them off. It's a shame. We used to love going there when we were kids, but we also understood the tides and how quickly conditions can change. It's not the same for people who just come visiting – they don't have the same respect for the sea.'

'People like me, you mean?' He sounded so forlorn that she took a minute to remind herself how young he was, and how easy it was for words to be misinterpreted. Fitting in anywhere new would be hard; all the more so in a small community like the Point where some didn't welcome those they deemed to be outsiders.

Nerissa paused to tug his hood up over his already wet hair before she smoothed a hand over his cold cheek. 'Not like you, because the Point is your home now.' When he brightened, she knew she was on the right track. 'You listen to what you are told, and you're becoming more aware of the risks living so close to the sea can pose. Like just now, you knew it wasn't safe to be too close to the water because of the storm.'

'And the tide is coming in? That's what it means when the water covers up more of the beach, right?'

'That's right. I've got an app on my phone that tells me each day what the tide times are, and what the weather and sea conditions are going to be. Remind me when we get home and I'll help you download it.'

The darkening sky lit up suddenly as lightning streaked across the clouds, followed moments later by a huge clap of thunder which echoed off the buildings, making them both jump.

'I don't want to be out here,' Max said, a little tremble in his voice.

'Me neither.' She held out a hand, an instinctive act to offer comfort. When he took it with a grateful smile her heart swelled with affection. Things might be complicated when it came to his father, but this boy she would cherish for as long as it was within her power to do so. 'Come on, let's run!'

21

Tom tried to concentrate on his documentary, but he couldn't settle. After he'd lost the thread of what was happening for the third time in ten minutes, he gave up and switched it off.

Tossing the remote on the coffee table, he stood and crossed to the large bay window and stared up at the darkening sky. Maybe he should've gone with them after all. He shook the thought away almost as soon as it formed. Nerissa was sensible and smart, and a damn sight more familiar with the weather conditions than he was. The worst that could happen was they'd get soaking wet and need a hot bath or shower to warm up when they got in.

On the heels of that realisation, he went upstairs and opened the airing cupboard to switch on the immersion heater. There'd been a few mornings when the four of them hadn't spaced out their morning ablutions quite enough and the unlucky last one in the bathroom had endured a cold shower. Tom now made a point of setting his alarm a good forty minutes earlier so he could be in and out before he had to worry about getting the children up for school. He grabbed an armful of spare towels while he was at it and took them down to the kitchen, where he set about filling the kettle and laying out things to make hot chocolate. Lastly, he retrieved a couple of the older towels Nerissa kept stored in the cupboard under the stairs with various other bits of doggy paraphernalia. He spread one out across Toby's basket and laid the other across the threshold of the back door. There wasn't much more he could do, so he wandered back upstairs to check in on Emily.

When he knocked and entered, she was sitting cross-legged on her bed, laptop balanced on a pillow in front of her and her headphones in.

'I'm making hot chocolate for when Max and Nerissa get back – do you fancy a mug?'

Emily glanced towards the window where the rain was now hammering against the pane and pulled a face. 'They went out in this? They must be mad.'

'Well, it wasn't quite this bad when they set out, and Toby needed a walk.' Tom found his gaze wandering back towards the window. It wasn't quite four o'clock but the sky was almost pitch black with the heaviness of the cloud cover.

'Still. Rather them than me. And yes to the hot chocolate, please. Do you want me to come down?'

Tom shook his head. 'I can bring it up if you're busy.' It was the most diplomatic way he could think of to ask what she was up to without seeming to pry.

'I'm watching a version of *Twelfth Night* I found on Sky Arts.' She turned her screen so he could see the paused programme. 'It's one of the set texts, and I know it's one of the questions I messed up so I thought this might help me.'

'That's a great idea. But don't forget it's Saturday night, sweetheart. You don't have to study all the time.' She was really getting to grips with what she needed to do to prepare for her resits, and he was proud of the way she'd taken control of it. 'And you know if there's anything you want to talk through with me, I'm more than happy to help.'

'I thought you did *Macbeth* when you were at school?'

'I did, but I downloaded *Twelfth Night* onto my Kindle and I've been reading it. It's a lot more fun than I remember, though it's taking a while to get my head around the language again. It's been a long time and my poor old brain isn't what it used to be.'

She ducked her head, then looked up at him. 'You didn't have to do that.'

Tom came to sit on the edge of her bed, reaching out to tuck a stray strand of her long hair behind her ear. 'Yeah, I think I did. I left you to manage on your own too much, Em, but not this time.'

'Thanks, Daddy.' She leaned forward to clasp her arms around him in a quick hug. 'I can save this on the planner and then maybe we can sit down and watch it together?'

'It's a date.' He kissed her forehead. 'Speaking of which, don't forget it's movie night tonight.'

Emily rolled her eyes. 'But it's Max's pick and it'll be some terrible superhero movie. Can't I stay up here?'

He'd instigated movie night as something he'd hoped they could do as a family, but so far it'd been a bit hit-and-miss as they'd argued over film choices. In the end, he'd set up a simple rotation policy, but even that didn't seem to work very well. If he insisted she join them, it would only get Emily's back up and she'd sulk through the whole thing. She'd also do her best to spoil Max's enjoyment of it with a barrage of snarky comments. She seemed happy enough with what she was doing, so while he wished she didn't spend quite so much time in her room, there wasn't much point in rocking the boat. 'Okay then. But maybe we can put our heads together and come up with something we might all enjoy next time?'

'I'll make a list,' she promised. 'Thanks, Dad.' She pecked a kiss on his cheek, then gave him a sly grin. 'Do I still get popcorn?'

'Now you're pushing your luck,' he said, but knew he would make her a huge bowl of it just to see her smile like that at him again. He stood up, resting a hand on her head. She was growing up so quickly, he felt like he needed to pause and take a mental snapshot of little moments like this before she was off and flying her own path away from him. 'Marshmallows in your hot chocolate?'

'Ooh, yes!'

He left her then and she was already tucking her headphones back in before he'd gone. When he came back a few minutes later, he tried not to disturb her, just set the mug down on her bedside table, then closed the door quietly behind him.

He milled around in the kitchen for a few minutes, not quite sure what to do with himself. The rain was still coming down in sheets and he was tempted again to throw on his coat and go out searching for them. Surely they'd have started making their way back as soon as it had turned really bad?

Deciding he'd give it five more minutes, he tugged open the fridge and contemplated its contents. Nerissa had bought some home-made burgers from the butchers after the kids had pestered her for them. They wouldn't be as good as when Andrew had done them on the barbecue, but Tom could handle the grill. He rummaged in the freezer and found some rolls. They probably wouldn't defrost in time, but he could split them and stick them in the toaster. A bit of salad, a few oven chips and everyone would be happy – and Nerissa would be free to enjoy her evening in peace.

The windows lit up as a bolt of lightning flashed followed by a huge boom of thunder. Right, that was it. Slamming shut the freezer, Tom marched to the hallway to grab his coat and shove his feet into his boots. He was still zipping it up as he yanked open the back door only to come face to face with three drowned rats – well, two drowned rats and a very soggy retriever.

'Get in, get in.' He stepped out of the way, holding the door for them as they scrambled in, just managing to grab Toby's collar before the dog got away and covered the kitchen floor with paw prints. He was rewarded for his pains with an absolute drenching when Toby gave himself a vigorous shake.

'At least you had the foresight to put your coat on,' Nerissa said with a rueful grin as she stripped off her own, followed by her very droopy hat.

'Lucky me.' Tom managed to get the door shut, then urged Toby towards his basket. 'There's towels on the table.' He pointed to the stack he'd left as he bent down to wrap the ends of the one he'd put in the basket around the dog's back and began to rub his coat dry. Content to be pampered, Toby lay on his side only raising his head when Tom showed any signs of stopping.

Nerissa took charge of Max, stripping off the jumper he'd been wearing under his coat, which was wet across the shoulders and down his back.

'I guess we need to look for a proper waterproof jacket for you,' Tom said as he watched Nerissa bundle his son into a big towel, then use a smaller one to rub the water from his hair, much the same as he was doing to the dog's fur. Her own hair was plastered down her back and around her face. Rivulets of water ran from it across her reddened, windblown cheeks, but she paid them no mind until she was sure Max was sorted out.

Tom couldn't help but notice the way his boy was grinning up at her, or the way she tapped his nose with a finger when she finished. The back of his eyes started to burn, the threat of tears taking him so off guard he had to look away and blink hard to ward them off. When he was sure he wouldn't make a complete fool of himself, he gave the dog one last rub before tugging free the damp towel and chucking it on the floor near the back door.

Going to the sink, he washed his hands, then flipped the kettle on once he'd dried them. 'I put the immersion on if you want a hot bath,' he said to Nerissa, leaning against the kitchen worktop. 'And I've got stuff ready to make hot chocolate, or a cup of tea if you want to take a hot drink up with you.'

'That sounds heavenly.' She'd picked up a towel and was squeezing her long curls through it, the pale cotton already darkening from the amount of water in her hair. 'But I'll probably just jump in the shower as I'll need to think about dinner soon.'

'Already covered,' Tom said with a grin as he folded his arms across his chest. 'Burgers and salad and oven chips.'

'Yes!' Max fist-pumped the air. 'Can I have two burgers?'

Tom laughed. 'One and a half – I'll split the spare one with you. Run upstairs and hop in the shower quickly so that Nerissa can have a bath, and then you might as well put your pjs on. It's just you and me for movie night – your sister has spurned the offer of our company.'

'Are we having popcorn?' Max asked, before he turned to Nerissa. 'Will you come to movie night? We're watching *Avengers Endgame* – it's amazing! All the superheroes are in it – Captain America, Iron Man, Black Panther, Hulk—'

Tom cut him off before he could bore poor Nerissa to death with a list of the entire cast of the movie. 'You've taken up enough of Nerissa's time today when it's supposed to be her day off.'

'Oh.' Max's face fell and Tom felt about as good as he might after kicking a puppy. He was delighted with how well the pair were getting on. It was clear Max had been starving for a bit of female affection, but he also needed to make sure they didn't take advantage of her good nature and kind heart. His children were not her responsibility, after all.

'Thanks for the invite, Max, but you two should enjoy a boys' night together. I'll be fine upstairs. I've got a new book I want to start.'

'But...' Max looked between the two of them, a pleading expression on his face.

Tom shook his head. 'Not everyone likes superhero movies, bud. Go on and get your shower.'

Max sighed, but did as he was told.

Pushing away from his spot by the kettle Tom retrieved the wet towels his son had abandoned and tossed them next to the others by the back door. 'I'll stick them all through the wash later.'

'You don't have to do that.' Nerissa twisted the towel she'd been using between her hands. 'And you don't have to make dinner, either.'

'And you don't have to wait on us hand and foot. That's not the deal.' He eased the towel she was clutching from her hands and tossed it aside. Her hair was a wild riot framing her face, and her cheeks still glowed from being outside in the cold. The long-sleeved shirt she wore was plastered to her shoulders and upper body, the pale material see-through enough that he could make out her sun-darkened skin, the hint of lace edging her bra. She looked other-worldly – like a siren blown in on the storm, and as tempting as one. He wanted to cup her cheek, to test the silky softness of her skin beneath his thumb, he just plain wanted... 'Nerissa.'

She swayed towards him for a moment, before pulling back. 'No.'

She was right. Of course she was right. What the hell had he been thinking? Shoving his hands in his pockets, he swung back towards the kettle. 'Sorry. I'll fix you that tea and then we'll all leave you in peace.'

Stupid. Stupid. Stupid. He silently berated himself as the kettle hissed and fizzed. It was the only sound in the room, and he wasn't sure if she was still there or she'd taken her chance and done a runner. And who would blame her? Just when things were starting to settle down and the kids seemed like they were adjusting well to their new life, here he was threatening to destroy all that new-found peace because – what? He had a hard-on for their pretty housekeeper?

A soft touch on his shoulder interrupted his mental litany of self-loathing. 'Tom?'

'I'm sorry. I don't know what I was thinking.' He shook his head, not daring to look around.

'Well, what if you're not the only one who's been thinking the same kind of things?'

He spun around, sure he must've misheard her. She was almost toe-to-toe with him. So close, too close. His treacherous hands itched with the need to circle her waist and drag her across those last remaining inches. 'You've been thinking about me?'

Nerissa bit her lower lip, then nodded. 'A lot more than I should've been, probably.' She looked away, then up through her lashes at him. 'I wasn't going to say anything because I thought it was nothing more than a silly crush. I mean, it was almost bound to happen with us spending so much time with each other.'

'You're probably right.' He gripped the worktop behind him to keep his hands from doing something unconscionably stupid. 'I haven't been around a woman this much since Anna. And with the enforced domesticity of our situation...' He shrugged a shoulder. 'Well, it was bound to generate a false sense of intimacy between us.' There was nothing false about the pressure in his body, but he was grasping for any straw of logic he could get hold of right now.

'Exactly.' She sighed in what sounded like relief, then smiled. 'I'm glad this happened and we're able to talk about it. Now we've acknowledged it, it's something we can both be on our guard for. I've been on my own for a long time, too, so it's only natural if our feelings are a bit confused.'

'Yes.' His eyes strayed to the dip of her throat where the ring she wore on a chain had rested earlier and saw it had gone. He'd seen her reach for it several times and wondered at its significance. And now he was wondering at the significance of her taking it off. *Step back, for the love of God, step back.* He was hemmed in against the work surface and if she didn't put some distance between them, he was going to dash all these sensible intentions to hell and do what he'd been aching to do since the moment he'd first laid eyes on her.

She swallowed but didn't move. 'Well, I'm glad we've got that settled then.'

'Yes,' he repeated, because anything else was beyond him at that point.

'I'd better go and have my bath.'

Don't think about it, don't think about it. But it was too late, he was already picturing her sinking down into the deep, claw-footed tub he'd seen in her bathroom when they'd first toured the house. 'What about your tea? I could bring it up for you?' Knock on the door and then let himself in to the fragrant steam-filled room and—

Feet thundered on the wooden stairs, heralding the imminent arrival of one or other of his children. Nerissa leapt back like a scolded cat, as Tom spun to press the front of his body against the cupboards, shielding the evidence of where those very dangerous thoughts had been taking him. He heard an exchange of words between Max and Nerissa, but he couldn't make sense of the conversation over the roar of blood pumping in his head. Acting on autopilot, he turned the kettle on to boil for the third time and set about making two large mugs of hot chocolate. By the time he'd loaded the top of them with whipped cream and marshmallows, he had himself back under enough control. When he turned around, he told himself it was a relief that only Max was present, sitting at the table with his face buried in his phone and seemingly oblivious to any lingering tension in the air.

22

Awkward. That was the only way Nerissa could describe the next few weeks. The end of the month had at least brought a change in the weather, and November was promising to bring with it the kind of crisp, bright weather where lots of long walks on the beach would at least give her the excuse to be out of the house. Tom was so unfailingly polite and formal it was almost grating. They revolved around each other like the moon orbiting the earth, distance negating the magnetic pull of attraction.

He was doing the right thing, the thing they'd both agreed was for the best, but the way he'd looked at her that afternoon in the kitchen haunted her. There had been so much intensity in his eyes, and the muscles on his forearms had been rigid from gripping the worktop so hard. If Max hadn't come in when he did, she wasn't sure what might have happened. She'd lain in the tub afterwards, almost breathless with anticipation as to whether or not Tom would act on his suggestion and bring her a cup of tea. The minutes had stretched, and the water cooled as her book lay ignored on the floor beside the tub and her eyes remained fixed on the tiny gap where she'd left the door between her bedroom and the bathroom ajar. It was good that he hadn't come up, she'd told herself as she'd dried off and pulled on a pair of leggings and a baggy sweatshirt over her oldest, plainest underwear. Even if she lost her mind and dared to throw herself at him, the thought of him seeing her in a pair of granny pants and a sports bra would hopefully be enough to check herself.

But the under armour hadn't proven necessary because he'd barely glanced her way as he and Max made supper together. Feeling like a bystander, she'd taken her dinner and disappeared off upstairs to watch *Avengers Endgame* on her own. She hadn't wanted to say anything in front of Max when it had become clear that Tom wanted some one-on-one time with his son, but she was a huge Marvel fan. The rest of the family had zero interest in the franchise, so she'd made many pilgrimages alone to the big multiplex in town to watch her favourite superheroes vanquish their many foes. How much fun would it have been to enjoy the film through Max's eyes? To experience his wonder and discuss all the theories she had about the series and its epic finale. Instead, she'd curled up on her sofa, letting her burger go cold as she worked her way through a bottle of wine, wishing she was downstairs.

It was all for the best, she reminded herself for the umpteenth time as she sent the next patient to sit in the waiting area and picked up the phone. 'Molly and Samuel are here,' she said to Tom when he answered. The rushed visit to A & E had unsettled Molly so Tom had made space for a weekly check-up, hoping a bit of extra support and reassurance would help rebuild her confidence. The baby had suffered no ill after-effects from his virus and his mother's handling of him was growing more assured after each visit.

'Thanks. Give me a minute and then you can send them through.' He'd stopped coming out to receive new patients.

Stopped those little moments of banter when he'd asked for the low-down on a new patient, or brought her a cup of tea because he was so damn considerate and didn't want her to think he expected her to do everything. When he wasn't dealing with patients he was closeted in his office with Doc as they made plans for the new men's health initiative they were piloting at the surgery. Anything, it seemed, to avoid spending any time alone with her.

'Okay. Umm, there's only a couple of appointments left and I could do with nipping out to Laurie's if that's okay with you?' It was Max's birthday this weekend and she'd commissioned her niece – with Tom's approval – to make a special cake for the occasion. His family were also expected to arrive later that evening and, although she thought she had everything ready, an hour to do some final checks before the children got home and the guests descended would ease her mind.

'That's fine. Put a note on the door and redirect the intercom to my line.'

Trying not to feel dismissed, Nerissa responded in the same cool manner. 'Of course.'

'Nerissa...'

Her pulse started thumping the way it did every time he said her name. 'Yes?'

'Thanks. You know, for Max's party and, well, everything else.' He gave a nervous laugh. 'I don't expect you to hang around this weekend, I'll see to everything.'

Well, if she'd been under any illusions about whether she was invited to join the festivities, she knew now. 'Message received.'

She hung up the phone before she said anything that might betray the turmoil she was feeling. Clearing the air had seemed like such a good idea at the time, but now she knew Tom might be feeling some of what she was, it was exponentially worse.

Although given his attitude lately, he seemed to be doing a much better job of getting over it than she was.

'You can go in now,' she called to Molly, waited for the woman to steer a grinning, gurgling Samuel in his pushchair towards Tom's surgery and then logged off her computer. She had a ready-made, laminated sign for the door asking patients to press the intercom for admission, so in a matter of moments she'd locked the front door and was heading towards her room to get changed.

Screams and shouts greeted her as she opened the door into the kitchen, followed by the heavy thunder of feet overhead and the slamming of a door. *What on earth?* Tossing her handbag and keys on the table, she ran for the stairs and hurried up to the landing where she found Emily hammering on Max's bedroom door.

'Get out here, I haven't finished with you yet!'

'Go away, I hate you!' Max's muffled yell came from the other side of the door.

'I hate you more, you little shit! You've ruined it! I'm never speaking to you again.' Emily slammed her fist into the door and yelled his name in total contrast to her previous declaration.

'Stop that!' Nerissa said, raising her voice to be heard over the banging and screaming. 'Emily, what's going on?'

The girl spun to face her, her red cheeks streaked with tears and her mouth twisted in an angry snarl. 'Mind your own business. This has nothing to do with you!' She went right back to banging on the door. 'Open up!' She aimed a kick at the wooden base, her shoe leaving a dark scuff on the white-painted wood.

'Enough!' Nerissa grabbed Emily and pulled her away before she could do any more damage. 'Calm down and tell me what the problem is.'

'You can't tell me what to do!' Emily's face was twisted into an ugly, angry snarl. 'You're not my mother. You're just the cleaner!'

Nerissa stepped back as hurt by the words as if they'd been delivered with a physical slap. She caught herself, though, because she was damned if anyone was going to speak to her that way, least of all an angry child. 'No, I'm not your mother, because if I was you'd speak to other people with more respect!' she snapped. 'Now stop this ridiculous carry-on and tell me why you are so upset.'

Emily shot her a mutinous expression, but her voice was quieter when she muttered, 'You wouldn't understand.'

Nerissa followed Emily's glance towards a bundle of material scrunched up on the floor by the opposite skirting board. Recognising it, a sick feeling filled her stomach as she bent to scoop it up. 'This is your mother's blanket, isn't it?'

Emily nodded, tears flooding her eyes once more. 'He's ruined it,' she whispered, her voice breaking on the last word.

With delicate hands, Nerissa held the blanket up so it unfurled to its full size. To her horror, a section at the bottom had come away and was trailing towards the floor. 'Oh goodness,' she said, turning it around in her hands so she could examine the damage more closely. 'What happened?'

'He happened!' Emily thumped her fist on Max's bedroom door once more. 'He stole it from my room!'

The door flung open to reveal an equally angry, equally red-faced Max. 'I didn't steal it! It doesn't belong to you, it was Mummy's and I have as much right to it as you do!' His fists were balled at his sides and Nerissa moved quickly to step between them, fearful they might come to actual blows.

'Stop it, both of you!' Her head swivelled between the two of them as she wondered what on earth she could say to defuse the situation. 'Your grandparents and Uncle Alex will be here soon, you don't want them to see you fighting like this, do you?'

'I don't care.' Max's words might have been defiant, but the way he dropped his head and scuffed his foot on the floorboards said otherwise.

'Go back in your room and try to calm down. You don't want to spoil your birthday now, do you?'

He shook his head, still staring at the floor.

'You're just going to let him get away with this?' Emily demanded. 'I might have known you'd side with him!'

'I'm not siding with anyone,' Nerissa said, her tone calm but firm as she gave Emily a gentle push towards her own bedroom. 'And it's not up to me what consequences arise from this, I just hate to see the two of you fighting. Please, Emily,' she said when the girl stood her ground. 'Let's go in your room and see what the damage is in a proper light. You never know, I might be able to fix it.' She said the last more in hope than expectation as her sewing skills had never been that great. Oh, she could fix a hem and sew on a button, but the kind of delicate, skilled work she feared it would take to repair the blanket was likely far beyond her meagre talents.

Emily cast one last baleful glare at Max before she turned and marched towards her bedroom. Nerissa followed a few steps behind, holding the blanket carefully to make sure the awful tear didn't rip any further. Emily flung herself down on her bed, her arms hugging one of the pillows close to her chest. Nerissa's heart ached for her – ached for Max too. They'd been through so much, and were far too young to have to cope with such a dreadful loss.

Holding up the blanket to the light, she winced. The damage was as bad as she feared. She'd have to wrack her brains – and Sylvia's too – and try to come up with someone who might be able to repair it. For now she settled on folding it carefully, making sure the damaged section was tucked inside and protected as much as possible before setting it to one side on the stool in front of Emily's dressing table. 'I'm so sorry, Emily. I know how upsetting this must be for you.'

'You couldn't possibly know.' Emily burrowed her face deeper into her pillow.

'While it's true I was a fair bit older than you were, I still understand how awful it is to lose someone who means everything to you.'

Emily raised her head. 'Your mum's dead too?'

Nerissa nodded. 'She passed a few years ago and I still miss her every single day.' She recalled what Emily had said earlier. 'No one can ever take her place. Just like no one can ever take your mother's place. If I've overstepped the mark, then I am sorry, it wasn't my intention. But you still have no right to speak to me the way you did earlier.'

'You shouted at me.' Emily sounded shocked at the very idea.

Nerissa bit her lip, suddenly amused. 'And you were so very calm, how dreadful of me.'

Emily made a funny noise, half-laugh, half-sob.

'I know it seems like the end of the world, but if you'll give me a chance to ask around, I'll try my best to find someone who can repair the damage.'

'It'll never be the same. It's ruined.'

'Only if you choose to believe that. Accidents happen, and no matter how hard we try to protect things, sometimes they get damaged.'

'It's Max's fault. He took it when he shouldn't have.' There was less hostility in her voice at least, though her eyes still burned with angry tears.

'And why do you think he took it?' Nerissa raised her hand when Emily's mouth opened immediately. 'Wait. Look past your feelings and think. I know how special the blanket is to you – the connection it gives you to your mum. Does Max have anything like that?'

Emily paused for a moment, then shook her head. 'I don't think so.'

'Then perhaps,' Nerissa said, using the gentlest of tones, 'he was looking for a way to connect with her too.'

'He still ruined it.'

'It got damaged while he had it.' Nerissa hoped the subtle correction would sink in, maybe not now, but once Emily had a chance to calm down. 'I am sure that's the last thing he would've wanted.'

'Maybe.'

It was as much of a concession as Nerissa could hope for and she felt like she'd done what she could for the moment. Tom could deal with the aftermath once he'd finished with his patients, and at least the children were no longer screaming bloody murder at each other. 'I need to go and collect a few things for Max's party. Will you be okay until I get back? Your dad won't be long.' Emily nodded, so Nerissa risked a gentle hand to Emily's leg, desperate to offer comfort but so very mindful of the barriers between them. 'Why don't you rest up for a few minutes until everyone gets here?'

''Kay.'

Nerissa glanced at the folded-up blanket. 'Do you want me to leave that here or shall I put it upstairs for safekeeping? I promise I'll take the very best care of it.'

'You will find someone to fix it, won't you?' Emily's eyes were as pleading as her voice.

'I'll do everything I possibly can.' Nerissa picked up the blanket with careful hands and tucked it against her body as she walked out of the room. It was as close to a promise as she dared to make.

She'd just placed the blanket in the bottom drawer of her dresser when she heard Toby barking, followed by a voice she recognised calling out. Hurrying downstairs, she entered the kitchen to be immediately enveloped in a bear hug. Alex followed the hug with a smacking kiss on her cheek, leaving her red-faced as he opened his arms and turned her to face the older couple who'd entered the kitchen behind him. 'Pop, Mum, this is Nerissa. Nerissa, these are my folks.'

Stepping free of his hold, Nerissa took the hand offered by the big, smiling man she'd have recognised as Tom and Alex's father with no introduction. 'It's a pleasure to meet you, Mr Nelson.'

'You too, my dear.' Mr Nelson ignored her hand and swept her into a similar hug to his youngest son, though he abstained from a kiss at least. 'Call me Archie, and this is Philippa.'

Philippa, all easy elegance in a pair of pale pink jeans teamed with a white T-shirt and matching cardigan draped over her shoulders, also hugged Nerissa, pressing her perfectly made-up cheek to hers. 'Lovely to meet you. I hear you've been doing a wonderful job looking after everyone.'

Nerissa blushed and tried not to think about how much of a fright her hair must look. She always started the day with good intentions, but the wild curls had a mind of their own and she could feel several strands tickling her neck where they'd escaped from her now-drooping bun. 'I do what I can, but really they're very easy to look after.' Given the absolute scenes a few minutes ago, she added a swift crossed fingers behind her back.

'Pop! Pop!' Max came charging down the stairs and leapt into his grandfather's arms.

With Archie and Philippa distracted, Nerissa tugged Alex's arm and drew him away to quickly apprise him of the drama between Max and Emily.

He grimaced when she'd finished. 'Thanks for letting me know, I'll do my best to keep them apart for a bit.'

'I haven't had a chance to tell Tom, he's still next door and I really need to go out and run a few errands.' Nerissa glanced at her watch. If she didn't get going soon, she wouldn't have time to pick everything up.

'Leave it with me,' Alex assured her. 'Go and do what you need to do and I'll wrangle the family.'

'Thank you.' She gave his arm a quick squeeze, then edged past the others to collect her coat and bag before escaping through the still open back door.

It was one of those perfect autumn days – bright skies, crisp air and a gentle breeze carrying the taste of salt. This was her favourite time of the year. The season of gloves and sun-warmed faces. Not exactly Wordsworth, but that's what this often quiet period before the onslaught of winter meant to her.

She was halfway to the café when she tugged the beret from her head and stuffed it in her pocket, letting her hair flow free after a day of being confined in a tight bun. It felt like a weight lifted, both figuratively and literally. Emily and Max were in good hands and it wasn't her responsibility to handle the aftermath. All she could do was oversee the preparations for Max's birthday party as best she could. It was up to the family to keep the peace and make sure the children made up so that they could enjoy themselves. With any luck, the café would be quiet enough she could sneak a quick cuppa with Laurie. Spending time with her lovely niece always restored her equilibrium.

Feeling better about everything, she reached to push open the door of the café, missed and almost stumbled as someone pulled it open from the other side.

'You're looking very pleased with yourself.' The frigid tone told her who it was before she even had the chance to look up.

'Hello, Margot. How are you?'

Gareth's mother shrugged. 'Not as good as you, from what I hear. Making yourself very much at home with the new doctor, eh?'

Nerissa glanced past Margot and spotted Bev, Kitty and several other members of the knitting circle. She straightened her shoulders. Whatever might be going on in her heart, she'd done nothing improper. Nothing to warrant the wagging of tongues, which had apparently been going on between sips of tea and mouthfuls of cake. And if there were problems lurking beneath the surface, that certainly wasn't the business of this bunch of busybodies. 'Tom and the children are settling in well, if that's what you mean.'

Margot snorted. 'If that's what you want to call it, then who am I to say any different. If it stops you playing the martyr after all these years, I'll be glad of it. You've milked this town's sympathy for too long.' Brushing past Nerissa, she stuck her nose in the air and started down the street.

Let her go. Let her have these spiteful little victories, it's not worth it.

Any other day and she might have listened to that internal voice of reason, but today her edges were just a bit too frayed. She was bone-tired of Margot and twenty-odd years of her ugly little snipes. 'It wasn't me who wanted to leave the Point,' she called out.

Margot's step faltered a second before her shoulders stiffened and she marched away.

Guilt and regret washed over Nerissa. She might have scored a point after all these years, but at what price? Feeling sick, she trudged into the café.

'You look like someone's burst your favourite balloon,' Laurie said as she gave Nerissa a quick one-armed hug. 'Grab that table by the window and I'll be with you in two ticks.'

After that nasty little run-in with Margot, she didn't feel like talking to anyone, even her beloved Laurie. 'I really ought to just collect Max's cake and get on.'

'Not with that face, you're not. Sit down.'

'You're as bossy as your mother some days,' Nerissa grumbled, but she slipped out of her coat and did as she was told. Laurie joined her less than five minutes later, setting two steaming mugs and a plate containing an enormous slab of chocolate cake on the table between them. 'I can't eat all that,' Nerissa protested.

'That's why I've got two of these.' Laurie produced a pair of forks from the pocket of her apron and handed one to Nerissa. 'Dig in, you look like you need cheering up.'

The first mouthful of the rich cake sent Nerissa's eyelids closing in pleasure. The second was even better, and by the time she dug in for a third, she was telling Laurie all about what had transpired over the past couple of hours. 'I just wish I'd kept my big mouth shut,' she sighed, then placed her cake-laden fork between her lips. 'God, Tom should dispense this on prescription,' she said around the cake.

'Speaking of... how is the divine Dr Tom?' Laurie's grin was positively wicked.

'Divine.' Nerissa sighed. 'And completely off limits.'

'Oh, boo.' Laurie pulled a face as she pressed her thumb to the plate and started picking up crumbs of chocolate cake. 'Are you sure?'

'We agreed it was for the best.' Nerissa couldn't keep a note of disappointment from her voice. She could talk to Laurie in a way she rarely did with Sylvia – admit things she'd otherwise keep to herself.

'When was that?' Laurie leaned across the table. 'Tell me *everything!*'

With a quick check to make sure no one could overhear, Nerissa leaned in too and quickly related the not-a-kiss incident from a few weeks back.

'But he wanted to kiss you?' Laurie insisted.

'I... He certainly seemed like he was going to for a moment.'

'And you wanted him to kiss you?'

Feeling a blush creep up her cheeks, Nerissa nodded, then glanced away.

'God give me strength.'

When she looked up, Laurie had rocked back in her chair, arms folded across her chest, eyes wide as though she couldn't believe what she was hearing.

'It's for the best,' Nerissa found herself saying.

'For who?'

'Shh!' Nerissa flapped her hand at Laurie who'd spoken far too loudly.

'For who?' Laurie repeated in a much quieter but no less demanding tone.

'For everyone.' Nerissa shoved the plate aside with a sigh. 'It's too messy and complicated to even think about.'

Laurie reached across the table and took her hand. 'Life is messy. Look at me and Jake. Neither of us was looking, and I for one wasn't at all ready to fall in love, but I was even less ready to let him go without taking a chance. It's still a bit messy. I probably shouldn't have moved straight into the cottage with him, but we're finding our way with a few bumps in the road.'

'That's different.' She'd been fearless at that age, too. 'I've got too much to lose – my job, my home...'

'Both of which are replaceable,' Laurie said, dismissing every-thing Nerissa had worked for with a wave of her hand. 'If you need a job, you come and work here with me, and if you need somewhere to live, then Mum and Dad would take you in until you found a place of your own.'

'I'm a bit too old for family charity.'

'Bollocks.' It was all the more shocking because Laurie wasn't one for swearing. 'You're just scared, which is understandable after all this time, but come on, think about what you might have to gain if you took a chance?'

Laurie made it all sound so easy that Nerissa found herself close to losing her temper. 'I didn't come here for a lecture; if I'd wanted one of those, I'd have gone next door.'

Laurie shrugged. 'I am my mother's daughter.' She released Nerissa's hand with a pat. 'I love you, and I want you to be happy, that's all.'

'I am happy,' Nerissa protested. Happy enough, anyway.

'If you say so.' Laurie stood and began to clear the table. 'I'll go and get Max's cake.'

Nerissa watched her walk away, wondering if there was something in the air, because it seemed like a day for disagreements and misunderstandings. When Laurie returned bearing a huge white box, Nerissa had put on her coat and was ready to go. Leaning forward, she pressed a kiss to Laurie's cheek. 'I love you too, let's not row.'

Laurie placed the cake down, then put her arms around Nerissa's waist and hugged her tight. 'I'm sorry for pushing instead of listening. I just think you and Tom would be so good together.'

Nerissa pulled back to regard her niece. 'You're a good girl. But sometimes we can't have the fairy-tale ending. That's not anybody's fault, it's just the way things are.'

Laurie looked like she wanted to disagree for a moment, but she settled for a single nod instead. 'Hey, on a complete change of topic, I was thinking about poor Emily's blanket and I was wondering if it was something Ivy could take a look at.'

Ivy had been Laurie's best friend since they were children, until a foolish argument over a man who couldn't hold a candle to Laurie's gorgeous Jake. Things had never been the same between them afterwards, and Nerissa knew it was a source of quiet regret for her niece. 'Do you think you could give her a call for me? I'd do it, of course, but things are going to be hectic, what with Max's party and Tom's family being here and everything. I'd really like to give Emily some good news.'

Laurie nodded. 'I've been looking for an excuse to talk to her, actually. Leave it with me and one or other of us will send you a message later.'

'You're a darling.' Nerissa kissed Laurie once more, then gathered the cake up into her arms.

As she carried the cake from the café, she sent up a silent prayer that things would be more peaceful when she returned to the surgery, and that there'd still be a party to cater for.

23

Tom let out his final patient of the day, then stood in the empty waiting area for a few moments as he decided what to do next. There were a handful of tasks he could justifiably pretend needed to be done before clocking off for the weekend, but he knew none of them were urgent and it would be easy to snatch half an hour on Saturday or Sunday to sort them out. If he did them now, he would be doing so only to delay the inevitability of spending time with his father.

Regardless of his personal reluctance, he was pleased Archie had agreed to make the trek down from London. He was even more pleased that Alex had come with them, because he would step in when things inevitably got strained between Tom and their father. It would do the children good to see him, and Philippa, too. Hopefully, it was the first of many family weekend visits, and would help everyone feel more settled in the Point.

And who knows, Tom thought as he wandered into his office to shut down his computer and lock up, maybe this time things would be different. If he resolved to stay on Archie's good side, to not let the thin-skinned boy who still lurked somewhere inside him out too much, perhaps the weekend would pass without a hitch. Max deserved Tom to be at his best, to make this birthday as special as possible. He was on that cusp between a child and a teenager. All too soon his innocent delight in superheroes and silly games would be buried beneath a hormonally driven wall of moodiness and self-consciousness. This might be the last time Max would still rather spend his birthday surrounded by family than hanging out with his mates.

He was growing up.

The realisation of it stole Tom's breath to the point he had to pause in front of the kitchen door and run through a couple of calming exercises before he could reach out and open it.

Stepping from the hushed semi-darkness of the surgery into the bright chaos of the packed kitchen was like crossing a portal into another dimension. Alex was the first to spot him, coming over to greet him with a bear hug and a quick whispered, 'Kids have had a bust-up, I'll tell you about it in a minute.' More loudly he said, 'About time you showed up, we can now officially declare it beer o'clock.'

Tom flicked a quick glance at Emily, who was leaning against the worktop next to the sink where Philippa – God bless her – had tugged on a pair of rubber gloves and was washing up. Em looked a bit peaky, but she seemed calm enough as she chatted away to her Mimi, as the kids called her because Philippa had never wanted to be Granny or Grandma, which she thought sounded too old-fashioned. Max was sitting at the table next to Archie, grinning at a handful of what looked like new superhero action figures – and had the look of someone who had wheedled a few early presents. 'Bad?' he muttered to Alex from the side of his mouth.

'Defcon One.'

Tom winced. 'Definitely beer o'clock.' He headed for the

fridge and retrieved three bottles, then crossed to the drawer near the sink where all the little kitchen gadgets were kept to find a bottle opener. 'Everything all right?' he asked Em, making sure he used the same tone as always.

When she nodded but didn't quite meet his eye, he hid a frown by kissing her temple, then turned to Philippa. She'd always been kind to Tom, even when loyalty to his mum had made it difficult at first to accept her place in his father's life. If he was going to make more of an effort with them both, now was as good a time as any to start. 'Hello, lovely Mimi. I hope the journey down wasn't too awful?'

She started a little at the affectionate term, before smiling and leaning over to dash a quick peck on his cheek. 'Bumper-to-bumper traffic getting out of London but plain sailing after that. Of course, your father and Alex had a huge shouting match about the best route to take.' Tom grinned because both hated to cede any kind of control and were therefore terrible passengers. 'Luckily I'd downloaded a fantastic audiobook onto my phone, so I stuck my headphones in and let them get on with it.'

'Very sensible.' He glanced into the bowl and was relieved to see there were only a couple of mugs still lurking under the water. 'You should be doing that,' he said to Emily. 'Mimi is our guest this weekend, she's not here to wait on us all.'

'Oh, I don't mind pitching in,' Philippa said, scrubbing the textured sponge around the rim of one of the remaining mugs. 'Emily's helping with the drying up, aren't you, darling?' She cast a pointed look at the folded, so far untouched tea towel on the draining board and Tom decided to leave them to it. Philippa might be soft-spoken, but she hadn't survived – and thrived – being married to Archie for thirty years without a backbone of steel.

Handing one of the now uncapped beers to Alex, Tom set the

other one down in front of his father and placed a hand on his shoulder. 'Good to see you, Pop.'

'Nice to be invited.'

Tom bristled, assuming it was a dig because they'd been here nearly two months and this was the first time he'd asked them to visit. Or maybe Pop meant exactly what he said, and he was reading too much into it.

'First of many visits, I hope.' Tom clicked his bottle against the one he put in front of Archie.

'I'll drink to that.' Archie raised his beer and took a mouthful.

'Can I have some?' Max asked his grandfather.

'When you're twenty-one and back from the war.' Tom had no idea where the saying had come from, but it was something Pop had said to him too when he was younger than Max was now.

'You can have a Coke,' Tom said, bending to kiss the top of Max's head. 'And then it's squash after that.'

'But it's my birthday.' Max stuck out his bottom lip.

'Not until tomorrow, and there's still time to cancel if you start any of that nonsense.' Archie tapped a firm finger on Max's nose. 'Do as your father says.'

Tom exchanged a look with Alex over Archie's head. Seemed like he wasn't the only one who was trying to make an effort. Alex flicked a glance towards his mother, then lifted his beer for a drink and Tom was even more glad he'd been extra affectionate in his greeting of her.

'I'm going to nip upstairs and get changed. Nerissa's not back yet?'

Alex shook his head. 'She was just heading out as we arrived, I'm sure she'll be here in a minute.'

When Tom went upstairs, Alex followed him. While he stripped off his shirt and tie and changed into a long-sleeved T-shirt and his most comfortable pair of jeans, his brother updated him on what had already been christened Blanketgate.

'Bloody hell,' Tom said, sinking onto the end of the bed. 'Emily will be devastated.'

Alex sat next to him. 'She was pretty upset when I had a chat with her, but I'm more worried about Max. Pop had a go at talking to him, but the poor kid point-blank refused to say anything other than it wasn't his fault.'

'I should've made sure he had something of Anna's too.' Tom scrubbed a hand across his eyes, feeling wretched and utterly useless. 'I never even thought about it because the blanket has been Em's thing for years. I did memory books with them.' It was something the counsellor had suggested and he'd found it incredibly therapeutic to go through the hundreds of photos on their cloud storage and help the children choose their favourites to print off and mount in a pair of albums. The children had each written their memories under the pictures. Tom had made one for himself – but he hadn't written anything in his. He hadn't needed to, because each and every one of the memories was etched into his heart. 'I got rid of the last of her clothes before we moved because keeping them felt too bloody morbid, but there's a couple of boxes in the back of my wardrobe with things I couldn't bear to part with.' He'd shoved them in behind his shoes and other bits and pieces, not ready to open them up again. 'I'll go through them with Max sometime soon and see if he wants to take anything for his room.' It was all he could think of to do.

'Don't fret about it,' Alex said, slinging an arm around his shoulder and tugging Tom in for a hug. 'You've done amazingly well with them. Give yourself a break. Besides, Emily seemed to think Nerissa was going to find someone to repair the damage, so hopefully they'll be able to put it behind them.'

Tom allowed himself a moment of indulgence to absorb the

comfort and deep abiding love he and his brother shared before he straightened up. 'Enough of that. Let's make this the best bloody weekend we can.'

'Sounds like a plan.'

When they returned to the kitchen, Nerissa was home and any lingering upset Max might have been feeling had been dispelled by his awe at seeing his birthday cake. Laurie had outdone all expectations and produced a perfect replica of the Black Panther's cat-like mask. She'd even iced the character's catchphrase of 'Wakanda Forever' onto the silver cake board. 'Can I have a bit now?' Max was asking Nerissa, who hadn't even had a chance to take her coat off.

'Remember what Pop said,' Tom warned him as he took him by the shoulders and bodily removed him from where he was crowding Nerissa. 'Besides, I thought we could have fish and chips tonight and I don't think that will go very well with birthday cake.'

'Fish and chips!' Max raised his arms overhead in celebration. 'I'm having curry sauce on mine, Pop. What about you?'

'Curry sauce?' Archie scoffed. 'And ruin a big fat portion of mushy peas? I think not!'

'Gross!' With Max suitably distracted asking everyone what they were having and then pulling faces of disgust whenever they chose something he disagreed with, Nerissa was able to put the lid back over the cake. 'I'm not sure there's room in the fridge for it,' she murmured to Tom. 'I didn't expect it to be quite so big.'

Overhearing, Philippa gave Nerissa's arm a pat. 'I'll help you sort it out, shall I?'

'Thanks. We're picking up most of the party food from the deli tomorrow, but I've still brought more stuff than we can possibly eat in a weekend. And now we're having a takeaway tonight.'

Tom frowned. 'I thought it would make life easier. Have I messed up your plans?'

She smiled at him and shook her head. 'Not at all. A bit of creative thinking and we'll find room for everything in either the fridge or the freezer. I haven't had fish and chips for ages, so I'll add something to the order, if you don't mind? I can take them upstairs with me.'

Of course he didn't mind. As she usually ate with them, he hadn't expected her to scurry off to her room just because his family was there, either. 'Stay down here with us.'

'Oh yes, do,' Philippa said. 'There's far too much testosterone when these three get together, and I can't escape upstairs like Emily will no doubt do when they get that blasted PlayStation out.'

'Max can go without his games for one evening,' Tom said to her, knowing she was right. It wasn't only his father and brother who were hideously competitive when they got going. Tom was just as bad, and Max showed every sign of the trait passing into their third generation.

'And disappoint your father?' Philippa laughed. 'He'd never forgive me! You boys can make a racket and Nerissa and I will find a comfortable corner and get to know each other. I brought a couple of bottles of Prosecco with me because everything's more fun with bubbles,' she said the last to Nerissa and they shared a grin.

'We'll definitely find room for those in the fridge,' Nerissa agreed.

* * *

After a couple of hours of noisy game-playing, which included the most outrageous insults they could come up with that didn't involve swearing, Tom tossed his controller down and declared it game over. It was already past Max's usual bedtime, and he would need a bit of time to unwind if Tom had any hope of getting him into bed and asleep before midnight.

'We can play again tomorrow,' Archie said, taking the controller from a protesting Max while Alex switched off the game. 'Give your poor Pop a break, I'm worn out.'

He did look a bit tired now that Tom thought about it, but he'd put it down to the long day and several hours in the car. He found himself studying Archie now, his medical brain kicking into autopilot even after several beers as he catalogued the lines of strain around his father's eyes, the larger than usual bags under his eyes.

'I can feel you watching me, boy,' Archie said as he pushed himself up from the depths of the sofa. 'And you can knock it off.'

'I was just...' At Archie's quelling look, Tom opted for discretion over valour. 'Wondering if you wanted a cup of coffee,' he finished.

'Like hell you were.' Archie patted his shoulder. 'Nothing to worry yourself about, and yes, I wouldn't mind a coffee. I'll give you a hand with them once I've had a pee.'

Tom headed out to the kitchen and switched on the coffee maker, which had already been set up by some fore-thinking soul – Nerissa, probably. He also filled up the kettle for anyone who wanted tea and put a few stray plates in the dishwasher. Deciding there was room enough for the cups once they'd finished, he popped a tablet in the drawer but didn't switch it on, making a mental note to do it before bedtime. Archie joined him in the kitchen and when Tom directed him towards the cupboard with the cups and mugs, they worked quietly side by side for a few moments.

Don't say anything, don't say anything, Tom told himself over and over, but the instinct inside which had driven him to be a doctor wouldn't stay silent. 'Pop...'

Archie sighed irritably. 'I might have known you wouldn't let it go. I've had a bladder infection, that's all. Been on the antibiotics to sort it out and it left me a bit drained. I'm getting bloody old and stuff doesn't work like it should, any more. Satisfied now?'

Knowing what it must've taken for a proud man like Archie to admit a weakness, Tom nodded. 'Thanks for telling me. I worry about you, that's all.'

'Well, there's no need,' Archie said, gruffly. 'I'm not ready to turn my toes up yet.' He reached across Tom for the sugar canister, which he set on one of the trays Tom had put out on the kitchen table, deciding they'd just ferry everything next door and let people help themselves to whatever they wanted. 'That girl of yours is a pretty piece.'

'Don't start,' Tom said, raising a warning finger towards his father.

'I'm just making an observation, no need to overreact,' Archie protested. 'Unless there is...' he added, slyly.

'There isn't. Besides, she works for me.' Tom hadn't meant it as a barb, but he saw the moment he said it that Archie felt skewered none the less.

'Ah, yes.' Archie's tone dripped with sarcasm. 'I forgot about that halo of yours for a moment. Couldn't possibly sully your morals and get off with an employee like your monster of a father, eh?'

'Pop, come on. That's not what I meant.'

But Archie was off on one and wasn't prepared to be reasoned with. 'Christ, you're like a dog with an old bone, boy. It's been thirty bloody years, but you're never going to forgive me for leaving your mother, are you?' Archie banged a couple of mugs down harder than necessary as he added them to the tray. 'Never mind that your mother gave up on me years before I gave up on her – oh no, that doesn't fit the narrative, does it?'

'Pop.' Tom put a placating hand on Archie's shoulder, replacing it and clamping his grip when his father tried to shake him off. 'Pop, look at me.' When Archie relented and turned to face him, Tom did his best to keep his tone gentle, to push down on the protesting inner child who was ready to leap once more to his mother's defence. It was the second time Archie had made that kind of cryptic comment, he should at least try to hear him out. 'I swear that I meant no slight to you when I said that about Nerissa and me working together. I promised myself I would try harder this weekend to get along with you – and I really want to do that. I'm sorry if I upset you, I didn't mean it.'

Archie glared a moment longer before his features softened. 'Mimi will have my guts if she finds out we've been quarrelling again.'

'There you are then. No one wants to face the terrible wrath of Mimi.'

They both laughed at the absurdity of it. Even at his most resentful horrible teenage stage, Philippa had been the soul of patient kindness with Tom.

'You'd be surprised.' Archie shook his head. 'I'm just tired of fighting with you about the same old things, boy. None of us are getting any younger.'

'I'm tired of it too. And it sounds like I don't know the full story.' Tom let it hang, an opening rather than a direct question. Something Archie could pick up or choose to ignore as he wished.

'We were never suited.' Archie turned away and started fiddling with the coffee pot, which was still hissing and dripping through the final stages of the brewing process. 'We were in lust, but never really in love and then, well, we got married because that's what you did in those days.' Abandoning the coffee pot, he turned his back on it, folding his arms as he contemplated Tom for a long moment. 'She was always such a free spirit – more interested in the world she wanted to capture with her paint-brush than the mundanity of real life. She found the pregnancy hard-going too.'

'I never realised.'

'That's because she never wanted you to. Postnatal depression didn't get the same kind of care it does today and it was the best part of eighteen months before she could bring herself to pick you up. I think she always felt guilty about that because once she turned that corner she doted on you. She found her love for you, but never for me.' Archie looked old, and so incredibly sad. 'I tried, but there's only so long a man can be pushed away before he gets the message. I never so much as looked at another woman though, not until Philippa. I don't want you to think I was catting around on your mother. I've loved exactly two women in my life – and married them both.'

'Pop.' Tom choked on the word, swallowed and tried again. 'I'm so sorry. I had no idea.'

Archie shook himself the way Toby did after splashing around in the sea. 'What's done is done. I'd just like there to be peace between us.'

'I promise.' Tom wanted to hug his father, but he was so moved by what he'd learned, he feared he'd start bawling. And Archie was looking a bit watery around the edges himself. 'Let's get these drinks next door before they send out a search party.'

24

At the first sound of raised voices from the kitchen, Alex had risen and closed the lounge door, pausing to give Nerissa a reassuring smile as he passed on his way back to resume his seat on the sofa.

'Pay them no mind, dear.' Philippa's tight expression didn't quite match the lightness of her tone, but Nerissa just nodded and let it go. 'Now then, you were telling me about the origin of your pretty name.'

'The women in our family have been named after mermaids for generations,' Nerissa said.

'Mermaids?' Max jumped up from where he'd been sprawled on his belly across the rug and came over to lean against her chair. 'Like the one that visited the Point?'

'Not exactly like that.' Nerissa shifted around in the oversized armchair so she could look more directly at him, creating an inadvertent space next to her, which Max squirmed his way into so they were wedged hip to hip. Twisting even further on her side, she crossed her legs and made a bit of room between herself and

Max's hot little body. Nerissa reached out to brush a damp strand off his forehead. 'You're roasting.'

'I was sitting right next to the fire.' Max shoved an impatient hand through his sweaty hair so it stood up all over like a hedgehog's prickles. 'Don't fuss.'

Well, that's me told. Biting back a grin, Nerissa returned to what she'd been saying. 'The mermaid over the summer was a publicity stunt, but Aurora Storm chose the Point because the village has such a strong connection with mermaids. Including my family. We have a story that says one of my ancestors brought a mermaid back from a sea voyage and made her his wife, that's why we have the names that we do. Now, I'm sure the truth of it is he probably married a woman from the Caribbean or somewhere like that and she was so different to everyone else here that a rumour started about her. Folks believed all sorts of things back in the day. Still, there's lots of other legends and lore linked to the Point. We have a saying that when we need them the most, the mermaids will come to our aid. And I suppose that's true for Aurora – because without her videos going viral, we wouldn't have had half the number of visitors we had over the summer. She stopped a lot of people from going out of business, so I guess you could say she saved us when we needed it most.'

'And where do they live?' Max prompted. 'The mermaids, I mean.'

Nerissa smiled at his eagerness. 'Some say they make their homes out on the Seven Sisters. They're the string of islands out beyond the bay,' she said to Philippa, who'd probably never heard the reference. 'Others say they live in the caves underneath the Point.'

'The ones behind the fence?' Max asked, eyes growing wide.

Worried she'd reignited his interest in the caves, she patted his leg. 'It's all just silly rumours and superstition. The caves aren't safe, remember? That's the only reason the fence was put up.'

At that moment, the door swung open and Tom and Archie staggered in bearing two laden trays. Tom cast a quick look in her direction and though he didn't say anything, she was suddenly conscious of how she must look. He'd been really kind including her in the family's dinner plans and it had been lovely to chat with Philippa, who she already liked, but she was overstepping the mark again.

Stretching her mouth open, she simulated a yawn. 'Well, I don't know about the rest of you, but I'm done in. I'll say my goodnights and leave you to it.'

'You don't want a cup of tea?' Tom swung around with a mug in his hand. 'Not even to take up with you?'

'I'm fine, thanks though.' And with that she beat a hasty retreat and left them to enjoy what was left of their evening.

The following morning, Nerissa barely had time to think as they launched into the final preparations for that evening's party. Max was the most hyper she'd ever seen him, and the recycling bag stuffed with discarded wrapping paper that was waiting by the back door for someone to put it in the outside shed was testament to the incredible haul of gifts he'd received. Nerissa's own gift of some book tokens she'd tucked inside his birthday card looked modest in comparison to the stacks of clothes, games and even a brand new bike Tom had been hiding in one of the spare rooms in the surgery for the past week, but she'd felt it was appropriate. Enough for Max to know she cared without being intrusive. When she'd mentioned they could take a wander over to

Cavendish's, the village bookshop, he'd beamed and given her a quick hug.

When a knock came at the back door, she rushed to open it, expecting to see Luca from the deli with their party food delivery. She yanked it open and stopped in surprise at the sight of a slender redhead dressed in what looked to be a gentleman's velvet smoking jacket belted over a pair of faded jeans tucked into fire-engine red wellington boots. Ivy Fisher had always had an individual style, which was most easily summed up as eclectic. Nerissa remembered when Laurie had been a dedicated follower of whatever had been the must-have trend when the girls had been growing up. In contrast, Ivy had gone her own way, her clothes a mixture of hand-me-downs and charity-shop finds which she'd altered to fit. 'Oh, hello!' Nerissa stepped back to let Ivy into the kitchen.

'I'm sorry to just show up like this, but I was passing, so I thought I'd pop in.' Her eyes strayed to the stacks of paper plates, cups, family-sized bags of crisps and other party paraphernalia piled up on the kitchen table. 'Sorry, it looks like you're busy. I can come back another time.' Pale cheeks flushing, Ivy retreated a step towards the door.

'Stay.' They both turned at the sound of Alex's voice, who'd just entered the kitchen and was staring at Ivy like he wanted to devour her. 'Forever, if you like.'

'Oh, do shut up,' Nerissa chided him fondly before turning back to Ivy. 'Ignore Alex, he's a terrible flirt, and you're not interrupting anything.'

'I'm a marvellous flirt,' Alex protested. 'And it's not my fault that Mermaids Point is full of so many pretty women to flirt with.'

Nerissa rolled her eyes. 'Ivy is here because I'm hoping she can do something to help with the damage to Emily's blanket.'

'Oh.' The teasing laughter in his eyes was replaced by a

serious expression. 'Then I'll leave you to it. Nice to meet you, Ivy. If you can repair the damage, then we'll all be in your debt.' He turned to Nerissa. 'Give me a shout if you need a hand with anything.' And with that he wandered back out again.

'My goodness, he's a bit much,' Ivy said, raising a hand to her heated cheek.

'He's harmless.' Nerissa laughed. 'Come on upstairs and I'll show you the problem.'

Nerissa sat quietly while Ivy carefully opened up the blanket, spread it over her bed, then crouched down to study the jagged rip. Nerissa could tell it wouldn't be great news just from the depth of the groove etched between Ivy's brows as she stroked gentle fingers over the delicate wool, lifting it periodically for closer inspection before laying it back down with a sigh.

'I'll do what I can,' she said, eventually, as she carefully folded the blanket into a neat square. 'It might take a bit of time though.'

'Whatever you can do,' Nerissa assured her as she led her back downstairs to the central landing. 'And don't worry about the cost.' Tom had already told her he'd pay whatever it took.

'I've got a few other projects I must finish first, but then I'll give it my full attention.' She paused to glance back at Nerissa. 'If you're that way inclined, then a prayer or two won't go amiss.'

'It's that bad, then?' Nerissa asked, voicing her worst fears.

'Well, we're not quite in need of a miracle, but we're not far off it either.'

A movement to her right caught Nerissa's eye and she spotted a stricken-looking Max standing in the doorway of his room, his eyes fixed on the bundle in Ivy's arms.

Ivy spotted him too, and obviously realising he'd overheard her comment, she gave him a smile. 'Don't mind my nonsense, I'm just talking it up so I can charge your dad a fortune for the repair.'

He didn't look convinced, but Nerissa didn't want to make any more of a big deal of it than it already was, so she hurried Ivy down the stairs and out the back door.

'I think I put my foot in it,' Ivy said, her blue eyes bracketed with concern.

'It's fine, don't worry about it. Just do whatever you can and we'll all be very grateful.'

Ivy bit her lip as she nodded. 'I've got your number from Laurie, so I'll send you an update in a few days.'

'Well, well, two of my favourite ladies together, must be my lucky day!' It was Luca from the deli, his arms full with two huge paper sacks overspilling with food. Happily married with a bundle of children to boot, he could give Alex a run for his money in the flirting stakes.

'You say that to all the girls,' Nerissa teased as she reached to lift one of the bags from his grip.

'Ah, but I only mean it when I'm talking about you.' He pressed a kiss to Nerissa's cheek. 'And you, pretty Ivy,' he added.

Laughing, she waved him off. 'I know all your tricks. I'll text you,' she said to Nerissa and headed off down the path, her cap of red curls bouncing.

'You wound me!' Luca called after her, eyes dancing in mischief. 'Right, then Nerissa, my love. Where do you want me?'

'On the kitchen table.' She laughed.

'Kinky. I love it!' From a different man, it might have been unsettling, but she knew he'd cut his arm off before he touched another woman. He set the bag down, his tone changed, and he was all business again. 'There's one more in the van, I'll be right back.'

* * *

Once everything was set up, Nerissa escaped to her bedroom for a lie-down before the party. The house below her fell quiet as the others did the same.

She must've fallen asleep, because when she opened her eyes, it was starting to grow dark outside and a heavy weight pressed on her chest. Setting aside her Kindle, which had fallen from her hands when she nodded off, she sat up as another knock sounded from her door and she realised what had woken her. 'I'm awake. Give me five minutes.'

The handle twisted and the door opened to reveal Tom's worried face. 'Have you seen Max?'

'No. Not since this morning.' She'd been so busy getting everything ready, she hadn't given him another thought since she'd seen him on the landing. 'He might have overheard something he shouldn't,' she added, recalling his upset face. She briefly explained her exchange with Ivy. 'We had no idea he was there.'

Tom dropped his head for a moment. 'It's not your fault.' He looked up, caught her eye and reiterated, 'It's not your fault. I put off talking to him about it because I didn't want to spoil his birthday.' Raising a hand, he scrubbed it across the stubble darkening his chin. He had to shave every day for work, so had a tendency to leave it over the weekend to give his skin a rest. She quite liked the look of him when he was like this – a bit rumpled, a bit less Dr Tom.

'It was one of those things.' Nerissa found herself moving to offer him comfort and forced herself to stop and focus on the matter at hand. 'Maybe he's with Archie?'

Tom shook his head. 'Pop hasn't seen him either. Maybe he's playing silly buggers and is hiding in the surgery.' He didn't sound convinced.

Nerissa washed her face and cleaned her teeth as quickly as

she could, still feeling a bit groggy from her unexpected nap and the swift awakening. By the time she got downstairs, Tom and the other adults were gathered in the kitchen looking increasingly concerned. 'No luck?'

Tom shook his head. 'We've looked everywhere – I even checked the shed.'

Nerissa checked Toby's empty basket. 'Did he take the dog out for a walk?'

Tom shook his head again. 'Nope. He's made himself comfortable on the sofa.' He flicked a quick look at Archie, who held up his hands in protest.

'We were having a quiet snooze – no one told me he wasn't allowed on the furniture.'

'Max tried to apologise to me earlier.' They all turned at the sound of Emily's soft voice. She was standing on the threshold, hands twisting awkwardly in front of her. 'I told him to leave me alone and he said not to worry because he was going to fix it.' Tears filled her eyes. 'I didn't mean anything by it, he just keeps bugging me about it when I've told him it's okay.'

'Oh, Em, it's not your fault.' Tom strode to his daughter and gathered her close. 'I should've spoken to him about it. It's not for you to sort out.' Tucking Emily into his side, he turned to face them. 'Anyone got any ideas?'

'I can go and check the beach?' Alex volunteered.

'I'll give Laurie and Sylvia a call, see if either of them have spotted him,' Nerissa said, reaching for her phone. She had a niggling worry in the back of her head, but she wasn't quite ready to give voice to it.

While Tom and Alex made plans, she spoke briefly first to Laurie, then Sylvia, both of whom confirmed what she feared, they'd seen no sign of Max. They promised to keep an eye out and extracted promises she would call back if there was anything else they could do.

As she hung up, Nerissa caught sight of the tide and weather app on her front screen. The same app she had added to Max's phone the other week. Feeling sick, she opened it and checked that day's information. High tide was in less than an hour. There was no time to lose. 'I think I know where he might have gone.'

Leaving a distraught Emily in the care of Mimi, the rest of them bundled into coats and hats and headed out into the afternoon gloom. Tom carried a rucksack, into which Nerissa had hastily shoved torches, towels and a blanket. She'd texted ahead and her brother was waiting on the footpath outside the café with a large flask of tea and a grim-faced Jake beside him.

'Nick and Tony have gone for one of their boats. They'll come around from the seaward side in case the tide's too high for us to get through on foot.'

Tom gave him a sharp nod, but didn't speak as he quickened his pace and headed towards the steps.

'It'll be quicker if we stick to the road until the other end,' Andrew called, halting him in his tracks.

'I'll check the beach from this end,' Nerissa offered. 'Archie, will you come with me?' She would only hold them up, and though Archie was in good shape, he would be slower too.

'Of course,' he agreed. 'Don't wait for us.' And as though that was all the permission they'd been waiting for, the four younger men started running.

She had to keep a tight grip on Toby's leash or he would've taken off after them. Not wanting to leave the dog with Philippa, who was a bit nervous around him, Nerissa had had no choice other than to bring him along. Hopefully he'd be a good distraction when they found Max.

When they found him. She would not contemplate the alternative.

Trying to stay calm, Nerissa swept the length of the beach, Archie beside her. They didn't speak, neither wanting to give voice to the fears gnawing at them, but there was no sign of Max. The few people they passed hadn't spotted a boy on his own either. By the time they reached the steps at the far end, a small crowd had gathered, including Pete Bray from the pub and Doc, who was clutching the handle of his big brown doctor's bag.

'I wasn't sure if I'd be needed,' he said when Nerissa flung her arms around his neck and gave him a hug.

'Tom's got blankets, a hot drink but nothing else. We were in too much of a rush.'

'Sylvia said something about the caves,' Pete said, his expression all business. 'I've got some rope and a few other bits.' He half-turned to show a bag flung over one shoulder. 'Whatever I could lay my hands on.' He cast a worried glance at his watch. 'Tide's getting in.'

'I know.' And it was getting darker too. And colder. Nerissa caught sight of the flash of beams up ahead. 'There they are, come on.'

Their ragtag party set off at as quick a jog as was safe in the quickly failing light. Doc and Archie said they'd catch up when they could, and one of the men who'd answered Pete's call for volunteers said he would stick with them and carry Doc's bag.

Toby's pull on his lead was making her arm ache now. No matter how quickly she went, the dog wanted to go faster. Giving up trying to control him, she paused to unclip him and the retriever hared off towards the lights, barking to announce his presence.

As they neared the fence, a torch beam waved from up near where it connected with the steeply rising wall of the Point.

'Here.' It was Jake. 'There's a hole in the fence. We made it as big as we can, but you'll have to crawl through.'

'Go,' Pete said. 'We've got it.'

Jake took off, the light of his torch bobbing as he ran to catch up with the others. From the water, a bright spotlight shone out illuminating the rocks at the base of the Point. Nick and Tony had arrived in their boat.

'Here you go now, darling.' Pete helped Nerissa through the hole in the fence, stretched much wider now by a couple of helpful hands. 'Don't worry. We'll get there in time.'

'If he's even there at all,' she said, though her gut told her she was right.

Panting, they scrambled over the rocks and had almost reached the others when a streak of blonde fur shot through the beam of the spotlight as Toby plunged into the water and started paddling.

As she reached Tom's side, he was already shouldering off his backpack and showing every intention of jumping into the icy waves after the dog.

'Wait.' Nerissa clung to his arm when he would've shaken her off.

'We heard him shout,' he said to her, face taut with strain. 'I have to get to him.'

'I know. Pete's got a rope, at least let him tie you on.'

Tom nodded grimly as he shed his coat, boots and jumper – anything that would weigh him down. Raising his arms, he stood still long enough for Pete to tie the end of the rope around his waist and then clambered over the last of the rocks and launched himself into the water.

As he stroked away, his arms churning hard to fight against the ebb and flow of the tide, Nerissa tried not to think about how cold it must be.

'Sod this,' Alex said, stripping off his own heavy layers and tossing them behind him as he followed his brother's path.

'Hold onto the rope!' Andrew yelled after him, having taken position at the front of the line of men who were spooling out the length of it between them, ready for a sign from Tom to pull him back.

Almost sick with fear, Nerissa could do nothing but watch as the heads of the two men bobbed in the water, their slow progress illuminated by the ever-brightening beam of the spotlight as Tony inched his boat closer and closer to the treacherous rocks. She could see a dark shape clinging to the front rail of the boat – Nick keeping watch as best as he could, and her fear spiked once more.

Please, please. It was the only word she had, a prayer, a supplication to gods both new and ancient as she watched first Tom, then Alex disappear into the darkness beneath the Point.

'They'll be all right.' Archie placed a hand on her shoulder, his words a statement so firm even fate could surely not disobey him.

'They have to be.' Because her heart was in that cave, and if she lost anyone else, she didn't think she'd be able to bear it.

You took Gareth from me, you can't have Tom. He's mine.

Time stretched. Each passing minute felt like an hour, and though she tried to hold onto her resolve, she could feel it ebbing away.

'I feel something,' her brother shouted, and everyone fell silent. 'Yes! That was definitely a pull on the rope. All right, lads, let's bring them in.'

Hand over steady hand, the gathered men pulled the rope in. Their progress was so slow, Nerissa wanted to scream at them to hurry up. Unable to look, she turned her face into Archie's chest, his arms closing around her.

'Shh. It's all right,' he murmured into her ear, but she could feel how tightly he was clinging to the back of her coat. She could feel his fear and uncertainty, a painful echo of her own.

'I love him,' she said into his shoulder.

'I know, darling. I know. You'll be able to tell him that yourself in a minute. Be brave now.'

She nodded, unable to speak for the tears choking her.

A cheer went up from the men around them, followed by her brother shouting, 'That's it, lads, pull!'

Spinning in Archie's hold, Nerissa was just in time to see first Tom, then Alex stumbling through the shallows to grasp the base of the rocks, Max held between them. A bark came from the water, and she spotted Toby scrambling onto dry land as the men shoved Max up onto the safety of the rock before hauling themselves out. Alex made it barely more than chest out, but it didn't matter as helpful hands were there to support him, to lift him to his feet and help him onto the safety of the sand.

Nerissa would've rushed forward, but Archie held her back until both Tom and Doc had a chance to give Max a once-over and the shivering, crying boy was bundled into a blanket and into the safety of her brother's strong arms.

Unable to wait a moment longer, Nerissa pulled herself free of Archie's hold and flung herself into Tom's arms. 'I was so scared! Are you okay?' She traced frantic hands over him, checking for injuries.

'I'm fine.' Tom captured her hands and held them against his chest, over his heart. 'I'm fine.'

She met his gaze, stilled as she registered the exhaustion and doubt in his features. 'He's okay. You got there in time.'

His hands tightened around hers. 'Say it again.'

'He's okay.' Pulling free of his grasp, she flung her arms

around his waist, uncaring of the cold water soaking through the front of her coat. 'He's okay, and so are you.'

Tom tugged her closer until she could feel him shuddering from more than just the cold. 'He was looking for the mermaids. Said something about them coming because he needed their help to fix that bloody blanket. I thought I'd lost him. I thought...'

'I know. I know.' She smoothed her hands up and down his back, peeking past his shoulder to see Jake wrap Alex's shaking hands around a mug of tea from the flask Andrew had brought with him. Archie stood behind his youngest son, using a towel to blot the worst of the water from his clothes. Andrew still held Max in his arms, rocking the boy gently. Knowing her family would take good care of them, she turned her focus back to Tom. Stretching up, she pressed kisses to his neck, his jaw, any part of his face she could reach. 'It's okay. I'm here, Tom.'

'Are you?' he whispered against her cheek before he turned his face and his lips captured hers and there was no more room for words as they sought and gave the comfort and reassurance each needed. When they finally broke for air, he lifted his hands to cup her face. 'It's too soon.'

'I know.'

'We agreed we weren't going to do this.' She felt a brief flutter of panic until she saw the corners of his mouth twitch.

'I know.' She said, a matching grin stretching her cheeks.

He pressed his forehead to hers. 'I need you. Not because you are the best receptionist I've ever had, or because you're amazing with the children, though both those things are true.' Pulling back, he smoothed the curls the wind had picked up and sent dancing across her face. 'I need you for me. I want you for me.'

So much was wrong – the timing, the losses they both needed to finally reconcile. Living and working together when they were only just now taking the very first steps towards a relationship together. Everything about their situation was wrong – except for him. Deep in her bones, in the very marrow of her being she knew that Tom Nelson was right.

For her.

Reaching up, Nerissa tangled her fingers in the soaking-wet hair at the nape of his neck and tugged his head down towards hers. 'You've got me,' she whispered against his lips. 'Always.'

ACKNOWLEDGMENTS

Welcome back to Mermaids Point!

I am absolutely over the moon with the wonderful response from so many readers about this new series. I love all the messages and comments I get about my books. It really makes my day when someone takes the time out of theirs to let me know they've enjoyed something I have written. I do this for you as much as I do it for myself.

A special mention to Dr Euan Lawson from *The British Journal of General Practice* (@BJGPJournal) for being kind enough to answer a random tweet and guiding me through how GP partnerships work so I could make sure Dr Tom made it to Mermaids Point in the first place. Not much always makes it onto the page, but it's impossible to write about something without at least a basic understanding of the process, and Euan made that incredibly easy. Thank you.

I don't have enough words to thank my wonderful editor, Sarah Ritherdon. I am so lucky to have you in my corner xx

Thanks to Jade Craddock (Copy Editor) and David Boxell (Proof Reader) for their hard work and eagle eyes. It takes a team.

To Amanda, Nia, Claire and the rest of the Boldwood team who are the ones who make sure this book finds its way into your hands (or on your e-reader, or into your ears via your favourite audio app!) – thank you.

#TeamBoldwood! I've said it before, but they really are the most supportive group of fellow authors I could hope for. Thanks for all the shares, the fabulous Facebook live events and generally being lovely. Watching you all shine is (almost) as much fun as when my own books do well.

My Party People who are the very best friends anyone could ask for – Jules Wake, Bella Osborne, Rachel Griffiths, Phillipa Ashley. I love you all xx

To my writing group – the Ass-kicking Word Wranglers – thank you for keeping me company, for sprinting with me, and commiserating with me and for getting successfully from the first page to the last in another book. I couldn't do it without you xx

Huge love goes to Rachel Burton, who always talks me down when I'm ready to quit this mad thing we do xx

To my fellow Criminal Minds addicts – Lynsey James and Cressida McLaughlin. Thank you for making me laugh and for the inspirational GIFS! xx

MORE FROM SARAH BENNETT

We hope you enjoyed reading *Autumn Dreams at Mermaids Point*. If you did, please leave a review.

If you'd like to gift a copy, this book is also available as an ebook, digital audio download and audiobook CD.

Sign up to Sarah Bennett's mailing list for news, competitions and updates on future books.

https://bit.ly/SarahBennettNewsletter

Summer Kisses at Mermaids Point, another warm, escapist, feel-good story from Sarah Bennett, is available now.

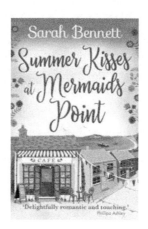

ABOUT THE AUTHOR

Sarah Bennett is the bestselling author of several romantic fiction trilogies including those set in *Butterfly Cove* and *Lavender Bay*. Born and raised in a military family she is happily married to her own Officer and when not reading or writing enjoys sailing the high seas.

Visit Sarah's website: https://sarahbennettauthor.wordpress.com/

Follow Sarah on social media:

- facebook.com/SarahBennettAuthor
- twitter.com/Sarahlou_writes
- bookbub.com/authors/sarah-bennett-b4a48ebb-a5c3-4c39-b59a-09aa91dc7cfa
- instagram.com/sarahlbennettauthor

ABOUT BOLDWOOD BOOKS

Boldwood Books is a fiction publishing company seeking out the best stories from around the world.

Find out more at www.boldwoodbooks.com

Sign up to the Book and Tonic newsletter for news, offers and competitions from Boldwood Books!

http://www.bit.ly/bookandtonic

We'd love to hear from you, follow us on social media:

facebook.com/BookandTonic

twitter.com/BoldwoodBooks

instagram.com/BookandTonic

Printed in Great Britain
by Amazon